Steady as the Snow Falls

FROM *USA TODAY* BESTSELLING AUTHOR

Lindy Zart

Steady as the Snow Falls

Lindy Zart

Published 2016 by Chameleon Writer

Copyright 2016 Lindy Zart

Cover by Cover to Cover Designs

Cover Photography Credit: Wendi Stitzer

Cover model: Kailey Dobson

Formatted by Nancy K. Mueller

Edited by Words and Alchemy

ISBN: 978-1-945164-02-6

This book is a work of fiction.

Names, characters, places, and incidents either are products of the author's imagination or are used fictitiously. Any resemblance to actual events or locales or persons, living or dead, is entirely coincidental.

Amanda,

I've come to realize that you should sur-
round yourself with people who make you
feel good, who laugh with you, and bring a
smile to your lips. The people who believe
in you. Thanks for being you.

Lindy

ONE

THE FIRST SNOWFALL of the season began as she drove her beat up and rusted forest green Chevrolet Blazer along the winding driveway to the house set on a hill. She'd never seen it up close before, even though she'd trekked the road that ran along its borders countless times. It was miles from town, alone and out of place in a small farming community.

Beth Lambert's gloved fingers tightened on the steering wheel, her breaths coming short and uneven. She felt insane, a sliver mad, but also excited. Life was an adventure, and in believing that, sometimes she jumped without knowing where she was going to land. Those around her who didn't understand said it was a regrettable part of her personality. But Beth didn't understand how anyone could expect great things to happen when they didn't go after what they wanted.

You can't stand still and hope to dance. You've been standing still for a long time now, Beth.

"This is me, going on a journey, how ever impractical it may be," she told herself, ignoring the swirling sensation inside her

1

stomach that said she wasn't as brave as she presently acted. Telling her she was beyond dancing, beyond second chances.

Beth scowled. No one got to decide that, not even her.

"Jumping without a landing in sight. I am a bad-ass." Beth's voice lacked conviction and she made a face as she pictured her ex-boyfriend. She couldn't get away from him in the compact town in which they both lived, and she couldn't get away from him inside her head. At least with her new job, she could physically avoid him for substantial periods of time.

Ozzy would smile patronizingly and tell her she had a better chance of cutting off her finger with a spoon than going on a great quest just a few miles outside of town. And Beth would smile in return and not say anything back, even as a thread of her joy unraveled.

Beth turned her thoughts back to her destination. Destination. Destiny. She was on a destination to find her destiny. A muscle beneath her eye went into a spasm, either in agreement or protestation.

Everyone said a man lived there—that he'd made Crystal Lake, Minnesota his residence two years ago. Whispers and slanted looks accompanied each vague, gossipy detailing. They talked about the wealthy recluse who'd been seen in public only a handful of times, and even that was rumored. No one could give an accurate account of his looks, or character. No one knew his age. Versions ranged from a man in his thirties to one in his eighties. No one even knew his legal name, the mailbox at the start of his driveway simply read 'C. Harris'.

It was said he was grotesquely deformed, and that was why he hid. It was said he murdered his wife when he caught her with another man, and that his money bought his innocence in a court hearing. It was said any who'd gone to his home never came back. She didn't believe the stories, and yet her whole body was stiff, as if seized by fear. No one really knew anything as fact, and that made people worry, and worrying people were the worst. They let their imagination overrun common sense.

Trepidation traveled with her, bringing the cold of outside into the vehicle, clutching her nerves. Freezing her. Beth turned off the radio, finding silence an appropriate passenger to make the journey with her. When the Blazer felt like the front of it was standing upright instead of flush with the road, and she could see nothing but frosty skies and the SUV's dash, the world evened out. She took her boot off the accelerator, the vehicle creeping forward as she stared.

Don't be scared. It's just a house—with a stranger inside. Her pulse shot into overdrive. *Don't be scared.*

The lightly falling snow made it seem like a scene out of a snow globe. A house painted clover green stood proud and sure, snow-tipped pine trees hugging either side of it, and white-cloaked hills beyond. If there were Christmas lights, or any kind of decoration, it would be inviting. As it was, unadorned and dark, it was eerie. She swallowed, straightening the wheel when the Blazer slid toward the lawn. Beth parked on the left side of the garage, as per the emailed instructions she had read one thousand times.

Weightless snowflakes fell upon her stocking cap and coat as she removed her laptop case from the passenger seat. The snow was coming down faster, and in bigger flakes. Beth didn't like to drive in snow, and the forecast for the upcoming hours and days did not look promising. There was no way she was going to cancel the meeting, not with the amount of money offered—money she needed to continue to have a house, heat and food for the house, and other necessities. She would take her time driving back home, and if it took an hour to travel six miles, she would do it.

Her fingers that held the handle of the laptop case were clenched tight, causing pinpricks of pain, and she relaxed them as much as she could without dropping her most prized possession. The whiteness of her surroundings hurt her sensitive eyes, and she blinked as she looked back toward the SUV, and escape.

There's nothing to be scared about. You're fine. You're here to do a job. Be professional. Here is your awaiting dream. Take it, and don't let go.

Taking a deep breath of icy air, she walked toward the house, looking for signs of disuse or abandonment. Everything was clean, updated. Well cared for. No dirt, no cobwebs. No broken windows or mold covering the siding. *No blood*, her conscience mocked. Beth's boots sank in the fast accumulating snow, the scent of pine fresh and welcome. She hesitated before the white door. The emailed instructions she'd received two days ago said to enter without announcing her arrival. That seemed ill-mannered to her, but she didn't want to mess up on her first day at the new job.

Beth gripped the doorknob in her trembling hand, and turned it. She stepped inside, quickly closed the door behind her, and looked around. It felt like a large, carnivorous cavern. A lifeless structure that swallowed those who entered. The pale coloring of the bare walls and uncovered windows allowed light into an otherwise dark foyer. On the outside, the house appeared imposing, but inside, it was empty. Where were the memories, the pictures—the personality able to be detected in a piece of furniture or decorative piece?

"It's okay," she whispered to herself, her throat thick and her mouth dry. "He's frugal, that's all. Frugal is good."

The scent of bleach and synthetic lemons entered her senses, and beneath that, something acridly sweet, like death covered up by the façade of life. *Leave, Beth. Leave and never return.* Her feet unconsciously turned to the door, and she forced herself back. The laptop felt heavy, the weight of her agreement dragging her hand to the hardwood floor. She tried to remember in which room she was supposed to set up, but the emails over the last few weeks jumbled up in her mind until they became indecipherable lettering with no meaning.

She removed her outerwear, including her boots that were leaving puddles on the black floor mat. A shelf with hooks covered part of the wall, and she hung up her coat, setting her hat and gloves above on the shelf. With panic racing over her back in chilly sweeps, Beth turned right and walked through a wide hallway to a kitchen. It was pristine, without a single item out of place. She lingered long enough to note the black appliances and cream-painted walls before turning and heading the other way.

It was too quiet. Beth's palms sweated, and she rubbed her free hand against her blue jeans, switching hold of the laptop case to do the same with the other. Her pulse was churning out a beat that was pure mayhem. She wondered if she was alone in the house. It felt like she was. She didn't want to call out, because then it would be obvious she was lost, and then her reliability would be put in doubt. He'd given explicit orders, and she was unintentionally disobeying them.

Beth cursed under her breath, staring at the stairway that ran along one wall of the entryway. Had anything been mentioned about an upstairs or a second level? She couldn't remember, but she didn't think so. She had two options. She could go forward through the closed French doors across the spacious room, or she could go through the hallway to the left.

The outrageous, and of course, untrue, tales, told by family and friends, and even Ozzy, shot through her brain, dizzying in their forceful clarity. Crystal Lake was full of yapping jaws and not enough logic. She knew—she'd had her share of mistruths and lies spread about her over the years without much thought to her feelings. Beth shook her head at the echo of the words, clamped her lips shut, and marched for the French doors. She opened the right side of the doors and went still.

All the materialistic items lacking in the other rooms were arranged in the space before her. Though the walls were painted a cold gray, the furniture set up invitingly in the middle of the room was the bluest of blues, the kind of bold hue of blue found in peacock feathers. A bookcase was built into one part of the wall, filled with a rainbow of books—more books than she could read in two years, maybe three. Beth's favorite books were the kind that made her want to write, and that made her wonder how someone else could write in such an impactful way.

The smell was of strong, black coffee with underlays of spices and hazelnut. Her eyes followed her nose to the stand where a coffeemaker rested, half a pot's worth of the delicious brew inside, beckoning her forth. Creamers and sugar abounded from a basket beside it, spoons and cups nearby. Beth's mouth watered and she swallowed, turning away before she was tempted to help herself without asking.

Windows lined the farthest wall directly from her, showcasing the winter scene outside. A wooden bench with a plump cushion in cream rested beneath the row of windows, abundant with light and dark blue pillows—all the different variations of the sky found in the paddings. It would be a perfect place to snuggle up and enter another reality in the pages of a book.

She looked up, and her breath caught at the beauty of the snow on the trees and earth, sparkling like millions of tiny diamonds littering the terrain. It was simple, and majestic. She inhaled deliberately, deeply, committing the sight to memory to later attempt to bring forth in words. Words were her friends, the truest form of understanding herself available to her.

Caught up in the wonder on the other side of the windowpane, it took her a while to realize she wasn't alone. Beth went still, feeling the heated look of someone watching her a moment before a voice spoke.

"You're late."

Beth froze at the sound of the raspy male voice and then she carefully turned, her heart following her body at a slower pace, and stared. In the one corner of the room where shadows played and teased, sat a man. His legs were long and clothed in jeans, sprawled out like he was carefree, or bored. The biting quality of his tone countered that. He didn't have the voice of an old man, but it was hard to place his age without a clear view of his face.

More curious than afraid, she took a step toward him, wondering why he'd watched her for as long as he had without letting his presence be known. His legs stiffened, as if silently telling her not to come closer. Beth opened her mouth to refute his claim, but a glance at the antique grandfather clock said it was true. It was eight minutes past one in the afternoon. She hadn't been late when she'd first arrived at his house, but by the time she entered this particular room, yes, she was.

Beth bowed her head. "I—yes, I am. I suppose. I apologize."

"You were scheduled to be here until five this afternoon." He paused. "Now it's until eight after five."

She shrugged nonchalantly, even as her pulse sped up in faint irritation. From the communication with him over email, she'd gathered that he was a control freak, a man who needed power to feel important. All the same, it chaffed being told when she was allowed to leave.

"We both know I'm paying you a more than adequate amount. Because of that, I expect you to be here when you're supposed to be. It isn't asking much."

Ignoring that, Beth gestured to the couch diagonal from the chair he occupied. Her face burned, her next words stiff and sharp. "May I sit?"

"You may," he bit out, his voice a low rumbling thunder.

Once seated, she unzipped the laptop case, setting it on the plump cushion beside her. She used the motions to calm the rampaging nerves within. His voice was harsh, as were his words, and yet, she wasn't entirely put off by them. There were undertones of velvet and power that spoke to her body, flipped a switch of awareness. It was easy to be attracted to someone's physical appearance—a voice that could demand the same took talent.

Notepad and pen out, she returned her attention to the enigma before her and asked a question she hadn't planned on asking. "Why did you?"

The entity paused. "Why did I what?"

"I don't have any references, no credentials, nothing really, other than college transcripts and awards to back up my writing. I'm a novice, barely out of school, and other than a part-time job, I'm pretty much unemployed. You could have hired anyone. And you're right—you are overpaying me. Why?"

He leaned forward, revealing pale forearms covered in fine red hairs; his facial features were blurred, just edges without distinction. All she caught was a flash of black, hollow eyes with dark smudges beneath, and a glimpse of a long, proud nose. The slice of a hard mouth before he resettled against the back of the chair, away from her eyes. She let out an uneven exhalation. It disconcerted Beth, made her feel like she was looking at something out of focus with the shades claiming most of his face.

Something feral, something magnificent.

"You said it yourself."

Beth went over her words in her head, but nothing she'd said made it obvious why he'd hired her. If anything, it made it that much more ridiculous, when spoken out loud. "What part do you—"

"We're wasting time," he interrupted, his hand lifting and lowering as if pulled by an invisible cord.

Focusing on the lined white paper on her lap, she nodded. She wondered if her face showed exactly how put off she was by his attitude. Beth hoped she adapted quickly to his rough demeanor, or it was going to be a long, tense winter. She understood control, and

9

the need for it. She hadn't had enough of it in her life. It was her own fault—she gave it away.

But what about this man? What part of his life was so misconstrued in chaos that he felt he had to act in such a way to her? She was a stranger, and one with whom he'd initiated contact. Being rude didn't make sense, unless it was about power. Control. Was the control taken away, or given? Beth wondered. She wondered too many things.

"Still wasting time," the man mocked, causing Beth to drop the pen as her thoughts were interrupted.

"I thought it would be beneficial for you to tell me about yourself, your views on things." She scooped up the pen and looked in his direction, her eagerness to begin hurrying the tempo of her words. "What are your goals? Where do you want this book to go? What parts of your life do you want to cover? What do you have to say? What do you want the world to know about you?"

He flicked his wrist before raising a hand to his forehead, the gesture absentminded. He didn't speak until his arm was lowered at his side once more. "How about I show you the trophy room?"

Trophy room? Why would he want to show her a trophy room? Without knowing his real name or what he looked like, anyone could be reclined in the chair a few feet away. She knew he had money, and now she knew he was exceptional at something. Beth stood on legs that felt heavy and uncooperative. She supposed if he didn't want to talk about himself, she could get a feel of him from the objects that made up his world. Of course, maybe the trophy room would be empty of anything, much like the entryway. A trophy room without trophies. It wouldn't surprise her.

"Okay. Whatever you want."

"Whatever I want," he repeated slowly. A bitter sound left him. "If only it were that easy."

His response was puzzling. What did he mean by that? The longer she was in the same room as him, the more peculiar he seemed. Beth didn't like anything that could not be explained. To her, there had to be an answer for everything. Even this man whose face and name she did not know.

He placed his hands on the armrests in preparation of standing. His muscles bunched, repressed strength visible in the forearms. His form hardened to stone. "When you signed the contract, you agreed to keep my anonymity. No one is to know you're here, or who I am."

She wanted to tell him that in a town like Crystal Lake, his identity probably wouldn't remain a secret for long. The town was like a swarm of aggressive bees, and they stung before they were aware of what they were stinging.

"Do you understand?"

Beth's lips parted at his words, more because she was finally going to be able to put a face, and possibly a name, to the voice. She stared at his arms, noticed the faint tremble as his muscles held a pose they no longer wanted to. *Who are you? What face do you hide?* Her heart pounded a dull, heavy beat.

Around a dry throat, she said quietly, "Yes. I know. And I won't tell anyone who you are. I promise."

In the silence that followed, she knew he weighed her words, her tone, deciding if he would trust her. And then when she felt like she would go mad from the stalemate, he stood, revealing unkempt red hair that was sun-streaked with lighter shades of red, blond, and a hint of gold. It was like looking at fire. Rumpled waves hung over a high forehead, a bit of mutiny on an otherwise reserved man. Pale eyebrows were presently lowered over empty eyes—black eyes.

There were lines around his chiseled mouth, darkness beneath the fathomless eyes staring at her. He dissected her as she did the same to him. The air got colder, as though his gaze sucked everything warm from the room. Beth swallowed, and swallowed again, fighting for air that wasn't there. Her stomach swooped, settled, and dipped again. He was lovely, like the sharpest blade, the agilest panther. The most destructive tornado. Lovely and deadly.

The man's cheekbones were slanted slashes of bone across an intimidating face, his jaw narrow yet strong, proud. He was cuttingly attractive, but the coldness evident in his face detracted from it. And he was too thin, the height of his frame making it more so. Beth was five and a half feet tall, and he had to be close to a foot over that. She guessed him to be in his mid to late thirties, the hardness of his appearance possibly adding years that weren't there.

Beth felt like she should know him, recognize him from somewhere, but there was nothing there.

Something happened to his eyes. They narrowed, lightened to the darkest brown, crinkles forming around them. If eyes could smile, she'd say his were, faintly, grudgingly. "You have no idea who I am, do you?"

Brushing a hand over the top of her blonde hair, she shook her head and dropped her hand. "Other than you obviously being a guy...I mean..."

His eyes narrowed.

Not knowing what she was trying to say and deciding the least she said, the better, she ended with, "Not a clue."

A grin, crooked and unexpected, flashed across his mouth. "That's what I was counting on. Follow me."

It took her ten seconds to remember to draw air into her lungs, the hint of boyishness she'd witnessed in his smile making her stomach swoop and fog form in her head. It tossed away years from him, and built up a wall of ammunition against her sensitive bearing. She'd always been a sucker for a pretty smile—one twist of Ozzy's lips and Beth forgave him almost anything. This man's smile was more disarming than pleasant, and she instinctively knew he wouldn't do anything that he felt necessitated an apology.

Beth tugged at the hem of her shirt that was down as far as it could go, needing a shield that wasn't available, and hurried after him. He made her feel inside out and upside down. She didn't want to get lost in the house, fearing if she did, that would be the end of her, and any future contact with the outside world. She'd be stuck with a brooding, intimidating, unstable man. She didn't want that unless it was by choice.

ℴ ◆ ℴ

"HOW DO YOU like the area?" Beth asked lamely as they walked.

He shot a look over his shoulder, showing swooped down eyebrows and a frown. Without a word, he faced forward, clearly dismissing her and her question.

"I take it, really well then," she muttered to his back. The stranger's shoulders stiffened and released within the span of a second, but she caught it.

"I've lived here my whole life. The most entertainment we have is trying to determine if the current gossip of the day has any truth to it or not. It usually doesn't," she added.

He didn't reply.

Her mouth, without first asking her brain, had decided to fill the awkward silence with even more awkward conversation. Beth pressed her lips together and hoped they stayed that way, at least for a little while.

She studied his shoulders as they walked, her footsteps sounding uncannily like her pounding heart. His shoulders were wide, telling a tale of muscle, once known even if no longer there. Hair curled up on either side of his neck, like the strands were trying to hug his skin. He didn't walk—he ambled—a predator lazily prowling its domain, knowing prey was near, and his. Like Beth was his. She blinked. She wasn't completely repulsed by the thought. There was something about the broadness of his shoulders and back, the multi-faceted strands of his hair, the darkness in his eyes and the distance in his expression.

Everything about him told her to stay away, and yet, something in the man called to her on some level she didn't entirely understand, but also didn't think she should ignore.

"Stare any harder and maybe you'll get lucky and see all of my secrets," he taunted without turning.

Her eyes jerked away from him as he took a turn down the hallway she'd earlier avoided. She didn't want him to think she was watching him with such intensity because she was fascinated by his appearance of mystery and aloofness, although she was. Beth wanted to know his secrets. She wanted to delve into the blackness of his mind and find the light within, however small, however dim, and learn his thoughts.

They walked through a dining room with sky blue walls that housed only a rectangular table and six chairs, not even a picture on the walls. Every room was missing something, as if someone had started to set them up and then abandoned the mission. She wanted to ask why; and instead made a flippant remark. Damn her nerves that made her talk first and think second.

"I like your minimalistic decorating sense. It shouts; *space is underrated*."

The man paused and lifted an eyebrow, his expression telling her she'd have to do better than that to get a verbal reply out of him.

The tall windows let in blinding white light; showing a view of a snow-capped countryside. The outside was overtaken by a blanket of white fluff, like someone stood in the clouds and dumped powdered sugar on the world. Unease weaved down her spine and dwelled in her stomach, growing into a pool of worry. How would she make it home later?

"Do you know how much snow we're supposed to get?" Her voice was faint, scratchy. Beth cleared her throat.

"No," he replied abruptly, continuing through a doorway on the right.

She frowned. "Don't you keep track of the weather?"

"Do you? If so, you wouldn't be asking me if I know how much snow we're supposed to get."

His offhand answer was correct, and it put a sour taste in her mouth. She ignored his words. "How do you ever know if it's okay to go anywhere?"

"I don't need to know what the weather's like. There's no reason for me to go anywhere." The words were hard, and brooked no further discussion.

"Why not?" she demanded, pretending she hadn't heard the closed off tone in his voice. When he didn't answer, she went on. "But you have to have a radio, or a television…"

"No television."

Beth's footsteps momentarily faltered. It was inconceivable. Who would intentionally go without a television? Not that she watched a lot of television, but she liked knowing that if she wanted to plop down in front of it and vegetate, it was available. How did he know what was going on outside of his house? Maybe that was the point—maybe he didn't want to know. She opened her mouth to comment on it, but then she saw where they were.

The trophy room.

And it was full of trophies.

Stagnant air constricted her throat, thick from being still for too long. She tried to breathe through her mouth, but the unpleasantness made its way up to her nose. Plaques and statues took up most of the space, gleaming gold, copper, and silver under the gauzy overhead light. There was no order to them, almost like they'd been dumped wherever and forgotten. Uncared for, an obligated, unwanted display.

Beth tried to focus her eyes, to remove the fuzzy lines from everywhere she looked. She coughed, realizing it was dust. She was breathing in dust, smelling it, looking at it, being suffocated by it.

"There's a fan." He brushed past her, flipping a switch. His shirt sleeve barely touched hers as he swept by and it felt like a spark ignited in the space between them. Beth shivered and rubbed her arms in the chill that followed. The man paused, his eyes shooting to hers as if he felt the charge too.

The whir of blades sounded, pushing around the dusty air. Neither spoke, neither moved. It was a perfectly tense instant full of unmentionables.

Beth was the first to look away, training her attention on the mess around them as she fought to steady her nerves. She didn't have to ask how often he came here. Rarely, if he ever had. Why boast about a trophy room he didn't care enough about to enter? Why show her something he clearly neglected? Rubbing at her stinging eyes, Beth leaned down and squinted at the closest award. It said something about a national football league and was addressed to a name.

Harrison Caldwell.

"Your name is Harrison Caldwell." It was a question, but it came out as a statement. The name didn't mean anything to her, sparked no knowledge of who he was. It wouldn't, though, if he was a football player. She didn't follow sports.

Beth looked at his clenched fists, tried to imagine them wrapped around a football.

"Yes."

Harrison stared unseeingly at a spot beyond her shoulder. She studied his dark brown eyes; wondering what they saw, because it wasn't anything in this room. His eyes were glazed, like he was only halfway with her, the other part of him in some faraway place only he could witness. He was fractured. It seemed an apt description of the man.

"You asked why I hired you."

She started to nod, and then stopped. He wasn't looking at her.

"You had no idea who I am. You still don't, although I am smart enough to realize your ignorance won't be for much longer." His tone was faint, and then hard. He shifted his gaze to her. The singular focus with which he watched her was unnerving. "That's why I contacted you, and that's why I hired you."

Beth swallowed. "But…how would you know that? I don't—I don't understand." She heard the tremble in her words, and wished he hadn't.

He shook his head, nothingness replacing the heat of seconds before. He raised a hand, and just as quickly let it drop. "You don't need to. But when you leave here, Beth, and you do your research, just remember that you already signed a contract to write my story. There is no backing out at this time. It's too late."

Shocked to hear her name pass his lips, and not sure why, she lowered her gaze. Her pulse beat out of tune, electrocuted into a song it didn't recognize. Beth's name on Harrison's mouth sounded like an endearment to her ears, which was silly. It was her name. All he did was say her name. But that voice, with just the right inflection, and it went from a name to more.

"You're a football player."

"Was."

She crossed the room to put greater distance between them. Standing that close to him felt dangerous to her. He'd suck her up into his vortex, and that would be the end of Beth; she might not even care. She stopped near the door, her limbs steadier with an escape only a few steps away.

"I don't know a lot about sports, but aren't you young to be retired?"

He didn't reply, moving toward her. Beth went still, her pulse escalating. He got closer. And closer. His face was a mask, giving away nothing of his emotions, but his eyes did. They burned, scalded. Made her body weightless, spun her heart around and around in her chest. Her lungs were singed, and she feared if she didn't break eye contact soon, there would be nothing but a pile of ashes in her place. And yet her eyes remained a hostage of his.

When he was close enough to touch her, he abruptly turned and left the room. She blew out a noisy breath of relieved air and rubbed her forehead. He made her jumpy, and she couldn't breathe properly when he looked at her a certain way—the way he just had. Beth dropped her hand and frowned, studying how it trembled. She clenched it into a fist, refusing to consider what her reactions to him meant. They weren't all bad. His words told her to stay away, but his aura said otherwise.

"Are you coming?" Harrison called, irritation prickling his words.

She flinched at the barbed tone and went in pursuit of him, finding him back in the initial room in which they'd met. Her eyes flicked to the coffee in longing. Coffee was good on cold days, but coffee was just as good on all the days.

He stood facing the bookcase, his long fingers traveling along the spines of the books. It was a gesture that could be easily overlooked if someone wasn't paying attention, but she was. It was reverent, loving. Harrison was a reader, which meant he was a thinker.

She'd always felt a certain kind of loneliness, a trickle of sadness, with Ozzy, who didn't read. Beth was never able to discuss books with him and how she interpreted them, or find out what he thought they meant. She missed that connection, however small it seemed. It meant something to her.

Beth was a thinker as well, a dreamer. Knowing she and Harrison had something in common made her head spin. She was in the presence of an anomaly, a contradiction. There were words, and there was tone, and there were expressions, and there was body language. All of his were at odds with one another.

"Help yourself to the coffee."

Not needing anymore encouragement, Beth poured a cup of the steaming black liquid, adding a hefty amount of creamer and sugar. She stirred it, the coffee tone changing from black to milky chocolate. Biting back a moan of ecstasy at the strong, smooth flavor, Beth resumed her place near her laptop. The coffee warmed her, muted the cold clinging to her frame.

His fingers paused on a black, hardcover book, and he pulled it from the row, leaving a slim crevice to mark its spot among the others. He paused with the book in hand, his head bowed. Time ticked off a nearby clock, holding his large body enthralled. Though he stood stiff and unmoving, Beth noticed weariness about him, possibly bleakness. His shoulders weren't straight; a twist of discord seemed ever present on his mouth. She shook the illusion away. Her eyes were malfunctioning, probably from the lack of coffee needed to jumpstart her senses.

Harrison turned and outstretched his hand, nothing but shadows and blankness meeting her gaze. "I want you to read this until it's time to go."

"But I'm not—I'm here to write, not read." Beth set down the coffee cup and stared at the book. "I don't understand."

"Yes. You've said that. I remember, and I hope that isn't your favorite saying, but if it is, find a better one." He looked from the book to her, carefully motionless while the energy around him hummed with the need to move. "Take it. And read it."

"You're giving me homework?" Confusion formed a line between her eyebrows. Beth barely got through having to do homework during high school, and that was to graduate. Homework from anyone else was abhorrent, even if she was getting paid to do it.

"Think of it as a personality enhancer."

Beth studied his hand as she slowly accepted the book. The palm was wide, the fingers unbelievably long. It was a graceful hand, elegant and strong. A dusting of red and gold hairs covered the base of it. His hand fell away, like an unknown caress against fevered skin, and Beth swallowed, feeling the touch in the air between them.

Impossible, she told herself.

"Yours or mine?" Beth grumbled.

Harrison blinked. "What?"

The book was heavy, bulky with unread words. Beth took a much needed breath of air and trained her attention on the book. Her eyes traced the gold cursive letters that spelled 'In the Storm'. Just looking at it made her depressed. She was betting it was dull rubbish that made the reader either contemplate life a great deal, or fall asleep—not the kind of light, fun entertainment she went for. Beth wanted to read about happy things, because reality was full of a lot of unhappy ones.

"Nothing. Why am I reading this?" she asked, her eyes down.

"Before you can write about me, you have to understand me."

Beth looked up, found Harrison's dark eyes locked on her. There was tightness around his eyes, and again she noted the purple underneath them, the tiredness evident in the lines and bleakness of his face. He ran an absent hand through his hair, disrupting the vibrant red and blond locks and making his appearance more appealing. What kind of a life had he lived, to bring him to where he was? Secluded, shut off from everyone. By choice, or because he had none? He was giving her clues she could either ignore or chase down.

"I'm supposed to learn about you from reading a book?"

"That is my favorite book," he specified. "It could be worse. Don't make me point out that I am paying you to read."

"You just did."

One pale eyebrow arched, giving Harrison arrogant appeal. He had the features of an aristocrat, highbred and pompous. She fought to keep a smile from her face, somehow knowing he wouldn't appreciate her present characterization.

"I'd rather learn about you from asking you questions than reading a favorite book," she pointed out.

"Work with what you're given."

With the book in hand, Beth sat down on the couch, wiping away the scowl before it completely formed. She put everything she'd taken out of the laptop case back into it, closed it, and opened the book. The print was small, the first lines blurring as thoughts raced through her brain. What was the point of this? Reading a book wasn't going to help her learn anything useful. Confusion and frustration built inside, but she tramped it down. The questions wouldn't cease, and along with them, came anxiety.

If Harrison wasn't going to tell her anything about himself, how would she know what to write?

If she wasn't producing words, how would the book ever get written?

If the book wasn't written, how would she get paid?

"You'll get the first of six payments within the next two weeks."

Beth's eyes flew to his. He'd accurately read her thoughts on her face. "I haven't done anything yet. You can't pay me for doing nothing."

A flash of humor lit up his eyes. "I can do whatever I want. And you can relax and not worry about the money. You'll get it regardless of how fast the book gets written."

Respite loosened her shoulders, but her conscience wouldn't let her be okay with that. "No. It feels wrong. I can't accept it. Not until I've written something, even if it's only a few pages."

"Do you need the money?"

She pressed her lips together, not wanting to answer that.

Harrison waited, unmoving, his eyes locked on hers.

Sighing, she admitted, "Yes."

He took down another book, settled onto his chair, and opened it. Head bent, mouth formed in a thin slash of pale color, Harrison seemed to forget she was there. His pose was casual, but he sat stiffly, as if in minor pain or unable to completely relax. She didn't know which.

When the minutes ticked by and he didn't say anything, she realized the conversation was over. Beth closed her eyes, took a few deep breaths, and opened them, resigning herself to spending the next few hours reading a book in a room with a man she didn't know and was pretty sure she didn't like—even if she might like certain things about him.

Harrison glanced up.

His eyes.

She dropped her gaze to the pages of the book, her face burning with the knowledge that he'd caught her studying him.

Beth liked his eyes.

༄ ♦ ༄

EYES TRAINED ON the book in his hands, he told her, "Whatever you're trying not to say or ask, do us both a favor and get to it. Your fidgeting is distracting."

Beth lowered the book to her lap. Her coffee was long gone, the clock ticking off the minutes until it was time for her to go. There was half an hour left to her designated time of departure— and eight minutes, she silently added. It had gone by peacefully, quietly, the periodic sound of flipping pages the only shared conversation. Occasionally she'd glance up to find him watching her, and he'd do the same, each of them studying the other in the way something shiny and new was considered. Hesitantly. Raptly. Obsessively.

"Do you ever get told you're rude?" Softly spoken and shaky, the words were out before she could bite them back.

24

Half of his mouth lifted, and seeing that made her glad for saying it. It was the promise of a smile, at some point. "Not by anyone who matters. That isn't what you wanted to ask me."

No. It wasn't.

She wondered what he thought when he looked at her. Did he see her blonde hair and blue eyes, and if so, *what* did he think or see? Beauty, indifference, plainness. Did he find her appealing? Did he not? Did he think her features were too childlike, too unoriginal? Did he even really see Beth at all? She didn't want to think the things she was, or wonder what he thought of her, but she did. He was intriguing, mysterious. Far too fascinating with his standoffish attitude and his secrets. A box of mystery and ribbon she itched to untie.

Without really knowing Harrison, she knew she had never met a man quite like him before.

"I'm not getting any more interesting while we wait," he said.

Startled by his voice interrupting her unfortunate thoughts, she hastily said, "Don't biographies usually get written when someone's life is about over? When they're old and gray and think it's time to get the good stuff down before it's too late? You can't be over thirty-five."

"Age has no bearing on death." The words were low, flat.

Beth's fingers tightened around the book, the hard edges of the cover digging into her flesh. Wow. She hadn't expected those words, or that lack of emotion. They resounded with emptiness, vibrated with whispers of unspoken discontent. Told her the barrenness was a lie. Life, and death, and everything in between—that was Harrison Caldwell. She inhaled sharply, tipped upside down by his comment.

His eyes were chips of black ice and she forced her gaze away, her chest tight.

"We're done for the day. Come back tomorrow."

She turned her head and stared at him. *I want to know you more. I don't want to know you at all.*

"What?" he demanded harshly.

"I don't..." Beth watched as his eyes hardened, the impatience in them causing her cheeks to warm.

"If it's going to take you five hours to produce one sentence, this association is going to become quite tedious. I don't have time for timidity. Say whatever you're thinking."

Anger sparked through her, the words fast and loud as they left her. "I don't think I like you. You're rude without being provoked and you act like everything I have to say is a chore for you to listen to." Her eyes went wide at the unintended confession.

Satisfaction bracketed his mouth as his lips relaxed from their hard line. "Just the silence. The silence I can do without. And I'm your employer. You're not supposed to like me."

"I—I'm sorry. I didn't mean...I'm sorry," she finished quietly.

"Don't apologize either. Goodbye, Beth."

He got up abruptly, a sick look passing over his features as his face turned ashen. Lurching to the side as if he had no control over his body, Harrison's legs crashed against the end table near his chair, his palms landing hard on the top of it, a slap of something pliable against something unrelenting. His fingers gripped the sides of it as he stayed hunched over, arms trembling and sweat beaded on his skin.

She was on her feet and to him before her brain realized what she was doing. Beth reached out to help him, not sure what she should do, and also alarmed that she wasn't already doing something. Her fingers grazed his arm and he jerked away. "Harrison? Are you okay? Are you sick?"

His voice filled the air, a lash of cold, striking words hot against her skin. "Don't touch me."

Beth snatched her hand back, fear rushing through her veins, pulsing with her heart. She tried to swallow. A warning of peril swept through her mind, told her to keep her distance. Beth backed up a step. "I'm sorry. I just...do you need me to call someone? Are you okay?"

"I'm fine," he bit out.

"You don't look like you're fine," she commented wryly, crossing her arms to keep from reaching out to him again.

His head slowly turned and he lifted his gaze to hers. Harrison's mouth twitched. "I look like shit," he agreed.

She allowed a small smile. "I wasn't going to go that far."

"Don't try to be nice. It doesn't do either of us any good." Inhaling, he straightened and stood motionless, the color returning to his face. "I'm fine," Harrison said again.

"What happened?"

"Nothing. I got dizzy. It happens. You can go now."

He wouldn't look at her and fallacy rang through his words. She didn't press the issue. Shrugging, Beth said, "Okay. Same time tomorrow?"

Harrison nodded, his gaze refusing to hold hers.

Beth picked up her coffee mug. "I'll wash this in the kitchen quick and be on my way."

"Leave it. I can get it."

"And I can clean up after myself." She didn't want to create extra work for him, not even for something as small as an unwashed cup. He tried to hide it, but there was frailty to him.

"Don't," was all he said, his attention finally locking on her.

The air crackled with tension and challenge. Beth's skin prickled as Harrison's eyes connected with hers. She didn't have something to prove, but he did. She could tell by the stiff set of his shoulders, the hard angle of his jaw. He was embarrassed. Angry. He probably wanted a fight, needed to prove he was in control to feel strong.

She carefully set down the coffee mug. Noticing how his shoulders relaxed, she avoided his gaze and nodded to the book. "I like it so far. See you tomorrow."

Picking up her laptop case, Beth didn't wait for words that wouldn't come. She walked from the room and quickly put on her coat, boots, and hat, but not so fast that if Harrison was to see her, he would think she was in a rush to leave—and she was. She regretted agreeing to write his book, she was unnerved by him, even a little scared. Beth was also riveted. She was as splintered as him, it seemed.

The compulsion to find out all she could about him was overwhelming, and when she stepped outside and into a foot or more of snow, even that didn't deter her. The snow had stopped, and if she was lucky, the plow trucks had already gone by. She let the Blazer warm up as she used the brush part of a scraper to remove the cold white fluff from the vehicle. Her eyes continually went back to the house, her thoughts on the man within. Beth shivered and set about going home, glad for brakes and four-wheel drive.

TWO

BYPASSING THE BAR where she worked part-time, and subsequently, her ex-boyfriend, Beth took side streets through the town of one thousand and something residents who liked to converge downtown in clusters of inquisitive eyes and flapping mouths. Anyone who didn't have anything better to do probably already knew she was in town, and from which direction she'd entered it. The chatterboxes consisted mostly of older, retired people, but Ozzy had his own clan of spies looking out for him too.

To her ever-loving frustration, nothing Beth did was unknown to him.

It was dark out, the streetlamps with their holiday wreaths adding light to the cold winter setting. A smattering of houses glowed with outdoor lighting from a porch or garage. She parked near her unlit house, not wanting to waste time shoveling the driveway even as she knew it was necessary. She wanted to research, and write. Beth did a sloppy job of shoveling, her arms aching and her skin damp inside the coat and gloves.

The call to find out details on Harrison was becoming irresistible, and she felt like one of the town's nosy residents in her quest to uncover all she could on him.

The growing roar of a diesel truck alerted her to a visitor, and with a groan, Beth set down the shovel and leaned against the handle, waiting. She watched as Ozzy jumped from the truck and sauntered over to her. A glance here, a stare there, his eyes took in the scene before landing and staying on her. His light brown hair was eternally in need of a trim and a brush, his wiry build deceptive to the strength he had. He wore blue jeans and a jean jacket most days, and on anyone else, it would seem outdated, but not on him. Ozzy owned that look. It was his.

Michael Oswald Peck, or Ozzy, as he went by, was the first boy Beth kissed at the age of nine, the first boy to hold her hand, the first and only boy she told she loved, and the first boy to intimately know her body. Both twenty-six, they had been a large part of each other's lives for the past twenty of those twenty-six years. His mark on her life was inescapable, even when she prayed for blankness. They had a history, no matter where they were in their lives, or what came between them—and a lot had.

Their history was thick, tangible. Constricting at times.

"Hey."

"Hey," she faintly replied.

"Why didn't you tell me you were on your way home? I would have shoveled before you got back." Ozzy's brusque words were sweetened by a blinding smile and a sweep of golden eyes.

"Why didn't you just shovel then? Why wait until I'm home?" Beth allowed him to take the shovel from her, her tone belligerent. Ozzy was a lot of talk and not as much action. "I'm done now."

30

"You call this hack job shoveling? Watch the master." Ozzy shrugged his shoulders and scraped the blade along the cement, whistling a Christmas song. Ignoring her questions.

"You know I wouldn't have told you I was on my way home." Her voice was low, but he caught the words, pausing to better listen. "You aren't obligated to know when I'm home or not. We are not together."

It wasn't hard to figure out how he'd known—Ozzy's brother lived across the street and two houses down. There wasn't much not known by others in Crystal Lake. How did Harrison Caldwell continue to remain elusive to the masses? How did he get his groceries? Where did he get his hair cut? What about clothes? So many questions. Too many questions.

"How was your first day at the new job?"

Ozzy, along with being a self-proclaimed shoveling master, was a master of delusions. If he didn't like something he heard, he pretended it wasn't said. If he didn't want something to be a certain way, to him it wasn't. At the moment, he wanted Beth and him to be together. At the moment, they were not. Her choice, not his, which added extra chaffing to his pride.

"It was work. Work is work." She hoped her tone didn't give anything away, hint at the energy she couldn't tramp completely from her voice.

He gave her a wounded look. "I can't believe you're actually following your dreams instead of wasting your talent in the bar like the rest of us. Where are your priorities?"

Beth's lips twitched and formed into a small smile. "I know, I really should work on my selfishness. How dare I want to have a career?"

"Right? That's what I'm saying. The plan was to get married and travel the world, live on love."

"One of us had to be sensible."

They joked about it, but there was an edge to the interaction. A glint was in his eyes even though his lips curved up, stiffness to Beth's voice even though she tried to hide it behind layers of friendliness. They both fell short.

Ozzy finished clearing off the short driveway and put the shovel inside the garage door. He turned and strode back to Beth, tapping out a beat on his thigh with his fingertips. There was a song in his head at all times. Even when Beth had wanted him to be lost in her, part of him wasn't hers to have, possessed by the songs in his head and heart. Music lived in Ozzy.

He stopped when only inches separated them. He quietly perused her features, searching, always searching. His animal eyes locked on hers, stole her air with that serene smolder. It was the kind of look that could steadily, endlessly burn until there was nothing left of its target.

"How did it go, really?"

Beth rolled her shoulders under his scrutiny, wishing away the familiarity that didn't seem to have a place to go. "It went okay."

"Yeah?" He touched a lock of hair near her shoulder. "Are you sure?"

She shrugged, stepping out of his reach so she didn't fall into it. "There were hiccups, but that's normal, being a first day and all. I'm sure it'll get better." She smiled, but she feared it wasn't convincing.

The only information Beth had divulged about her upcoming job was that she was hired to write a biography of someone not well known but who had money. It was assumed her employer was old. It was assumed he was a she. It was assumed they were in a different town.

Beth never said anything either way, because she hadn't even known who she was working for. And after knowing, she still wouldn't say anything, because she'd promised, with a contract, with her words. She wasn't naïve—she knew there was a good chance the truth would come out at some point, but it wouldn't be because of her.

He rubbed the small of his back and looked to the side. "You know, you didn't have to get another job so you had less time to spare for the bar." Ozzy dropped his hand and turned to her.

"Yes," she said evenly, her eyes unwavering from his. "I did."

With his mouth set in a hard line, he shook his head. "What did you do? Drink tea and reminisce about their younger days?" Ozzy smiled, but it was fake.

"Something like that." Beth put a hand in her coat pocket and jangled her keys, wanting to grab her laptop case from inside the garage and run to the warmth and solitude of her home. The cool air froze her lungs as she inhaled, showed in a visible puff of air as she exhaled. "It's been a long afternoon, and I'm tired. I think I'm going to make it an early night. So…I'll see you around."

"Oh." Ozzy's face fell, his charismatic looks even more interesting when there was a crease of dissatisfaction between his eyebrows. "I wanted to buy you a drink at The Lucky Coin, celebrate your new job. As friends, of course." He smiled when he said it, but it was small and didn't touch his eyes.

"You don't pay for your drinks at the bar," she pointed out.

"I've worked there since I was sixteen. They should pay me to drink their drinks."

"Don't they?" Beth laughed when his eyes narrowed.

Ozzy lifted his hands, his eyes entreating, and hopped back a step. "So…no? Yes?"

Saying yes to him felt wrong, but so did saying no. "Just as friends?"

"Yeah. Of course." He put his hands in his pockets and waited, a hopeful lift to his eyebrows.

"And just one drink?"

"Just one drink. Unless you want more." Ozzy's full lips curved up on one side.

"Um…" Beth looked behind her, back to the beacon of her house. Her computer waited inside the laptop case, beckoning her forth. All she really wanted to do was put on pajamas, snuggle under a blanket with a cup of coffee, and spend the night with her computer. Learning all she could about Harrison Caldwell.

Sighing, she tugged the stocking cap lower to her head. "Okay. Just one. Let me put my stuff inside quick."

"I'll be right here," he called after her. "Waiting. In the cold. Being cold."

Beth rolled her eyes. "Come on in, Ozzy."

He jogged past, smacking a kiss on her cold cheek. "I knew you still loved me."

She stiffened at the kiss and his words, and then moved quickly. She grabbed her laptop case and followed him inside. It had never been about whether or not Beth loved Ozzy. It had been about how many times, and in how many different ways, she would allow her heart to be broken. It always came back to one word: endless. End-less ways with him.

℘ ⋆ ℞

OZZY THRUMMED HIS fingers on the tabletop, his eyes taking in the scene around them before coming back to Beth. "When I said a drink, I was thinking of something more, I don't know, alcoholic."

"What's wrong with hot chocolate?"

His mouth slid to the side. "Nothing, if you're twelve."

Boisterous laughter and conversation vied for attention with the country song playing on the jukebox inside The Lucky Coin. With its walls painted pumpkin orange and antique and country décor, the bar and grill was a welcoming atmosphere that was family friendly and tame during the days and became rowdier as night approached. It smelled like fried food and buttered popcorn, reminding Beth's stomach that she hadn't eaten anything since lunch that day. Being a Monday night and with the town covered in snow, Beth was sur-prised by how busy the place was.

"Would it make you feel better if I told you your mom put a shot of peppermint schnapps in the hot chocolate?" Beth held the mug between her fingers, letting the hot liquid warm them. She low-ered her nose to the cup to better inhale the sweetly chocolate scent.

He perked up. "Did she?"

"No. But would it make you feel better?"

Ozzy gave her a look, smiling faintly. "Funny girl."

His parents, Dan and Deb Peck, owned The Lucky Coin. Their hope was that Ozzy would eventually take over the place, but he wasn't one to commit to anything for too long. He was content working there until he found something he'd rather do. Ozzy was an untethered being, prone to restlessness and wandering. A dreamer who was always finding a new dream.

Beth shrugged, looking over Ozzy's shoulder. Kelly Burbach, a fellow classmate of theirs, was watching them again. Her expression was guarded, as if she was fighting hard to keep what she was feeling and thinking from her face. Blonde and petite, she had the kind of looks Ozzy preferred. Beth didn't want to bring it up, sure she could guess at the woman's interest in the attention Ozzy was giving Beth.

She shifted her gaze to Ozzy, swallowing hard. Just because they weren't together anymore did not mean it didn't hurt to know what he did, and with whom. Everywhere she went, she had to be reminded of all the women Ozzy had been involved with at some point, a few even while they were together. He denied it, of course, but Beth's gut told her the truth. She was surrounded by his actions, no matter where she went.

"Why did you ask me here?" Her voice was quiet, shaky.

Ozzy's eyes softened and he reached across the table for her hand. His touch was familiar—once coveted, then hated. Now unwelcome. "I miss you. We hardly ever see each other anymore—I know you've been purposely scheduling yourself to work when you know I won't be. I was surprised you even came tonight." His countenance was calm, but there was hardness in his eyes.

"It's easier this way."

"Maybe for you," he shot back. Ozzy took his hand away to rub it across his mouth. "It's not easier for me."

"I know." Beth's disposition cooled, an icy layer of self-protection forming over her. "It's always been about you and what's best for you, not me."

Ozzy sighed and looked at the ceiling. "Are we doing this again? It would be nice to have just one conversation without bringing that up. It happened, it's over." He dropped his head forward to aim his gaze at her. There was anger in the thinness of his mouth, blame in the dark golden flecks of his eyes.

"What happened, and what is over? What exactly are you referencing?" *Which time you broke my heart are you talking about?*

His jaw shifted, the mask of calm and humor wiped from his expression like it had never been there. "You know I didn't mean to hurt you."

"That makes it okay, right?"

They weren't talking about breakups and infidelity anymore. They were talking about something else, something darker. Something neither could entirely block from their minds. They were talking about the end, their last night as a couple before Ozzy destroyed the last of her love for him. Sometimes she forgot, just for a moment, just enough to seriously mess with her head when she remembered, like now. She knew Ozzy was better at forgetting.

Rainbows of black and gray fell over him. Pain slipped into his countenance; regret broke through his shield of light.

"It was wrong to come here." Beth scooted off the barstool. "I need to—I should go."

"Run away like you always do, Beth. That'll make things better," he quietly mocked from behind.

37

Beth marched toward the exit with a stiff spine and lifted chin, knowing most eyes were on her, knowing most ears picked up on their conversation. There would be talk, there was always talk, most of it making her the villain and Ozzy the victim. She was the heartless one who refused to give him another chance, even though she'd already given him too many.

Her jaw ached from clenching it as hard as she was and she relaxed her mouth as she stepped out the door. The arctic temperature stabbed through her coat and attacked her skin. She paused, allowing herself deep breaths of frigid air. It wasn't about running away. It was about realizing some things would never change, never be the way she needed them to be, and choosing her dreams over someone else's dreams that included her.

But Ozzy wouldn't understand that.

She didn't get one block before he was there, grabbing her arm and pulling her around to face him. When she looked pointedly at his hand on her arm, he dropped it. She'd known he would come after her. She'd wished he wouldn't. He'd always fought the hardest for her when it was too late.

"You can't walk home." He bounced on the heels of his boots, either to stay warm or from restlessness. "It's too cold out. I'll give you a ride."

"It's not far." Beth shivered, hugging herself.

White Christmas lights adorned the straggly tree behind Ozzy, forming shadows and tiny stars across his face, making it look like the lights shone from his skin. His smooth jaw tightened. "It's twenty degrees out. You're not walking."

"I'll walk if I want to walk. I'd rather walk in the cold than sit in your truck anyway." She tried to sound firm, but the chattering of her teeth ruined it.

"Oh, really? Why is that?" He tilted his head and crossed his arms. "What's made my truck so abhorrent since the drive here?"

"You." Beth scowled, annoyed with Ozzy, but more so with herself. It was her fault for coming, for thinking for one ignorant instant that they could be friends. There was no friendship between them. There was old love and new bitterness. Shattered dreams and broken vows.

He laughed softly, dropping his arms to his sides. "I'm sorry for what happened at the bar, all right? I don't want to fight with you, but it seems like it's the only way we know how to talk anymore. I just wanted to hang out with you and act like everything was okay for a little while. I know it's not," he added, his throat bobbing as he swallowed.

Beth exhaled. "I'm sorry too. I should have just...I don't know." She should have said no to the drink, to the idea of them hanging out as if they could forget everything. She shook her head, not wanting to say anymore. She wasn't able to pretend like Ozzy.

"You don't have to like me right now, but at least let me give you a ride home. I don't want you to get sick. We all know how miserable you make everyone else when that happens." A teasing grin accompanied his words. Beth resented that he knew that tidbit about her behavior while ill, that he knew anything at all significant about her.

"All right, Ozzy. I'll take that ride home." She was tired, and cold, and hungry. And there was the call to find out about her employer—that one was the loudest. "Thank you."

Sitting in his truck was the same as submerging herself in flashes of the past. The smell of cologne and leather, the feeling of love swirled with infatuation. Two bodies pressed side by side but not close enough. Promises. Lies. Anger and passion. Their first kiss as a couple. Prom. How he knew her body as well as she did. Laughter. Dreams that were theirs, dreams that didn't happen. The disillusionment. The pain. Realizing some pieces of a person had to be let go, that even some people had to be.

And the final breakup over four months ago.

She fisted her gloves in her lap and stared straight ahead. The ride was quiet, Beth focusing on the sound of the classic rock song playing on the radio instead of attempting any conversation. Ozzy was the same, his eyes trained forward, his mouth closed. He absently drummed his fingertips on the steering wheel in time with the drums of the song.

She wanted to ask if he was as haunted by the two of them as she was.

"Don't be a stranger," he said when the truck rolled up to her house.

Her eyes flew to him, took in his blank expression. It was such a deficient goodbye. Short, dismissive. It minimized anything they'd ever been to one another, but Beth supposed it was necessary for them to move on from one another. She should be grateful.

She tried to smile. "Right. You...you either." Beth's tongue stumbled over the words. Was that the proper response? Was it misleading? She wasn't sure what to say, how to act. She hesitated with her hand on the door handle. Should she say more?

"It's okay."

Beth twisted to face Ozzy, taking in his fractured smile. "What?"

He looked at his hand, opened and closed it. "It's awkward... this...you and me...but it's okay. I mean, I understand. Or I'm—I'm trying to. I'll give you space. I just—I really do miss you. I meant that."

She met his gaze, her throat tight with unsaid words. Beth wanted to tell him she didn't want space—that she wanted an *end*, but that would hurt him. And she also wanted to tell him things would be okay, but she didn't know that they would. Ozzy with his bright eyes, selfish heart, and too much charm.

She said nothing.

"I didn't want to let you go," he whispered.

Beth blinked, pressing her lips together hard to keep from saying something she shouldn't. It would be so easy to tell him it was okay. It would be so easy to give in. Her teeth dug into the tissue, causing pain to ripple through her mouth. *Don't forget. You can't forget. Don't forget, Beth.* A single sentence, a certain look, and all the bad could be forgotten. Somedays she had to fight to remember.

Ozzy nodded at her silence, his eyes hidden from her. "Anyway, have a good night."

She mimicked the farewell, her steps slow as she heard the engine roar and fade away. Her heart squeezed at the thought of him hooking up with someone else, maybe even Kelly Burbach. It wasn't painful, it wasn't debilitating. But it stung, just a bit. *Not your business.* Beth took a deep breath, hurrying for the front door as the cold slithered up and down her body.

Once inside, she stood for a moment in the dark, collecting her courage as, not for the first time, she patched up the pieces of her frayed heart. Beth locked the door, reminding herself that however long she and Ozzy had been a couple, it didn't mean they should have been. It wasn't always an accomplishment to count the years spent with someone—it could be something to grieve as well. Lost opportunities and dragging something on that should have ended long ago.

Beth removed her coat, hat, and gloves, setting them on the small table located beneath the key hook. She turned on the lights and made her way through the living room with its cream walls and carpet, took a left down a short, dark hallway, and entered her bedroom.

When she'd first come to look at the house with hopes of renting it some months ago, she'd been overjoyed to see that the bedroom walls were painted gray with hints of lavender. It was a pretty, soothing color. She'd kept the decorating minimal—pink mini-lights strewn along the top of the walls, an eight by ten canvas of her with her mom, dad, and two brothers above the dresser.

A chest painted black with white and teal stars rested at the foot of her bed, and situated near the door, there was a wooden desk and lime green chair meant to be used for her writing. Most days she was either on the comfortable plum-toned chair in the living room or propped up in bed with her laptop.

The bed beckoned her forth, and she turned her back on it. Restless, she paced a small path before the desk, needing something to focus on so she didn't focus on the past. Finding out more about her employer would fill the space from consciousness to slumber.

Clothes removed and tossed in the hamper inside her closet, Beth tugged on a pair of soft red lounge pants and a black long-sleeved shirt. Hair in a loose ponytail at the nape of her neck, she made her way to the tiny kitchen with its sunshine yellow walls, smiling at the striking color. It was eye catching and demanded notice. She felt like that sometimes—insignificant but noteworthy, if anyone chose to really look at her and realize it. Overlooked, that was Beth.

Fighting to be seen without knowing how to shine.

Within minutes, she had a bowl of air-popped popcorn tucked in the crook of her arm and a large glass of chocolate milk in her other hand. Beth turned on the television, the low hum of it making her feel like she wasn't alone. After living with Ozzy for two years, living on her own was strange. Not exactly lonely, but different. It took some getting used to, the sounds of another person living beside her taken for granted until it was gone. She didn't miss him, but she missed the space he'd filled.

And more than that—more than that—Beth missed herself. That was something she hadn't realized until recently, and she was stumbling in her trek, but she was getting there. Learning about who she was and who she wanted to be. Slowly. Painfully. Beautifully. Like a caterpillar finding it had wings, and could fly.

Beth smiled with self-derision, wondering if she should have designated herself a poet instead of a novelist.

She paused with the remote control in her hand, her thoughts turning to Harrison with his mysteries and black-fire eyes. Beth took in the solitude, the realization that she was a party of one, like him. What was it like for Harrison without a television, without anything

43

but the sound of his voice to give him comfort? Maybe there was a radio. He hadn't said there wasn't that. She turned off the television, the silence instantly consuming her. So quiet it was loud. Beth closed her eyes and tipped back her head, trying to put herself in his place, trying to figure out his brain.

Beth shook her head and opened her eyes, her lips lifted in the merest of ways. Did she want to know how his brain worked? Yes, and no. It seemed to be a dark, endless corridor. Beth opened the laptop, braced it on her lap, and waited, her pulse jumping around inside her veins. Once the screen was up and she was on the internet, she froze with her fingers posed over the keys. Whatever she found, she couldn't go back and unlearn it, she couldn't unread the words.

He knew she was going to look him up. He'd told her whatever she learned, she was obligated to remain in his employ. What was left unsaid was what would happen if she tried to break the contract. She would be sued. It was plainly written on the paper she signed. Maybe she should have thought everything out in a more detailed manner before taking the job, but she didn't want to be stuck bartending in Crystal Lake, Minnesota the rest of her life, and especially not with her ex-boyfriend. She wanted to use her degree. She wanted to *write*.

Beth's fingers shook and she swallowed, sweaty with indecision, her flesh clammy with foreboding. She chugged the chocolate milk like its cold goodness was going to give her a boost of fortitude, gnawing on a handful of popcorn when the glass was empty. She methodically chewed the buttered and salted popcorn, talking herself into Googling Harrison Caldwell as she did so. Wiping her greasy fingers on a napkin, Beth took a deep breath, straightened her shoulders, and typed his name in the search engine.

ʘ ✦ ʘ

HUNGOVER WAS AN apt description of how Beth felt, never mind that she hadn't had any alcohol the previous night. Her eyes felt heavy and gritty, and when she opened them, she quickly shut them, the sliver of light finding its way in around the window blind directed straight at her eyeballs. She'd spent hours late into the night reading articles, studying pictures, getting a fragmented tale of Harrison Caldwell.

She slapped her palms against her closed eyelids and groaned, her stomach churning in protestation of the information she now knew. Beth pressed hard against her face, a hitched breath all she could form as she tried to shove the knowledge she'd learned through the back of her head and out of her mind. She felt sick. And sad. Hopeless. All for a man she didn't know, and after last night, wished she'd never met.

Beth turned to her side, one arm hugging her midsection, and pointlessly tried to erase him from her brain. She thought of flowers, their silky petals, their scent, and somehow, her brain tripped to an image of him, lying in a meadow of sunflowers. Eyes closed, skin reflecting the sunshine. Still and somber. Dead or alive, Beth didn't know.

She counted instead, but only made it to thirty-one. Beth swallowed, her breath catching at the number. When her attempts to drive him from her thoughts did nothing but pull her further into despair, made him an even brighter beacon for her to dwell on, she went over facts in her head, something she did to calm herself. Some of them were already written down on paper, paper she'd stared at in disbelief as the night grew and turned into dawn.

> 1. Harrison Caldwell was born in Mississippi.
>
> 2. His family later moved to Illinois due to his father's work.
>
> 3. Generally seen with a football in hand since he was four.
>
> 4. He was thirty-one years old.

Beth tucked herself into a ball as her heart pounded faster. He was only thirty-one years old. She took a breath, her body shaking, and took another. *You barely know him. Get ahold of yourself.* It didn't seem to matter that she'd known Harrison Caldwell all of one day. All Beth could focus on was that she did know him, and that made him matter. He was a person. She tried to swallow and couldn't. He was a person and that made him important.

Never married, no children. There had been a woman—Nina Hollister—who'd been with him for years, and when he lost everything, she went with it.

He quit playing football five years ago.

Rarely seen in public for the past three, said to live in the Midwest, but that was unconfirmed.

Her mind tripped over the one fact she couldn't compute, not yet. She'd blinded herself to it. The truth was a dark taint, an oozing blob of black she couldn't outrun for long. And how did Harrison feel, living inside of it? Breathing in the darkness, choking on it. It was true that with the advancement of science and medicine, what Harrison had wasn't as life-threatening as it once was, but it was still there, working its evil magic. Destroying.

If Beth thought about it, dwelled on his reality, she wouldn't leave the house all day, and she would never return to Harrison's home. And that would be wrong, that would seem like she was judging something she didn't understand—plus there was the issue of being sued. Little things she'd noticed yesterday made sense where they hadn't prior, and it put an ache in her throat.

Beth uncurled from where she was lying and left the bed, her legs and arms sore along with her heart. Heavy. Sad. Flashes of him pictured and catalogued throughout the years besieged her as she stumbled to the bathroom. His happy brown eyes as a child, the determination in his jaw as a teenager. How he exuded confidence and drive during college. The cocky flare to his grin as his professional football team won and won and kept winning. When Beth's eyes were too exhausted to read, she watched clips of games, something she hadn't had any desire to do before. Harrison made it interesting, his movements graceful and strong, his form fierce and unconquerable on the football field.

He wasn't good at football—he was brilliant.

She brushed her teeth, staring at her puffy face and eyes in the mirror. The more recent photographs showed a broken man. Physically struggling, but also mentally, emotionally. Bitterness honed into his features, glaring from his eyes, thinning his mouth. Beth spit out the toothpaste and cursed, putting her weight on her wrists against the countertop.

She mashed a finger to her short nose and made a face at herself. "Stop feeling sorry for him. You have work to do. Get to it," she told her image.

Resolved to separate her emotions from her job, Beth spent the morning going over her notes, jotting down questions, rereading articles, all with a stiff face and a sick sensation in her gut. Even the two cups of coffee, hot and robust, fell flat against her taste buds. When it was time to go to Harrison's, she stopped in front of the door, her instincts telling her not to go. Nausea grew. Beth inhaled and exhaled. She'd told herself the same thing yesterday, but for different reasons. And she'd gone.

Beth left the house.

The drive took hours at the same time it took seconds. Hills and trees, all bedecked in glittering white, surrounded her. She could feel her heart pounding, powerful and filled with dread. Her fingers tightened and relaxed on the steering wheel, again and again. The sky was blue and cloudless, but she knew there was snow in the forecast again for later that day. Yesterday she was afraid because she hadn't known what to expect—today she was afraid because she did.

Everything was different. The house took on an ominous cast. The windows were eyes, the door a mouth posed in a shriek of horror.

The landscape turned barren. Tree limbs became arms, reaching for her, reaching for life to steal and keep as its own, until it was dead like the tree. It was all twisted, warped.

It was worse inside.

The walls cried with sorrow. Their pain could not be covered up with memories. Memories for no one to witness, or enjoy. She imagined Harrison coughing up blood, and that blood seeping from the corners of the ceiling to drip down its length. Pooling on the floor, alive and venomous. His skin broken out in oozing sores, red and angry and vengeful. Beth had a perverse impulse to check the cupboards and refrigerator, to prove there would be paltry supplies, barely enough on which to survive. He was waiting, biding his time. He'd given up.

She understood then—the house was a coffin, and he was the corpse within.

Beth stood in the foyer, imagining unseen disease crawling along the walls and floors, heading straight for her. She wanted to turn and flee, and she couldn't.

Harrison found her like that, still as stone, unable to move, her eyes continually shifting over her surroundings. He wore a red shirt that clashed with his hair, and black jeans. White socks covered his feet, but no shoes. His eyes seemed blacker, bleaker. Older. Like they had seen his destiny and knew there was no way to bypass it. She stared at his face, seeing beyond the skin and into his insides, picturing the rot. What was it like, living with something that was slowly killing him? Did he hurt all the time? Was he currently in pain? He had to be exhausted, mentally and physically. The thoughts he must have…

What was it like to meet his demons and know they could one day slay him?

"I wasn't sure if you would come back."

"I told you I would." Her voice lacked strength.

Understanding tightened his features as he studied hers. "But you thought about staying away."

"Yes." She clenched her hands into fists, an unconscious motion, the action that of someone illogically afraid of the unknown. Beth loosened her grip, immediately feeling bad.

His eyes dropped to her hands, a muscle bunching in his jaw. "You can't catch it by touching things."

"I know that." Beth's voice was a whip, sharp and striking. Her mind went back to the coffee she drank the day before, the mug she used. *Stop being crazy*, she told herself. It didn't change her thoughts. She didn't know him as a man, as a person, and therefore, she couldn't trust him.

Harrison's expression scorned, even as it said her reaction was one he'd endured before. "What's changed from yesterday? I'm the same. You're the same."

"It's not the same," she denied. Weakly. Shamefully.

Shadows shifted over his features, drifted into his eyes. "And now you know why I'm here, without a television, without contact with the outside world. You're the embodiment of every prejudice I got tired of dealing with."

"I'm sorry, I just—I've never known anyone before with…it."

"That you know of. Most people don't announce it."

"I'm sorry," she said again.

His upper lip curled, telling her what he thought of her remorse.

Beth took a deep breath and continued. "You said you hired me because I didn't know who you were."

"Yes." His eyes went back to her hands and stayed there. "And that's true."

"But that isn't the only reason, that isn't why you specifically contacted me. You tricked me." The words sounded petulant.

"How did I trick you?" His gaze hadn't left her hands. He seemed fascinated with them.

"You must have researched me. How else would you know about my degree, that I was freelance? How else would you know that I had no idea who you were? How many others have you done this to?" Her pulse was out of control, in tune with her thoughts. She didn't know what to think, what to say.

Harrison's gaze finally lifted, and it was bitingly blank.

"You lied by omission. You had me sign a contract under false pretenses. What is this—some kind of sick game to you? A way to pass whatever miserable time you have left?" Beth had gone too far. She knew it as soon as the words left her mouth, as she watched the color leave his skin. What she said was cruel, and she stunned herself by it.

"I'm s-sorry," she stuttered. "I don't know why I said that. I didn't mean that. I shouldn't have said it. That was mean to say." Beth shook her head. "I don't know what to think, what to do."

"Nothing."

Beth blinked. "What?"

"You think nothing. You do nothing."

She laughed shakily, running her eyes along the bare walls and empty spaces. Looking everywhere but at Harrison, and then she did, and she couldn't turn her eyes past him. "You make it sound easy, like my world wasn't just rocked by being introduced to yours."

Other than a flicker in his eyes, Harrison had no reaction. "Would you have said yes to writing the book if you knew who I was beforehand? If you'd known what I have, would you have even considered working for me? Would you be here right now?"

"I don't..." Beth looked down, swallowed. Her throat had a lump in it that seemed to grow as he spoke. "I don't know."

Harrison stepped closer, a thoughtful look on his face as he casually crossed his arms. He was mocking her. His stance, his expression. Calling her a fool without saying a single thing. "Let's look at it this way then—who in their right mind would agree to write a book about a person they know nothing about? Who would sign a contract on nothing more than assumptions and promises? Who would show up at a stranger's house in the country, knowing nothing about the person inside?

"I could have lied about having money, about needing someone to write my story. I could have been any kind of monster, and you willingly stepped into my lair." Harrison's chest raggedly lifted and lowered, belying the calm he'd strived to exude, but his eyes were unwavering from hers. Drinking in her unease, sinking into her soul. His look demanded an answer.

"You're right. It was stupid of me," she said quietly.

He expelled noisily, swiping a hand across his mouth. "Not stupid. Desperate. Hopeful. I understand them both."

Beth looked into his deep eyes, the disquiet fading from her bearing as she did. He looked harmless, a shell of the man from the pictures. She tried to put herself in his place, but her brain refused. It was too close, he was too close. A dying man stood before her, talking to her, his breaths already counted beforehand by some invisible plague. It was eerie, and wrong. Not for her, but for him.

Strangest of all, she wanted to touch his face, wipe the hidden pain from it. Beth clenched her fingers, then locked them before her, making sure she didn't reach for him. She couldn't stand others hurting. It made her heart cry. And Harrison would probably deny it until he no longer could, but there was a crack in him, and it was full of an unhealable ache. She felt it, in the air, in his words. It reached for something, anything, to ease it, and there was Beth. Standing so close, feeling more than she should.

He dropped his gaze. "I hired you to write a book. My health should have nothing to do with that."

Beth straightened. "What do you want me to write about then?"

Harrison lifted his eyes to hers, and they were laced with emotion, dark and light and raw. "Me. I want you to write about me. I am not what's killing me. I am me."

Beth's shoulders slumped. Never had she heard truer, rawer words. He'd opened his chest and given her a tiny chunk of his heart in telling her that. The book—he'd told her to read his favorite book because she couldn't write about him if she didn't know him. *Him.* He showed her the trophies because he'd earned them. Harrison Caldwell. There were hints of the man before her, shown in the barrenness of rooms, and broadcasted in others.

Guilt crawled up her throat, heated her face. She was as bad as every gossip in town, basing opinions on some truths, but not all, and not the important ones, the ones that should matter. She was prejudiced like all the others she told herself she was different from.

Beth knew what it was like to have lies and half-truths told about her, misconceptions that hurt.

Look at the man, she told herself, and when she did, she had to look away. His expression was calm, but his eyes were stricken. She couldn't bear to see it, and Beth wasn't ready to wonder why.

"You would think, with how long this has been around, that people would be more open-minded about it, or at least act accordingly. This isn't the eighties or nineties anymore, and yet, not much has changed as far as preconceptions. I've hired others who'd known, before I moved to the area. Many refused, some wouldn't come to my house, others would, but they didn't last long. The few who actually agreed wanted to turn the book into the disease."

He made a sound of frustration, swiping fingers through his hair. "They wanted the story of my life to be about something I might eventually die from. What kind of a book is that? That isn't what I want. I had years and years of life before I was diagnosed. I want to be remembered for what I was, who I was, before."

Harrison swallowed and shifted his eyes to her. "Can you do that for me? Will you write my story?"

"Do I have a choice?"

Harrison fisted his hands at his sides as he angled his head away from hers. He seemed to fight to speak, his voice rough and graceless when he finally did. "If I tell you that you do, what will be your answer?"

Beth's breaths came faster. "Are you saying you'll let me out of the contract?"

"Yes. Today." He looked at her, and she swore his eyes were painted in sadness. It humanized him, turned him from an arrogant man to one with vulnerabilities. It made her see him clearer, and that made him more dangerous.

Look away, Beth.

"Today is your one chance to rip up the contract without fear of retaliation. Walk away now, if that's what you want." Harrison angled his face away, but not before she saw his jaw harden. "I'll be in the reading room."

Beth watched him leave the entryway, a seemingly invincible man brought down by an unseen adversary. The reading room. He'd named the welcoming room full of his books the reading room. His sanctuary. The one place in the house that she knew had the care it took to make a room more than walls and space, to make it a haven.

His footsteps were measured, his trek stable. It was a façade. His personality demanded action, not the slowness with which he moved. Did he hide how tired he was? Did the side effects of medicine, if he took it, cause his muscles and joints to ache? *Did* he take medicine? How far had it progressed since he was diagnosed? Was it still in the beginning stages, or much worse?

Beth had questions, endless questions, and she didn't know how to ask a single one.

The door was right there, a reachable escape. Two steps and she could open it and go. She would be free of any obligation to him. And what would Harrison do? He would sit in a structure full of lost hopes and dreams, alone, his story untold. It wasn't her problem, and yet empathy kept her where she was. Empathy, yes, but what else?

She lowered her head and covered her face with her hands, her eyes tightly shut. She tried to breathe normally, but her breaths came out shallow, raspy. If she stayed, she was agreeing to submerge herself in a reality she didn't know, didn't understand. If she left, she would feel like she'd abandoned him to his bleak fate. He had a story to tell, and he was asking her to tell it. Maybe this was her chance to do something meaningful, however altered she became in the process.

Beth didn't think she could write his story and not be affected by it.

With a sigh of resignation, Beth dropped her hands. She couldn't do it. She couldn't go. Beth lifted her head and pulled back her shoulders, turning new eyes on the situation. Her decision was made, and determination stiffened her spine. Once Beth committed to something, there was no giving up. His story was worth something, and she would write it. Beth would not give up on this, on Harrison.

THREE

TODAY SHE DIDN'T bring her laptop, knowing there was three-quarters of a book waiting for her to read it. The story of a boy losing his mother at the age of seven took on a different meaning. It became real, formed depth. And Beth knew when she picked up that book again, she would read words different from the ones she'd read yesterday. The story changed because the person reading it changed the way they saw it. Perception was a powerful tool.

Harrison stood with his back to her, looking outside much like she did the previous day upon first entering the room. "It's snowing again."

She was surprised by the comment. He didn't seem the type for idle conversation. Neither was she. She wanted to know about a person's childhood, what scared them, what is was about the first person they fell in love that made them do so. If they preferred candy to chocolate, or the opposite, and why. Beth wanted to know what made a person the way they were, what gave them their individualism, what scars they carried, what life was to them. What dreams they had.

In Harrison's case, what was it like to have a countdown to his mortality?

And yet, she replied, "It's supposed to snow all week."

He turned then, his expression giving away nothing of his thoughts. "You stayed."

"I stayed."

"The disease is not to be discussed." When she opened her mouth to protest, he added, "Unless there is crucial information you should know."

Beth shifted her feet, her jaw tight. Sighing, she nodded. "Fine."

Harrison nodded to the stand beside the couch. "You have a book to read."

She moved to the couch, her eyes not leaving his. "What are you going to do?"

"I'm going to go for a walk."

"In the snow?"

One pale eyebrow tipped up. "Is that not permissible?"

"Well, yeah, you can do whatever you want, but…" Beth trailed off, not wanting to ask if she could come along to keep an eye on him. What if he got too cold and couldn't make it back? What if he fainted? She grabbed the book and turned it over and over in her hands, needing to keep her hands occupied. What if something happened to him out there in the middle of nowhere and he was all alone?

Harrison's expression darkened. "Help yourself to refreshments. If you get hungry, there are snacks in the kitchen."

Beth held her breath until he walked away, releasing it when he was in the doorway. He paused there, and she stared at the book in her hands, feeling his eyes on her. They were inescapable, prying into her head, accurately reading her. She knew he had some idea as to her thoughts, and he was irritated with her.

"Beth."

She looked up and turned her head to meet his eyes, an electric shock zipping along her skin as their eyes connected. A muscle throbbed in his jaw, his body taut as his eyes trailed over her face, ended on her chin, and swept back up to her eyes. The look made her breaths uneven and her hands clammy. When Harrison looked at her a certain way, he stripped away everything until all that was left was her truth, hidden deep inside, not meant for anyone but her to know.

"Don't act like I'm dying and you're not. I just have a better idea of when it's happening to me."

Beth exhaled noisily when he turned the corner and disappeared, stunned by his words, even if they were true. Her mother always said people began dying the moment they were born, as soon as they took their first breath. She'd found it a morbid observation and tried not to ponder the validity of her words. Her mom might be right, but that didn't mean Beth wanted to think about how quickly her life could be gone. But Harrison—he thought about it. How could he not?

She poured herself a cup of coffee with hands that shook, pausing as she watched the black brew move from side to side in the cup. Harrison hadn't touched it yesterday or today. Did he make it specifically for her? And if so, how had he known she liked coffee? *Stop it. You're glamorizing things you should not. It's coffee. Even if he did make it specifically for you, it means nothing. Except that maybe he isn't quite as rude as you first thought him to be.*

Coffee made milder and sweeter with cream and sugar, Beth took a sip before setting the cup on the window sill near the bench. She was more eager to continue the tale of the motherless boy than she would have guessed. With the accumulating snow to watch, and a book in hand, Beth enjoyed the peaceful scene as she read about a boy who didn't know how to give up, even when every aspect of his life told him it would be easier to.

Motion outside the window drew her attention to the white hills. Sitting up, Beth moved to her knees and set her elbows on the window ledge, her eyes locked on Harrison's lean form as he journeyed through the snowy waves, heading toward the hills farther back. He wore a bright orange jacket, and a black stocking cap on his head. The sight of the clashing colors brought a small smile to Beth's lips. His progress was slow, and he stopped every few feet, but she had to admire the way he kept going.

Chin in hand, Beth observed a sick man wordlessly dare the elements to tell him he was anything but healthy. What lies he must tell himself, his truth clear in the discoloration of his skin, the lines of strain and exhaustion evident in his face. The bleakness of his eyes. It was sad, and beautiful, and inspiring, and before she knew it, Beth was on her feet, searching the room for paper and something to write with. She found a napkin near the coffee, and a pen in a drawer of them, and plopped back down on the settee to write.

She wrote about the snow being on all sides of him, and how small he looked against it, even as he fiercely faced it with a challenge clear in his rigid stance. She mentioned the conflicting colors of his coat and hair, as if he was defying fashion as well as anything else that told him the way things were supposed to be. Harrison disagreed with his fate—that she could tell. And he wasn't giving up. She'd been wrong about that. But what was he doing?

Beth tapped the pen against her chin as she thought.

What are you doing? He was higher up on the hill, moving slower than he was moments ago. Clearly, his body was tired, and that disgusted him. Harrison pushed himself, relentlessly, determinedly. *You're fighting, any way you can.* That's what he was doing. Beth dropped her gaze, an eerie chill sweeping across her skin. Emotions swirled around her, building and building, and Beth found that she desperately needed to know Harrison, every detail of his life, his thoughts, his feelings.

She wanted to know *him*, the seemingly broken man who refused to shatter.

He fell.

Beth made a sound of dismay, her arms stretched out as though to catch him as she watched him tumble down the hill. She was to the front door before she stopped, her hand tightly squeezing the doorknob. She stared at where her flesh met the metal, her heart pounding like she'd fallen with him, and she let it go. Closing her eyes, Beth took deep breaths, shaking off the fear, steadying the trembling in her hands. He was okay. He wasn't a child, and he wasn't an invalid. He was okay, she repeated to herself.

She went back to the reading room, and she watched through the window as he picked himself back up. He stood unmoving, not wiping the snow away, his sharp face angled toward the hill that tried to defeat him. She couldn't see, but she imagined his features would be carved with determination, and anger, and they would be fearless.

If it were her, she would stop trying. She would go back inside and change her clothes, warm up. Possibly cry about her fate as she wallowed in self-pity. But it was Harrison, and however foolish it might be, whatever consequences he was bringing to fruition with his actions, he started up the hill again. Beth cursed, her blunt fingernails digging in her palms, and then she grudgingly smiled.

It wasn't long before a frown claimed her face. With his weakened immune system, it might not take much for him to become ill, and it could become serious. Beth snorted. She could tell how much he cared about that. She chewed on her lower lip, wondering what medications he was on, wondering how often he went to the doctor. Wondering all kinds of things Harrison refused to talk about.

The urge to research the disease more grabbed her, and she knew how her evening would be spent. Beth picked up the book, tried to read, and immediately set it back down, only a word or two registering in her brain. Harrison was the only book she wanted to read, and write, and then reread.

℘ • ℭ

IT SEEMED TO take hours, but was closer to one when he finally made it to the top. Beth pumped a fist in the air when he peaked the incline, grinning. Harrison tossed both arms up, his head thrown back, and declared himself the champion of the hill without uttering a word. She would love to know if he was smiling, and if he was, she wanted to see it.

What would a full, genuine smile from Harrison look like? Would there be teeth, or not? Would it touch his eyes? Would it creep up on one side more than the other? Would it brush aside the shadows from his face for a moment?

Harrison dropped his arms, and his whole body seemed to crumple inward, though he didn't move. His shoulders slumped, and his hands dangled at his sides. Beth's smile faded, along with her joy. Whatever he was trying to prove to himself, reality could only be ignored for so long. Proving that he could do that had cost him something, and she wouldn't know what until he came back.

She scowled. Beth was not going to wait around to see when that time came.

Knowing she was going to get reprimanded for bothering him, checking up on him, whatever he would call it, Beth flung on her coat, boots, and hat, and stomped through the snow in the direction of the hills behind the house. Before she even reached the hill, she was spent, her breaths coming fast and ragged, sweat lining her body beneath her clothes. Her leg muscles burned from tramping through the thick snow and her lungs ached from sucking in frigid air.

Harrison seemed miles away, a pinpoint on a map high and far in the distance. She squinted her eyes against the bright whitish-blue sky, and the falling snow, pausing to catch her breath at the base of the hill. Beth put out a hand and let it collect snowflakes, the speed of them languid as if to be better enjoyed. They were dainty, and frail, unique. Beautiful bits of impermanence. She told herself to stop procrastinating, and with a sigh, she took the first step to reach her employer.

The path was treacherous, uneven, and unnecessary. Exercise was great, and she enjoyed walking, but not through difficult snow. Beth cursed Harrison as she journeyed the hillside, some of the names quite colorful. Butt-monkey quickly became a favorite, because only a butt-monkey would venture up an undisturbed hill of snow. She lost her boot once, fell three times, and twisted her ankle when she stepped down hard and met ground before she was ready for it. By the time Beth reached Harrison, she was out of words, and air, and she wanted to fall to the cold ground.

"I'm not paying you to take long walks," he said without turning.

"You aren't…paying me…to do…anything, really," she gasped.

Harrison glanced over his shoulder at her, his dark expression turning to amusement when he took in her snow-caked form. His gaze swept up and down the length of her, one corner of his mouth lifting. The humor she caught a glimpse of was refreshing. Dizzying. "Or to frolic in the snow."

"I fell," she admitted sullenly. "Three times. And I lost one of my boots. I now have a foot, frozen inside a layer of snow, inside my boot. I can't feel it anymore."

"Are you thinking amputation?" he asked, his head tilted thoughtfully.

"Did you just make a joke?" Beth quietly mocked.

He faced forward without comment, his arms rigid at his sides, and took in the view. Beth sighed, deciding they weren't quite to the teasing stage yet, if they ever would get there. She wanted to ask him if he was feeling okay. Even as he stood straight, the air around him crackling with life, it was clear he was fatigued, shadows under his eyes and all the color drained from his lips. She knew better than to ask it, biting her tongue when it became hard to keep the questions unspoken.

He was standing. She focused on that.

When the quiet got to be too much, Beth followed Harrison's gaze, going still as awe washed over her in tones of pink and blue and yellow, reminiscent of the scene before her. Down the hill was a forest of trees surrounded by water. The trees were silhouettes, dark and spindly against the snow, mirrored back from the dark waters below. A thin layer of ice covered parts of it, adding character. It was like looking at an image that couldn't be real but was, nature twisted in blackness and beauty. She glanced at Harrison, thinking of what life and death had decided for him, and seeing similarities between him and earthen artwork they studied.

"I didn't realize there was a lake back here," Beth mused.

"It's the main reason I bought the house, and the land. You should see it in the spring, when the ice and snow are melting." Harrison's voice went soft, turned lyrical. "It is life and loss, meshed together in green and brown. Like a goodbye, and a hello. And the smell—everything is fresh and new." He inhaled as if he was experiencing it. "It reminds me that I am nothing, and I like that."

He looked at her, a slash of emotion before blankness, and then he stared ahead. "I don't matter. I'll live, and I'll die, and the world around me will continue. Knowing my place, my irrelevance—it frees me."

Beth choked as she inhaled. She'd felt those words. She could see the seasons clashing, competing for dominance. All worthy, none relenting. A bitter fight until the water overtook the snow, or the leaves refused to not flourish. Until all the elements melded into one another and merged, life and death and loss and hope, together, as one.

She could hear his words in her veins, promises and confessions whispered to her soul. *I am much more than you see*, they said. *I am much more than you know. Dare to uncover all that I am.* They were Harrison's words, but they didn't come from his mouth. They came from his heart, from his center. The part of him untouched by the tragedy inflicting his body and mind, that innocent part of a person that remained unscathed, no matter what happened to the shell. The part that could see beauty even as an ugliness ate away at them.

"What did you want to be when you grew up?" It was a generic question, asked more times by society than should be allowed. Beth didn't expect an answer, her blue eyes trained on the horizon. It would be dark soon, the nights coming earlier with winter, and it would be time for her to go. She wasn't ready to go.

"An astronaut."

Beth turned to Harrison. "And why did that change?"

He shrugged, his head angled down. "It didn't seem possible, and my dad was big into sports. He had me play anything I could, as early as I was able. Football stuck with me. I liked football. That seemed possible."

"You were a linebacker, right?"

His answer was softly delivered. "Yeah."

Beth shifted her feet. The only details she knew about the sport were the ones she's found online, and she was aware her knowledge was less than lacking. She felt silly talking about things she didn't understand, but it was better than awkward silence. Maybe—maybe it was better than awkward silence.

"Chicago Bears?" When he didn't reply, she added, "You went to the Super Bowl a few times, even won one. That's impressive."

In a sharp tone, he told her, "I don't want to talk about it."

Harrison removed the black stocking cap from his head, revealing rumpled red waves. He seemed agitated, and she realized she'd pushed too hard, too soon. Beth stared at the strands of his hair, wondering at their texture. Coarse silk, that's how she imagined them to feel. Her stomach swirled as she pictured her hand lifting to find out.

"Okay." Beth blinked, the acidity of his voice stinging her skin. "Sorry."

He rubbed a hand against his head before resituating the hat. He sighed and glanced at her. "What about you? What did you want to be?"

She shrugged, a self-conscious smile hovering on her lips. "I wanted to be a writer."

Harrison frowned at her. "Always?"

"Always." Her smile grew. "Of course, I thought I'd write one book and become famous, all by the age of twenty-two."

"Why twenty-two?"

"I have no idea." She laughed softly, feeling him go still beside her. "I must have liked the number. Or I thought I'd be mature and responsible by then. Shows what I knew."

"You have a nice laugh," he said in a low voice, and it was her turn to go motionless.

She raised her eyes to his. They were dark, and deep, and said so many things. The snow melted, the sun faded, the cold never existed—all while she looked into Harrison's eyes. Time was a lock, but it was also a key. She understood that as they studied one another, and time held still. Beth swore she caught a shadow of fear, outlined in the furrow of his eyebrows, in the speed of his pulse at the base of his neck. Fear or something else.

"I'd like to hear your laugh," she said in a voice that wobbled.

He jerked his head to the side as if to clear it, breaking the stare. "How old are you?"

Beth shot him a look, her pulse racing and her throat tight. She strove for calm as she replied, "What, all your detective work and you don't even know my age?"

Two red splotches appeared on his cheeks and he turned his head away from her view.

"I'm twenty-six," she answered, her tone quiet.

"And have you written a book?"

Beth's face heated up, at odds with her cold cheeks, and it caused a burning sensation. "One or two. Nothing good," she said vaguely, looking down.

She studied the thick purple laces of her black boots. Her toes were turning into icicles. Beth hoped he wouldn't ask any more about her previous book endeavors. Writing was about baring her soul, and when others couldn't see how much of her essence was in her words, it stung. She'd asked Ozzy to read pieces of her work, and he'd always had an excuse. The one time he'd agreed, he'd acted like it was a chore, and his input consisted of a shrug. Beth kept her expectations low. There were fewer chances of being disappointed that way.

"How do you know if your work is good or not?" Harrison questioned.

Snorting, she shoved her hands in the pockets of her jacket and bounced on the balls of her feet, the cold stripping away the layers of her clothes to pierce her skin. She felt naked, as if no barrier at all stood between her and winter. "I know."

A pause, a glance. "Why did you come up here?"

"Why did you?" Beth retorted.

"Fresh air is good for you."

"So is being warm."

He faced her, tall enough to envelop her whole. His eyes were brighter surrounded by the paleness of his skin and the white world around them. Dark chocolate, brimming with unsaid ideas and uncertainties. "Did you stay up all night Googling me?"

Beth wanted to deny it, but she wasn't good at lying, and she didn't like it. She nodded, careful to keep from looking directly at him.

"Find out anything interesting? Other than the fact that I was a linebacker for the Bears and I'm sick," he added.

It felt like a trap. He was luring her in only to snap at her if she prodded too much. Beth shook her head. She wasn't falling for it. The questions stayed inside her head, tormenting her. What happened to Nina, his girlfriend of six years? Did she go, or did he? What about his parents? He was cut off from everything, everyone. Everyone but her. That detail shouldn't seem noteworthy to her, but it was.

"How..." Beth scowled at her timidity around him. It faded at times, but it always came back. Courage ran in the opposite direction when she was in Harrison's company. Straightening her shoulders, she started over. "How does your identity stay hidden? What do you do for groceries and other things you need? You completely stay out of Crystal Lake? I don't understand how you can live out here without someone knowing you're here."

"You know I'm here."

Her cheeks went unnaturally warm, and she didn't want to analyze what it meant. "Besides me." *Oh, come on, Beth, let's analyze. You feel special. Handpicked.* Beth stared at the white ground so she couldn't look at him.

"I shop out of town. I see a doctor out of town. My mail does not have my given name on it. My parents get me the things I can't, and bring them to me when they can. I don't go into Crystal Lake, no. It's a pretty town, but I can observe its beauty without entering it. Anything else you'd like to know?" Mockery was in his tone.

Yes. There were many, many more things she'd like to know.

"You see your parents?"

"From time to time, yes. They apparently didn't get the memo that all contact with me is to be avoided."

Beth looked at him from the corner of her eye, and then she turned toward the house. He said the words without inflection, and that was a telling sign. He'd secluded himself, yes, but maybe he wasn't as okay with it as he seemed. She wouldn't be. If Beth were in Harrison's position, she would cling to her parents more, not push them away.

"I'm going back."

She waited a beat, and when it was obvious he was done talking, and wouldn't be joining her, she started down the walkway her boots and Harrison's had made in the snow. What was she doing here? She brushed hair from her mouth and quickened her steps, sliding forward when she moved too quickly. She was hired to write a book, and instead she was reading and chasing after a sick man who wanted to be left alone. Life was rarely easy for Beth, and a lot of the time it was of her own doing.

Back inside the house, she stripped off her wet stuff, including her socks. Her jeans were damp, the chill of them driving right through her skin, but those would have to stay that way. Finding a heat register in the dark foyer where every move she made echoed around her, Beth set her pink socks on top of it, and shivering, she walked with determined steps to the reading room. She was going to finish reading that book, and then she was going to leave.

Reading is not a chore. Stop acting like it is, she scolded herself.

Book in hand, she stood before the window and watched Harrison carefully navigate down the landscape, repeatedly drawing her eyes back to the pages even as they longed to stay on his form. His voice was harsh, and his eyes were unfeeling, and still he captivated her. He made her think, and wonder, and that made him much too interesting. It was wrong, not only because she was his employee, but obviously because of his declining health. Beth's skin was ice-cold and yet her cheeks were on fire, more from emotion than her circumstances.

She thought him beautiful, darkly lovely.

Beth stood trembling when he appeared, her hands shaking around the book she gripped, making it hard to read the words. Her legs were icicles, her toes numb. Harrison took one look at her and paused, his face darkening as storms took up residence among his features. He turned and strode from the room, returning with a brown blanket.

Harrison motioned for her to take it, his eyebrows lifted.

71

She hesitated, and then shook her head. It didn't seem right to take the offering, and she'd only end up getting the blanket wet along with her. "I'm okay."

Shutters fell over his eyes and Harrison left the room.

Beth sank her teeth into her lower lip as her eyes shifted from the doorway to the book and back. She'd made him mad. Of course she had. Beth was starting to think her simply breathing was enough to irritate him. Whatever her intentions, she seemed to do everything wrong. Shoulders dropping, with a sigh she set down the book on the bench and went in search of him. If she explained herself, maybe he would understand.

The foyer whispered for her to halt, to step away from the staircase her feet were about to ascend. Beth didn't listen. This house wasn't living, and yet it breathed. Spoke. Listened. She wondered what confidences Harrison had unknowingly shared with it. Did the walls know of his pain, his sorrow, his anger? Had the windows watched him break down? Did the stairwell count each time he went up and down its steps, had it witnessed him stumble? And the floor— how many times had it felt him pace its length, alone and bitter?

As she walked up the stairs, they creaked in certain spots, alerting anyone nearby of her presence. Like they wanted to warn Harrison of her approach. No light shone over this part of the room, making the trek dark and foreboding. Beth was stepping toward something she shouldn't, and it made her want to run before it had the chance to disappear. Her brain told her she was reckless, and her heart told her it didn't matter.

She crested the stairwell, her heart hammering from the exertion and apprehension over what she would find. Beth paused at the long hallway before her, lined with doors. The first door on her left was open and she stopped, catching movement from within. It was Harrison, and he was in the process of putting on a shirt. A view of pale skin, lined with muscle, met her vision. She gasped at the unexpected sight of his upper body. Her eyes widened, tightened, and she couldn't look away. She didn't want to.

He was beautiful. Flawed, and ravaged, and beautiful.

Seeing him partially unclothed made her insides bunch up and her tongue go thick. She was surprised by her reaction to him. It froze her with its undeniable truth. Beth was attracted to Harrison, not just emotionally, as she'd already suspected. But physically as well.

Thin as he was, his body was corded with smooth muscle. Her hands fisted, her hands that wanted to trace the lines of his shoulders and back. He wasn't as bulky as he was in the pictures she'd seen, but Harrison had definition to his tall frame she wouldn't have estimated there to be. And then Beth felt stupid, once more, for passing judgment on something she didn't understand. She only knew surface details, and until Harrison told her anything—if he told her anything—she should think of him as being a blank piece of paper, free of words. An idea that was easier to think and harder to put forth.

Hearing the noise, he looked up. His cheek muscles flexed and then his expression went through a variety of hostile thoughts, all showcased in his sharply etched features. Harrison stalked toward the door, his eyes holding her in place even as she told herself to move. His face was contorted with fury, reds and blacks taking over the man and turning him into a beast. Without uttering a word, he slammed the door in her face.

Beth flinched and sank against the wall, unsure if she should leave or wait for the inevitable confrontation. When he slammed the door, he took her breath with him. She pressed her hands together and held them under her chin, her eyes glued to the closed door as though hypnotized. Her pulse spiked up in tempo, all the cold incinerated from her body from her overactive nerves.

The door opened a moment later. Harrison was in dry clothes, his hair matted down from the stocking cap, two black abysses passing for eyes. He looked lethal, awe-inspiring. "You are not here to gawk at me," he said in a deceptively quiet voice. It was cold, lacking any form of warmth.

"I...I know. I just..." she trailed off, words turning to mush in her head before she could get them out.

Something went flying at her, and she reflexively caught a pair of black pajama pants, clutching them to her chest as if they could lessen the force of his dark mood.

"Put those on," he commanded, moving past her and down the stairs.

FOUR

O N THE WAY back to the reading room, Beth decided some things. The first was that they needed to have a better form of communication. Constant misinterpretations of what each other meant was not the way to go about understanding one another. The second was that she needed to stop acting scared of him. Harrison was a man—a formidable, edgy, intense man; a sick man, but still a man—and it wasn't doing either of them any good for her to act like he was anything else.

The third, and the one that made her breath hitch and her palms sweaty, was that he had to be upfront with her about what he was battling. If she was going to be indefinitely spending her afternoons with him, he had to give her something of him. Beth needed her questions answered, because in spite of him saying his health had nothing to do with what he wanted of her, it did. She couldn't write a story without knowing all of him, even that unwell part he wanted her to pretend she didn't know existed.

Harrison wasn't in the reading room.

Beth sighed and stood indecisively in the doorway before turning and heading back to the entryway. Goose bumps covered her arms and legs, and she held the pants closer to her body. It would probably be in her best interest to not worry about Harrison and focus on the book she'd been assigned to read, but Beth feared if she waited to talk to him, she wouldn't. Her bravery was already diminishing, and she was trembling at the thought of standing up to him. Trembling, but resolved.

Once again she found herself traipsing through unknown parts of a lifeless, dark house. Beth entered the dining room, her eyes dipping to the table that mocked family dinners and what they represented. Life, love, a connection. It was uncanny, and she wondered why Harrison even bothered to have the table and chairs put in the room.

She stepped past the door that led to the trophy room, and walked the length of the hallway. At the end of it was a window, a beacon of light in a somber reality. The low thrum of sound pulled her to the last room on the right. Through the closed door, she picked out faint instruments playing a hauntingly slow tune. There were no words, no voices.

Beth carefully turned the doorknob and walked inside, gently shutting the door behind her. Her ears were assaulted by sound, it vibrating through her body like she was a piece of it instead of separate. Midnight blue curtains kept out the sun, darkening the tan walls. Harrison didn't have a radio—he had an entire sound system. The walls had to be soundproof, because inside the room was an orchestra so fierce she feared her ears would bleed. As she listened, it changed its beat, alternating its rhythm.

In the center of the room was a chair, and sitting on it was Harrison, his profile in view. Features cut from stone were alluringly resplendent in peace. His form was relaxed, molded to the chair in quiet, oblivious, seduction. Beth swallowed, her heartbeat fast and powerful. Witnessing his soul splayed open for all to see, and her eyes alone permitted to view it, made her veins tighten and release. She felt possessive, protective. She wanted to shield him from anything that tried to break him down. Even himself.

The music was loud, powerful. Instruments flowing like magic, pounding like the beat of a million hands. It floated through the room, sad and fast, slow and sweet, ripping open Beth's heart as she listened. Repairing it. Building her up and crashing her back down. She stared at Harrison, entranced by his stillness. His eyes were closed, his head tilted back, as he breathed in the melody, living in the music. He was breathtaking, a half man made whole in the storm of the song.

Lost in the rapture of the song and Harrison, Beth became unaware of time. She was no longer cold; the nervousness disappeared. She was an ember of life, on fire in the heat of the blaze. There was only Harrison, and he was a masterpiece. When the music abruptly shut off, her eardrums protested the silence. She fought to blink away the fog covering her eyes and mind.

The only part of her not blurred was her heart. It beat—clearly, powerfully—it beat.

Harrison was sitting up, his eyes on her.

Beth met his gaze, felt her pulse jump.

A small black remote was in his hand. He stood, his attention dropping to her arms. Harrison clenched his jaw and focused on her.

"You refused the blanket and you're refusing the pants as well? You insult me, Beth."

"No. That isn't it." Flustered, she lowered her eyes and squeezed her fingers around the article of clothing. It smelled freshly laundered, the scent of snow and rain emanating from it. "I just…I didn't know where to change. I don't know where your bathroom is." Her words were dipped in wariness and embarrassment.

Harrison paused, scrutinizing her with his all-seeing eyes. "And yet you managed to find me, upstairs and in here."

Beth's jaw jutted forward as she lifted her eyes to take in his derisive countenance. "I didn't want to get your blanket wet. That's all it was."

Time hesitated as he studied her, and then he gave a short nod. "There are two bathrooms." Harrison moved for the door. "One upstairs and one on this level. I'll show you where the downstairs one is—if you aren't too afraid to use it, that is."

She wanted to shout at him that he was wrong, she wanted to scream her denial through all the rooms, but he was right. She had thought about it, and she had questioned the smartness of using the same facilities as him. Beth cringed from the suffocating shame as it trickled over her in streams of scalding heat. She hated that about herself, loathed the ingrained prejudices she didn't want to feel. Enough time had passed, enough medical advancement had taken place that people didn't have the fears they once had, and still they acted as if no time at all had passed. As if the disease were new, and as deadly as it once was.

Beth followed him, silent and stricken.

He stopped near a door at the start of the hallway, opening it and flipping up a light switch while remaining outside the room. Harrison turned to her. "I clean as needed, but someone my mom knows comes over weekly to do a better job."

"It's—" Beth began, her face burning, but he cut her off with a look that told her not to bother with whatever she was going to say.

She hovered in the doorway of the spacious room, taking in the gray and white tiled walls and floor. There was a large, square-shaped tub near the far wall, illuminated by the light shining through from a high window. A shower with glass doors took up a corner. Everything sparkled as if recently washed. Even the toilet gleamed bright white, scorning her weak disposition.

Harrison opened a cupboard door and set a bottle of cleaning solution and a roll of paper towels on the counter. Glancing at her, he said, "We might as well be open about it. It's an ugly disease. No point in trying to pretty up the unpleasant facts. If it eases your conscience to clean everything before you touch it, go ahead."

Without waiting for her reply, Harrison left, closing the door after him.

Beth set her back to the door and covered her face with her hands, the pants sliding from her grasp. The coldness of the floor leached into the soles of her feet and up her legs. Her shoulders shook against the emotion coursing through her like an inescapable curse. She felt sick, not only in her stomach, but in her soul, and erroneous in a way she couldn't brush aside with an apology. Harrison was living with the illness, and her presence shouldn't make him feel worse about it.

Stop it. Stop reacting negatively to something you don't understand.

Straightening, she slowly removed her jeans, her skin cold to the touch. Beth slid on the soft cotton pants, tightening the drawstring around her waist. They were too long and too big, but they were warm, and they were dry. She folded her jeans and set them on the counter and looked at her reflection. Remorse pinched her features, made her blue eyes dark with the reality of the kind of person she was. Beth choked on air as she brought it into her lungs, turning from the image of someone she didn't entirely want to claim as hers. She didn't think he would accept it, but she owed Harrison an apology.

Harrison waited outside the door, on the opposite wall of the hallway. His face was angled down, his eyes lifting to hers as she stepped out of the bathroom. The darkness of his gaze pulsed with emotion. A single glance from him and her mouth turned to dust. He offered a pair of white socks and she gladly took them, his fingers unconsciously brushing across hers at the exchange. Harrison's fingers were long and warm and Beth blinked in surprise at the pleasant sensation of contact.

He snatched back his hand, his throat bobbing as he swallowed. He stood partially turned from her, as if to protect one of them from the other. The air around them radiated with awkwardness, thick with everything kept unrevealed. She quickly leaned over and pulled on the socks, the material ending halfway up her calves. Beth straightened, catching the direction of Harrison's attention.

Pulling his eyes from her legs in a way that suggested it took substantial effort, Harrison said, "I can put your jeans and socks in the dryer."

Beth bit back the need to tell him she could do it herself, not wanting him to do any more for her than was necessary, and instead nodded. "Okay. Thank you."

She gathered up her damp clothes and was led by Harrison to a laundry room located off the kitchen. Trying to keep her eyes from his shoulders and back proved difficult as she remembered the sculpted terrain beneath his cobalt blue shirt, but Harrison didn't comment on her inability to look elsewhere, and it was a small reprieve.

The laundry room had wood flooring like the majority of the house, and the walls were painted cream, lined with windows and cupboards. When he tried to take the clothes without touching her, Beth purposely made their hands touch. Convincing herself or him that it was okay, she didn't know which. Both. Dark eyes flickered to hers and away, a spark of light glowing tiny and distant in their depths. Beth wanted to grab his hands, and hold them, and force him to look into her eyes and see that her prejudices weren't by design. That she was trying, that she would understand, if he let her.

He paused before the dryer with his back to her. "I understand your reservations. I have them as well. I am a monster with poison living inside me. One wrong touch, one innocent mistake, and someone else is compromised."

The breath she exhaled was ragged and profound, unseen parts of her hurting for Harrison, for the way he saw himself. *Monster.* Beth flinched from the word, and what it implied. How could he think of himself that way? He was no more a monster than she.

"Don't call yourself that," she told him, her voice quaking around the words she almost didn't say.

81

Harrison looked to the side and down, a bitter smile caressing his mouth.

"You know it isn't that easily contracted."

"I don't know anything." Harrison turned back to the dryer. He closed the door and started the dryer. The clothes thumped around inside as the machine hummed. He faced her and crossed his arms. "You say you know it isn't easily contracted and yet you act like it is. Why should I think differently?"

"People react negatively to things they don't understand." Beth's voice was quiet, a silent apology for her actions clear in her tone, if he wanted to hear it.

"People react negatively to things that can harm them," Harrison corrected.

"Tell me how you got it," she implored. "Tell me what you thought, how you felt, how others acted around you. Tell me everything."

"No."

"You have to, Harrison," Beth insisted, the unknown bottled up inside her and scratching to be discovered. It seemed as if she was on a panicked, frustrated quest with no positive outcome. Even so, she couldn't abandon it—just in case there was a positive outcome. "Not because I want to know about it, but because I need to know about you. I need to understand what you're going through. Please tell me."

When he looked back, his expression indifferent, Beth continued, "You can't really expect me to be here with you when you won't divulge any of what you're going through to me. It isn't fair of you, and it isn't fair *to* you."

Tainted humor flared to life on his features, casting the facial bones in derision. "I see. You want me to dig out my heart for *my* benefit. Thank you for your selflessness. I appreciate it. Truly."

Irritation thinned her lips and brought heat to her cheeks. "It might be good for you to talk about it with someone. Do you have anyone to talk to?"

"Didn't you see the line of concerned people standing outside the front door?"

"Fine," she said, determination adding rigidity to her tone.

Harrison dropped his arms and straightened. "Fine?"

Beth nodded and turned to leave the laundry room. "Fine. If you won't talk to me, I won't be here anymore. I can't write about someone who won't tell me anything about them. I didn't say the information had to go in the book, but I need to know it, for me."

"Go ahead and sue me," she called over her shoulder. The hallway was fading away, the door and her exit out of Harrison's life getting closer. *Don't let me leave, give me a reason to stay. I want to stay. Why do I want to stay? I need to stay.* Beth's heartbeat was too hard, the forceful beat of it making her dizzy and disoriented.

"You won't get anything out of it—I'm broke. But you knew that, didn't you? Glad one of us gets to know something about the other." The hook where her jacket hung was less than two feet away, and she could feel the growing chill of her departure. It was wrong, bitter with all that should be and might not. *Stop me. Stop me, Harrison. Stop me!*

Harrison caught up to her as she was reaching for her jacket. She held her breath to keep from letting out a loud sigh. Beth's pulse was mad with fear and hope, and she pressed a palm to her flushed cheek. His hand lightly touched her shoulder, but it was enough to make her halt all movement. There was power in him, even now, even fissured as he was. It could be it was there now more than ever because it had to be.

He slowly turned her around; the face he showed her was awash with contrition. He released his hold as soon as she faced him. "You're asking something of me I'm not sure I'm ready to give, now or ever. Not even my parents, the two people in the world who unconditionally love me, know what it's been like for me."

"Tell me," she whispered.

The weight of a frown tipped down the corners of his mouth, and he shook his head, his movements at odds with his next words. Derision, and maybe a hint of resignation, coated them. "You make me want to tell you."

Beth's eyebrows lifted in surprise at the admission.

Light splintered through the dark of the man before her, only for an instant, only long enough to steal the air from her lungs and shove wonder inside her in its place. Beth couldn't breathe. She didn't fight it, relaxing into the allure of secrets, promises, a plane where thoughts had no purpose, and the only ability given was to feel.

Harrison stared directly into her as he said, "You're the one I want to tell my story to."

$\infty \bullet \infty$

THE SKIES ON the other side of the windowpane turned grim as he talked, the dim light of the lamps in the reading room creating an intimate setting. Although it had stopped at some point during the day, with the current pace of the snow, it didn't seem like it had. Thick and heavy, it dropped from above to coat below, turning their immediate vicinity into stark whiteness trickled through with gray.

"A little over five years I got really sick, rundown. It was like a never-ending cold or flu, and I was told it was most likely due to stress, and to take better care of myself." Harrison looked at the end table beside his chair, the hardness of his jaw belying the calm tone of his voice. "Except I didn't get better. I went back to the doctor. They ran more tests."

Beth's throat was tight. She wanted to tell him to stop talking, naïvely thinking that if she didn't hear him confirm what she knew to be truth, there was a chance it wasn't.

"I didn't believe them at first." Harrison made a bitter sound. "I told them to redo the tests. I got second, and third, and fourth opinions. Eventually, I didn't have any other choice but to believe it. I could only deny it for so long. And then it came down to how I contracted it."

Harrison clenched his fingers, his eyes down. "I don't have any tattoos, I've never done drugs, haven't had any blood transfusions, and the only person I had unprotected sex with was Nina."

He looked up, hollow-eyed. "She had HIV before I knew her, and she never told me."

A draft swept through the room, freezing Beth. She tried to inhale and it came out sounding choked. Frozen, she was frozen in the glare of his twisted story, a fairytale gone wrong, a life altered by a single choice.

"One sentence. One sentence could have made all the difference. It was so pointless, so easily avoidable," he whispered, his eyes on his fingers as he put them in a steeple, an absentminded prayer, and curled them inward, breaking the unspoken entreaty.

Harrison dropped his hands, and his gaze went with them. "Nina had a drug problem when she was younger, but as far as I knew, it was no longer part of her life when we got together. She told me about the former addiction, and how she fought it, and I stupidly believed her. I knew she liked to go out on weekends, but I was busy with my career, and I didn't know. I didn't know what was going on. How could I not know?" He laughed shortly.

"I guess reusing needles wasn't an issue for her, and somewhere along the way, she contracted HIV from her carelessness." He closed his eyes, his shoulders hunched. "People think they are invincible until they are shown they're not. I thought I was."

When the silence grew, shouting out its disquiet, he opened his eyes. "I hated her. For years, I hated her. She tried to apologize, and I was too bitter, too angry—I couldn't even stand the sound of her voice. The sight of her made me sick." Harrison looked up, bleakness stamped into the set of his shoulders. "Now I just feel… numb. A while back my dad told me she isn't doing well, that it's progressed to AIDS. When I found out, I felt empty."

Harrison stared at the floor and said, "I feel nothing."

Beth swallowed, her voice muted. She had no words of comfort, and if she attempted any, they would be insufficient. All the thoughts she had were silent, too many to try to navigate through. Harrison needed this moment to himself, and she gave it to him. She didn't talk until the murky haze slid from his eyes and he blinked at her.

86

"Were you sick a lot?" Her eyes followed the purple path beneath his. They told a story of tiredness even if Harrison never mentioned it. "Are you still?"

"It was a guessing game at first, trying to find out what drugs worked and which ones didn't. I tried multiple antiretroviral medications, and reacted badly to a lot of them, but it's stabilized for now. I check in with my doctor regularly, and for now, I'm as good as can be expected. I don't have the energy I used to have, and I'm tired a lot. I get dizzy, like you saw."

"You've had it for five years," she commented, because she didn't know what else to say, and that was something she could say without overwhelming emotion grabbing hold of her and twisting her up like metal wrapped around steel. Five years with HIV, and how many more until it turned into AIDS? If it did. Harrison's life was surrounded by 'ifs'.

"Five long years," he affirmed.

Beth held the blanket draped over her shoulders closer to her body, warmth evading her as Harrison confessed words that had to cut his throat as they were produced. "What have those five years been like?"

"Oh, you know, lollipops and sunbeams."

She trained her gaze on the coffee table, wondering how she would be if it were her with the disease. Beth rubbed her chilled arms through the blanket. She didn't think she would be handling it as well as Harrison. He'd had time to adapt, but how did a person really adapt to that?

A caricature of a smile lifted half of his mouth when she raised her eyes, and it was a taint against his pale skin. "The rumors have been hard, the outward shunning has probably been the worst. My sexuality was attacked, I was accused of using needles myself. After they found out, people I've known for years acted scared of me, or like they didn't know me."

Memories shattered him as she watched, Beth a silent bystander to a tragedy.

"I could see contempt in their eyes, blame for something I did nothing to contract. I resigned from playing football. I could have kept playing, but I felt like a pariah. A drop of blood and it would have been a threat to anyone in contact. I didn't want to make others uneasy, and I didn't need to feel worse than I already did."

Harrison glanced up at her. "For a long time, I felt hopeless, like I was always swimming toward something I knew I wouldn't reach, just as I knew I would eventually drown."

It was easy to remain unaffected by death when it kept its distance. Beth had never dealt with loss firsthand, not to this extent. Any family members who were gone had been so before she could recall, or she'd only distantly known. A person could feel sad about another's misfortune, but it passed, because it wasn't their world that was directly affected by loss.

But when a person was face to face with it, like Beth was, it was impossible to stay apathetic. Death touched her life, told her someone she knew could be taken at some point, and it shot her mind through with fear, and her heart with sorrow. It didn't go away. It didn't heal.

It stayed, staring her in the face, watching her through Harrison's eyes. She looked at Harrison's face and felt her chest tighten with the thought that one day in the near future he might no longer be. Beth blinked her eyes, but still they filled with tears, overflowing and trickling down her cheeks.

Harrison leaned forward. "Why are you crying?"

"Because it makes me sad."

"Don't waste your sadness on me. There are far worse sorrows worthy of your tears."

"How can you say that?" she asked in a wobbly voice, brushing away warm tears to allow room for more.

"You're sad because you're just learning about it. It's all new to you." He offered the hint of a smile. "I've had years to come to terms with it. I'm not sad anymore."

"I didn't realize you could move past the sadness."

"I suppose I could have chosen to not, but what would that get me? Nothing good. Sometimes I get sad, but I fight it. I've had a good life, I can still have the rest of one, even as compromised as it may be." Harrison looked at her. "I'm not scared to die, Beth. And I said all my goodbyes years ago. I made my peace."

"Now what? Now you just wait?"

He shrugged, showing her a side of himself that was softer, less harsh. As if her tears had the power to release the true man from his black tower of solitude. "I'm not waiting. I'm...convalescing."

"That means to recover."

"Yes." Harrison smiled faintly. "My body may be slowly breaking down, but my mind is flourishing."

"But I don't—I don't understand. You don't see anyone. You don't go anywhere. You don't do anything. It's like you're living half a life. You have this big house and it's filled with *nothing*. Why?"

Harrison leaned forward, his eyes on the floor. "I don't need things, Beth. Things are just that—things. I have my thoughts, and my memories. I have what I need."

"You also have family. Why aren't you with them? You don't seem happy."

Two pale eyebrows lifted along with his gaze. "Don't I? What you perceive with your eyes isn't always what's there."

He stood and approached the couch, sitting beside her but careful to keep space between them. Beth turned her upper half to face him, her lips parted in question. The tears, hot and damp, froze on her cheeks—dried by the heat his proximity produced in her. Harrison moved closer, his eyes stayed by hers.

Beth tensed, her fingers curling into the soft fabric of the blanket. She didn't know what he intended to do, but her pulse quickened in anticipation, not alarm. He leaned forward as if to kiss her, but angled his mouth away at the last instant. Her chest lifted and lowered from the might of her emotions.

He put his mouth near her ear, and his voice was a caress, deep and thick with emotion. "Sometimes, Beth, you have to look with your mind." Sitting back, Harrison tapped her head. "You have to look deeper than what is shown on the surface." His eyes dropped. "You have to see with your heart."

"Can I—" Beth reached out a shaking hand to him, knowing she shouldn't. Knowing he'd pull back. "Can I hug you?"

"Why?" The word was short, one syllable and yet chopped in two around his exhalation.

"I don't know. I just—I want to," she answered, letting her hand drop to her lap. Her fingers longed to touch him, to give him comfort. Beth wanted him to know she wasn't repulsed by him, that she didn't see him as a monster. She wanted to let him know he wasn't alone.

"You act like I'm going to expire before you. I'm not going to die in the next few months. You're safe." Harrison sat with his back to the couch and his eyes on the bookcase across the room. "I could have twenty more years."

"You could have ten."

He turned his head and regarded her. "I could have thirty. Stop thinking about my death. It's forbidden until it's actually here."

Beth snorted, but when he didn't relinquish eye contact, she nodded.

Harrison got up and she shot to her feet as well, her nerves unreliable and spastic. She fidgeted with the blanket, and then pulled it from her frame, quickly folding and setting it on the back of the couch. When that was done, she watched Harrison, taking in his fiery hair and fearsome eyes. He stood still, unyielding, thoughts flittering across his features as he examined her. Harrison looked at Beth like he was deciding something about her.

"I, um, I should get going," she explained when he gave her an inquiring look. "It's…" Beth turned to the clock and gasped. "It's after six."

Panic spun her in a half-circle and she fled from the room, blinking her eyes at the darkness she hadn't been aware was creeping up on them. Beth was on the schedule to bartend at eight that night at The Lucky Coin. That didn't give her much time to get home—especially with the weather—eat something, and shower. She sped toward the laundry room, flinging off the pants and shimmying into her jeans. Her hands trembled with the thought of being late for work, prolonging her clumsy attempts to fold the pants. Grabbing her socks from the dryer, she quickly exchanged Harrison's for hers.

Jogging into the foyer, Beth shoved her feet into her boots, put on her coat, and flung open the door with the intention of wiping the snow off the car and letting it warm up for a few minutes before leaving. Icy air blasted her face and stole her breaths, snow rushing toward her. She muttered a curse. Black and white met her gaze, stinging enough to cause her eyes to water, and she squinted against the elements. The SUV was barely visible, a mound of an unidentifiable object beneath layers of packed fluffy white substance, and it was still coming.

"I wouldn't advise driving home in that. The plows won't go by until it has stopped, and the driveway will be not be addressed until morning."

She slammed shut the door and turned to look at Harrison. The havoc outside was jarring in comparison to the quiet inside the house. "I have to. I'm supposed to work tonight. I should have been paying better attention to what was going on outside." *Instead of getting lost in you.*

"Call them, tell them you're stranded outside of town. I'm sure they'll understand."

Ozzy wouldn't understand, and he'd be the second person to know after she talked to one of his parents. Whether or not it was the smartest decision, she could see him being adamant about coming to get her. Ozzy couldn't know where she was, let alone risk his safety to come to her rescue in the tumultuous weather. He also couldn't know about Harrison, or his anonymity would be compromised.

And she couldn't stay at Harrison's. It was a familiarity they should not share. Beth had to leave. There was no other option.

Beth shook her head. "I have to go."

Harrison reached around her, grabbing his own jacket. "Let's get you home then."

She looked away before he could catch the protestation on her face, but Beth knew he sensed it anyway. Harrison was intuitive, and she was sure he'd had lots of practice garnering peoples' true thoughts even while they didn't voice them.

"Get over it," was all he said.

Exhaling slowly, Beth nodded. She would, somehow.

FIVE

PROPERLY ATTIRED, SHE stepped out and into what felt like a blizzard. Her legs were covered midway up to her calves in snow as she lumbered through the thick coldness. *What am I doing?* The wind whipped the strands of her hair not anchored down by her stocking cap up and in her face. She could see her breaths, and her nose and cheeks were instantly assaulted. It literally hurt to be outside. Beth zipped up the jacket to her chin, the material rubbing against her sensitive skin.

Harrison met her eyes, a question in his.

Beth shrugged and turned to the vehicle.

Small tremors ran through her body as she pried open the door of the Blazer. The metal was stuck together by ice, and it took multiple tries, her fingers aching by the time she got the door to cooperate. Snow tumbled down the side of the vehicle, landing inside the car and on her. The Abominable Snowman was not on her list of things to be today. Beth allowed herself a moment to calm down as she brushed aside the snow, but she was still stiff-jawed and irate as she went about retracting the scraper from the backseat.

When she straightened, her eyes unconsciously looked for Harrison. "Harrison?" The wind caught Beth's voice and sent away the word like she had never spoken.

She closed the door and turned, seeing the outlines of trees in the valleys below the hill line. Beth faced the house. It was hard to see more than a few feet in front of her, and when she didn't find him, Beth's pulse tripled its beat, and she hurried as fast as she could through the snow to the other side of the vehicle. She opened her mouth to call out again when she heard a scraping sound. Beth angled her head to the side and picked out a dark figure at the front of the Blazer, his form bent over at the waist and hard to distinguish.

"What are you doing?" she demanded as she stopped near him.

Harrison paused with a shovel in his hand and looked up. His eyes matched the shade of the night sky, his skin reddened by the below zero temperatures and powerful wind gusts. "I'm shoveling."

"I know that," she huffed, feeling silly.

He inclined his head and went back to work.

Beth started clearing off the Blazer, but as quickly as the snow was removed, it was substituted for more. After about twenty minutes, she admitted defeat, chucking the scraper to the ground. Her fingers and toes were numb, and her face ached from being so cold. She stared down the driveway, and all she saw was white. She looked up, and all she saw was more white. Beth turned her gaze to Harrison, seeing a man framed by white. Gripping the handlebar, he rested his chin on his gloved hands and waited, his eyebrows lifted.

"This is pointless."

"It is," he agreed.

"But you knew I had to find that out on my own, didn't you?"

He didn't reply, shoveling a path to the house. She couldn't fault his logic. People generally needed to see things for themselves in order to believe them. Beth picked up the scraper and put it back in the vehicle as Harrison finished up, meeting him at the side door to the garage. He was breathing hard, and even with the limited visibility, she could tell all the color was gone from his face.

"How are you doing?" she asked, examining his features.

His mouth twisted at the inquiry, but he spoke evenly as he said, "Well enough."

"Look at you, answering questions and stuff."

Harrison's eyes narrowed.

Smiling to herself, Beth stepped forward too fast and slid on ice hidden by snow, her arms shooting up and her legs flying out from under her. With a grunt leaving her, she landed on her back, her head thumping against the shoveled part of the ground. The air rushed from her lungs in a painful gasp. It didn't take long for the snow to chill her entire body. As she ascertained she was not seriously hurt, Beth stared up at the swirling snow, thinking it deceptive as the snowflakes swayed and swirled like mini, frozen tornadoes. It was beautiful to look at, but that's as far as the exquisiteness went.

Harrison dropped to his knees next to her, concern pinching the sides of his mouth. She shifted her eyes to him. His irises looked like two black coals in the dark. He touched her shoulder and immediately removed his gloved hand as if scorched. "Can you move?"

It took her a moment to catch her breath, her mouth ineffectively opening and closing. "S-stupid…s-snow," she got out around chattering teeth.

The skin around Harrison's eyes crinkled as he showed her how a full smile looked upon his face. Both corners lifted, and there were teeth. She lost her breath again. His eyes softened, light dancing in the black. "You should write winter a very stern letter, listing all your complaints against it."

"Number one...would be the stupid snow," she told him, smiling back.

His head tilted back as he laughed, dropping his gaze to her face. The mirth lingered on his features with sharp, masculine charm. All Harrison had to do was smile and laugh and Beth forgot all sense. Good thing it didn't seem to happen often. "Let's get you up before you turn into a life-sized Popsicle."

The process was slow and awkward, mainly because anytime Beth went to use Harrison as an anchor, he moved away. She was on her knees with him crouched next to her, gazing at him in exasperation when she finally said, "Are you afraid to touch me?"

He looked away. "I know you'd rather I didn't."

"You're wrong," Beth told him, conviction strident in her tone. "You told me to get over it and I'm over it. All of it. I wouldn't have asked to hug you if I wasn't."

Doubt lingered in his expression. "Just like that, huh?"

"Just like that." She nodded.

"Why?" he asked faintly.

"Why, what?"

"Why did you want to hug me?"

Her body flooded with warmth, and Beth felt her heart reach toward the man beside her. It wanted to designate all the hurting parts of him as hers, and heal them. "Because I think you needed one, and maybe I just wanted a hug."

He dropped his attention to the ground, the weight of a million invisible bricks resting on his shoulders.

For Harrison's benefit, Beth changed the subject. "Can we please do this already? I'm really, really cold."

Harrison swallowed thickly, giving a short nod.

It was much faster to get her to stand after that. With an arm around her waist, he helped her to the door. Beth leaned into him, enjoying his heat, and the firmness of his body on hers. She was lightheaded, and it wasn't from the fall. Harrison entered the garage and turned on a light. Beth stepped in after him, shutting the door on the seasonal chaos. Her body convulsed in tiny tremors, her face numb and her lips felt dry and cracked. A hot bath, fluffy pajamas, food, and a bed were all she wanted.

"What time were you supposed to be at work?"

The room was stark white, two shelves set up along the farthest wall to house tools and other items Beth couldn't name, but that she knew were mandatory to men. A sleek black Ford truck stood tall and proud, its monetary worth clear with a glance at its shiny exterior.

She focused on Harrison, her cheeks burning as their gazes clashed. "Eight."

He nodded, removing his stocking cap to reveal untidy hair. It gave him a hint of boyishness that made it hard for her to swallow. "You should call them. I'll get you some more dry clothes."

"Can I...would it be okay if I took a bath? And, um, do you have a long-sleeved shirt I can wear to...to bed? I get cold easily."

Beth shifted her feet as his eyes bored into hers. Her innocent questions somehow sounded like propositions to her ears and she hoped he didn't hear the same. She didn't even know where her bed would be.

"Yes," he said slowly, careful to keep his attention from her as he answered. "Of course. I'll fix us something to eat as well—if you're hungry?"

"Yes. I am. Thank you."

Once he disappeared through the attached door to the house, Beth tugged off her gloves and fumbled about in her pocket, searching for her forgotten cell phone. She stared at the screen, knowing if she called in to work under false pretenses, the culpability would hover over her for weeks. But if she called in to work with the truth, it would be worse. If she asked her friend and coworker, Jennifer Travis, to work for her, she probably would, but then Ozzy would wonder what was going on and try to investigate.

Phone clenched tightly in her hand, Beth weighed her options before coming to what she felt was the best decision.

Beth sent Ozzy a text saying she'd hurt her back and couldn't easily move and asked him to work her shift for her. It was a short one—only four hours—and hopefully, it wouldn't interfere with his plans for the night. She felt the pause in his response, but he agreed. Another text came, asking if she needed anything or wanted him to stop by later and check on her.

Beth swallowed down a sick sensation and told him thanks, but she was going to rest and wouldn't need anything. It was a partial truth, at least. Only the knowledge that she was protecting Harrison's identity helped salvage the guilt as it slashed down her back like sharp, ominous nails.

She was falsifying information to one man to keep another's secret.

Harrison waited in the large entryway, disengaging from the shadows as she entered the house. "Get everything taken care of?"

"I found someone to fill in for me, yes." Beth didn't meet his eyes, feeling unnaturally shy about staying over.

After a tense-filled minute, Harrison said, "There are clothes and toiletries in the bathroom I showed you earlier. Take your time."

When she reached the bathroom, her eyes went to the cleaning spray, sitting where Harrison had left it. The disease couldn't be spread by using the same restroom as someone with it. There were all kinds of ways it could not be spread that fear made people forget—made her forget. Beth shoved the bottle back to its spot in the cupboard and went about filling the tub. Lavender scented bubble bath was set out for her, and she smiled as she sniffed it, adding it to the water.

The room turned into a steam room as heat rose from the hot water, and Beth lingered in the relaxing bubble bath until the water turned cold and her fingers and toes were wrinkled. She was tired, and her lower back was sore from where she hit it as she landed. Beth fought to keep her eyes open as she dressed in velvety smooth gray and black plaid pajamas. There was a packaged red toothbrush sitting on the counter for her to use before bed. She carefully brushed her hair with the comb she found in a drawer, wiping a circle in the mirror to view her blurry face. With Beth as exhausted as she was, she imagined Harrison had to be doubly so.

Tracking down the sounds of movement, Beth walked through the hallway and veered to the right. Harrison was at the kitchen counter, clad in another set of clothes, his copper hair damp and curling up in spots. His back was to her as he prepared something to eat. She smelled the distinctive scent of tuna fish and her stomach contracted with hunger, making a rude rumble in the quiet. Beth set her wet clothes on the edge of the counter.

"Hungry?"

"Yes," she told him. There was no point in denying it.

"Do you like tuna fish? Onions, lettuce, pickles, tomatoes?"

"I'm not picky. I like everything."

Harrison glanced over his shoulder, the smallest of smiles evident.

She didn't look away, not able to break eye contact. Harrison did, his gaze dropping to her garments and quickly sliding away. Beth took a deep breath, telling herself that whatever she was feeling for Harrison, she needed to restrain it. Sometimes when she looked at him, all she saw was the disease. Other times all she saw was the man. Both were detrimental, but for different reasons.

"Avocadoes?"

"Yes," she answered.

"Beets?"

"Of course."

Harrison met her eyes. "Liver."

Beth brushed hair from her eyes and shook her head, fighting a smile. "You got me. No to the liver."

"I'm the same," he said. "No to the liver."

Without asking, she opened the refrigerator and perused its contents. It was surprisingly well-stocked with fruits, vegetables, cheeses, and yogurt. She chose orange juice for her, looking over the refrigerator door toward Harrison. "What do you want to drink?"

"Whatever you're having is fine."

"Glasses?" She put the container of orange juice on the counter. Following the direction of Harrison's finger, she found a set of clear glasses. She poured orange juice in each and refrigerated the container.

Beth took her damp clothes from the counter and carried them to the laundry room. The dryer was already running, and unsure what she was to do with hers, she stood in the center of the room and looked around. She turned, and not expecting to see Harrison, gasped as her pulse tripped.

Lightning scorched the pupils of his eyes as they came to hers. In the semi-dark, Harrison's countenance turned dangerous. Graceful, lupine. His hungry gaze stripped away her clothes and looked at her naked flesh. It was an illusion of the night, but her body felt the singe of his gaze upon her like handprints. There were at least half a dozen feet from him to her, but it felt like nothing separated them. Nothing but all the ugliness of the world.

"You can hang your clothes on the rack over there," he said in a voice like sandpaper.

"Okay," she answered faintly. Beth's heartbeat pounded loudly in her ears. "Thanks."

Harrison showed her his back and stepped away, into the dimly lit kitchen.

With careful movements, she set her jeans, shirt, and socks on a bar of the clothes rack, noticing the shakiness of her hands. Beth let her head fall forward and closed her eyes, her hair curtaining either side of her face. Her emotions and thoughts were a mess, going one way while fighting to go another. She felt sick, but it wasn't an entirely bad feeling. That look he'd given her, she couldn't get that look out of her head.

The scent of Harrison's clothes was embedded in her skin, and she welcomed it. Beth was afraid, and it wasn't because of Harrison—she was afraid of her response to him. He was compromised, and he was as exquisite as the darkest, deadliest flower.

She strolled into the kitchen, pretending whatever just happened hadn't happened. "I'll leave first thing in the morning, after your driveway is plowed. I, uh, have to, um—I'll be back in a minute."

Beth didn't look at him. She didn't need to, to know where he was—she felt him. The room smelled of him, was alive with his warmth, shrunken with his presence. Beth hurried her footsteps, needing space from Harrison in order to properly breathe. She was overheated, nervous and edgy. She didn't trust herself around him, something she'd never had to struggle with before. Beth felt out of control and wild.

"Beth."

The pull of his voice, more an entreaty than a command, halted her. She waited, her back to him.

"Whatever romanticisms or fantasies your imaginative mind is coming up with, stop them all. You'll only get hurt if you don't."

She pirouetted like a ballerina in slow motion.

Harrison stood near the sink, his jaw as taut as wire. It looked as if he physically fought an unseen foe, one who attacked him even as his eyes delved into hers. Was he fearful of *her*? Beth's eyes narrowed. No, not of her, but of his reaction to her. She understood that all too well.

"What did you just say?" she rasped, disbelief adding a breathless quality to the words.

"You're attracted to the forbidden element of our association." Harrison moved closer. "I'm your employer. I'm...unwell." His eyes drilled into hers. "All reasons to stay away, and all obstacles that can be viewed as a challenge to some."

"And you're crazy," she scoffed, even as her body hummed with awareness. She wasn't a daredevil, or someone who chased danger. If she was attracted to any part of him, it would be his strength, or his mind. Not the state of his health or what it represented.

Fire crackled within the depths of his eyes and half of his mouth crooked in a sardonic grin. "Not yet."

"I'm not like that." Her voice sounded weak. Beth cleared her throat, trying to speak firmly and failing again. "I wouldn't... wouldn't do that. That isn't—no."

"Good." Harrison stopped walking when there was an arm's length between them. Close enough to touch, close enough to kiss. "I must have imagined the look I thought I saw in your eyes."

Beth moved around him and grabbed one of the two plates housing a tuna fish sandwich, pretending like her skin wasn't flushed or that her hands didn't quiver. She sat down on a barstool at the island, taking a large bite of the sandwich. It was good, a lemon garlic taste smoothing the tuna fish flavor.

Swallowing, she said, "I must have imagined the same look I thought I saw in your eyes."

৪১ ◆ ৫৭

AFTER THEY HAD eaten their light meal in silence, Beth helped clean up the mess and was shown a spare bedroom down the hall from Harrison's. It was as far away as he could put her from his bedroom while having her remain on the same floor. She spent the hours until she fell asleep reading the book about the boy who, motherless and alone, grew into a man great enough to rule countries. It was a story of unparalleled drive, showing how obstacles had to be taken down from within before they could be overcome on the outside.

Her eyes drifted closed not long after the last word was read, the driving question of why it was Harrison's favorite book prominent in her mind.

As soon as dawn lightened the sky, she was up and out the door. Beth wanted to look back at the house before getting into the warmed up Blazer, and because of that, she wouldn't let herself. The roads were clear, and the open skies and fresh air righted her thoughts once more. She wasn't attracted to Harrison. It would be a horrible mistake to think she was.

It was simply because they'd been together for so many hours yesterday, just the two of them, and the circumstances brought on familiarity that wasn't really there. Confused her. Put hunger in his eyes and in her bones. Beth groaned, shaking her head in denial of what her body told her was true. When she went back that afternoon, everything would make sense again.

The undetectable wall would be back in place.

"Yes. Yes, it will."

Beth made a stop at the grocery store on her way home, stocking up on essentials that were running low. Ozzy's truck appeared outside her house as she was removing the grocery bags from the back of the Blazer, the loud and obnoxious rumble of it announcing his arrival. She softly cursed, not surprised by his appearance but aggravated just the same. His brother's wife worked at Chester's Grocer, and it made sense that she would inform Ozzy of Beth's stop at the store so early in the morning.

Anything out of the ordinary was suspect, and Beth grocery shopping at an hour she was normally sleeping qualified. There were spies everywhere, and if she ever truly wanted to be free from Ozzy, Beth knew she would have to move out of town. But her parents were here. She wasn't ready for that.

She set down the bags and waited for him to approach.

"You lied," were the first words he said to her.

His square jaw was tight and his golden eyes glittered with anger. He wore jeans and his jean jacket with a blue hooded flannel shirt beneath it. His brown hair swirled around his head like he'd jumped out of bed and raced to her house without brushing it—and he probably had.

"You weren't home with a bad back. I was worried about you and stopped by after filling in for you at The Lucky Coin. The Blazer was gone. You weren't home. Where were you, really?" The freezing air singed his skin, turning it pink.

"How do you know the Blazer was gone?" Her lips were stiff, frozen with cold and Ozzy's anger.

"The side door to the garage was unlocked." Ozzy shifted his eyes to the left, the motion announcing the lie.

Beth stared at Ozzy, a wave of dread sweeping over her. She always made sure every door was locked. Always. "You were in my house?"

"No," he denied, still not looking at her.

The landlord was a family friend of the Pecks', and if Ozzy showed up at his house with concern over Beth's welfare, would he give him a key? Her stomach spun with sickness. Beth didn't want to believe it. She was beginning to feel like she wasn't safe from Ozzy anywhere. She was beginning to feel like she needed to be afraid of him. Did he still have the key? Had he made a copy? What had he done inside her house while she was gone?

She took a step back, the sky swirling overhead and shifting to the side. Beth shook her head and put a steadying hand against the Blazer. "Please tell me you didn't break into my house," she whispered.

"I didn't. I saw your car was gone, and I left." Ozzy finally looked at her, a slash of eyes that showed no warmth. "But if I had, it would have been justified. I thought there was something wrong. I thought you were hurt."

Anger boiled through her, heated her skin from the inside out. All of Ozzy's actions were excusable, no matter if they were right or wrong. He was without blame, always.

"It's none of your business where I was or what I was doing."

"How can you *say* that? It is my business!" Ozzy swallowed and looked around to see if they had an audience. In a quieter voice, he continued. "It is my business when you ask me to work for you, and then lie about why you aren't going to be able to work. Where were you? Do you have a new boyfriend, is that it?"

Beth's cold skin blazed with fury and her mouth twisted with it. "I did hurt my back, and I couldn't work. I didn't lie about either of those things."

"Is there someone else, Beth? Are you—are you in love with someone else?" Ozzy demanded like she hadn't spoken, his voice vibrating with wrath, and something else.

An ache she recognized from her own heart, and voice, once upon a time. It was the startling moment when it became clear that the one she loved could be with someone else. It was disbelief and insanity and denial, all neatly packed together, all ready to unravel the person at the slightest provocation.

Ozzy realized that she could move on. She could love another. Her heart was not only to be his. He moved on, but he never thought she would. And he thought he could come back, every time. Because she'd let him, but not anymore. Beth deserved more than what he could give her. She deserved better.

"It doesn't matter," she told him, her eyes hot with disenchantment. "It's over between us. You need to admit that to yourself. And you have to stop showing up whenever you feel like it, and tell your family to quit keeping tabs on me. I don't appreciate it."

"You don't care about me at all, do you?" His expression was wounded.

Beth took a deep breath, trying to calm her speeding pulse. Arguing with him did nothing but give him power. She wasn't letting him have power over her anymore. Beth was taking it back. Ozzy was a manipulator, and he didn't even realize it. It took Beth years to see it. A manipulator, and a liar—two things that should be avoided in life, as they made people doubt their instincts. Instincts were always right.

"It isn't that, and you know it."

"Is there even really a job?" The anger faded to sorrow, and looking into his devastated eyes was like looking into her own a year in the past.

"Yes, there is a job," she hissed. Beth reached for the groceries. "This is *my life*, and it is separate from yours. Accept it. I have to get these inside. Go home, Ozzy."

Ozzy grabbed the remaining bags and hefted them into his arms. He looked defiantly back when she opened her mouth to tell him she didn't need help. Not wanting to keep arguing, but also knowing it was wrong to give in, Beth shook her head and walked through the plowed driveway. Her face reddened at the knowledge that Ozzy must have cleared the snow for her. Guilt tightened her throat.

She tried the doorknob. The door was unlocked, and that gave her pause. Had she been so upset over learning what she had about Harrison that she'd forgotten to lock the doors on her way out? It was possible. She took a quick breath and entered the house through the garage, kicking off her boots before stepping inside.

The warmth was appreciated, and as Beth took in her living quarters, she felt like she was home. She couldn't recall feeling that way before. The house was alien for so long, but now it was hers. Beth had missed sleeping in it last night. She'd been dependent on Ozzy for so long that it had taken her a while to realize she liked her freedom. The only thing wrong with the house was her ex-boyfriend's presence. She would talk to her landlord about Ozzy and make sure her privacy hadn't been violated, a task she wouldn't enjoy, but one that was necessary.

Ozzy's eyes were weights on her back as he followed her to the kitchen, and she wondered if that was how Harrison had felt when she'd stared at him as they walked. Dissected. She felt dirty in her worn clothes, like all of the activities of yesterday were visible in the wrinkles of the fabric and the unkemptness of her appearance. Beth's most secret thoughts and feelings were shouting from her skin, and Ozzy was observing them all.

"You missed it—there was a fight at the bar last night." Ozzy set down the bags on the counter and looked around the room. His moods switched without warning, the wrath absent and friendliness in its place. Beth never understood how he could do that. When she was mad, she stayed mad for a while.

Beth started putting away the food, glancing at Ozzy as she worked. She wanted him to go, and the best way to get that to happen was to be agreeable. "Who?"

He drummed his fingers on the countertop. "Denny Imhoff and Jason Hilton. They were playing cards and Denny accused Jason of cheating."

"Was he?"

Ozzy grinned. "Well, yeah, but he always does. Denny just decided to take offense to it last night."

"I'm sure drinking was involved."

"Of course." Ozzy handed the half-gallon of milk to Beth.

"Thanks." She put away the last of the groceries. At his raised eyebrows, she added, "For helping carry in the groceries. And plowing the driveway. Did you use your brother's plow truck?"

"Yeah. And it's no big deal. I didn't want you shoveling with your hurt back."

The allegation was covered in silk, but she caught it, and she resented it. Neither spoke as their gazes locked in place. Ozzy's eyes were hooded and dark.

Her jacket vibrated and Beth pulled out the cell phone, breaking the stare. She didn't recognize the number associated with the text message, but she knew who it was from. Harrison. He said she didn't need to come over today.

A frown tugged at her mouth. Beth couldn't remember if she'd given him her number, not that it mattered. He had it. Why didn't he want her to come over? Disappointment, shocking in its amount, engulfed her body. Her hand dropped to her side.

"What's wrong?"

Beth looked at Ozzy, saw the questions and suspicions in his eyes. "Nothing. I don't have to go to work today. It's an unexpected free day, that's all."

His gaze dropped to the phone. "Your boss sends you text messages? Isn't that a little unorthodox?"

"They don't like talking on the phone," she quickly told him.

"I guess anyone who doesn't want people to know who they are must be strange." Ozzy talked in an agreeable tone, but Beth knew it was a ruse. A calculated gleam darkened his eyes to burnished gold. He was digging for information.

Refusing to comment, Beth gathered the empty plastic bags and shoved them under the sink, her back protesting the motion. She didn't remember how much she'd told Ozzy about her job or boss, and she wasn't going to say more and indirectly give away something of Harrison.

"I have stuff to do," she said as she straightened, giving him a pointed look.

111

Ozzy looked at his boots and nodded. "Right. Me too. I guess I should get going."

He strode to her, pulling her into his arms before she could move out of reach. Beth remained stiff, not allowing herself to sink into his embrace and their history. Ozzy smelled like snow and a warped love. Once she was happy with him, once he had her heart. Once. It was dangerous to think of moments that no longer were.

"Let me go," she commanded quietly, careful not to move.

Ozzy kissed her forehead and caressed her hair, and her skin crawled at the wrongness of it. "I can't. I can't not have you in my life in some way, Beth."

"Ozzy, please."

He pulled away, pain adding grooves to his face, making it seem older and harder. "You've been part of my life since I was a kid. You're part of me."

"It'll get easier," she told him, trying to believe the words. Beth wanted him to forget about her, about what they used to have. Neither of them would truly be free until he did.

"It's been months. It hasn't gotten easier."

"But you're dating. I know you've had girlfriends. It's hypocritical of you to act hurt at the thought of me being with someone else when you're already there." Beth stepped away, putting her back to him as she crossed the room.

She looked into the living room, her eyes landing on the laptop where it rested on the coffee table. Already she craved a connection to Harrison, even if it was through a computer. Words. She needed to write about him. Anticipation shot through her with energy, and Beth felt the hum in her veins. She wanted to forget all the ways her heart had bled for Ozzy, and she could do that with the magnetism of Harrison's untold story.

Beth looked at Ozzy. "You've been with other women. Don't pretend you haven't."

His eyes shifted down and away, the tightness of his jaw admitting he had. "It doesn't change how I feel about you."

"But it changed how I feel about you," she told him, crossing her arms. "Too much has happened. We can't go back. That's wrong. It's wrong to try to live in the past, Ozzy."

"Don't say that," he pleaded, crossing the room to her. "Don't designate me to a part of your past, Beth. Please."

She looked to the right of him, her gaze moving to him as she spoke. "If you need a night off from the bar sometime, let me know and I'll cover it if I can. To make up for you filling in for me."

His mouth contorted. "I don't want your gratitude."

Beth didn't say anything.

Veils dropped over his eyes, and coldness descended. It chilled her blood, looking into Ozzy's eyes and seeing nothing. A stranger looked back at her, and trepidation unfurled in her chest. She'd seen him angry before, but only once, had she seen him furious. Beth had hoped to never see that side of him again. Rejection did not sit well with Ozzy.

"It didn't have to be this way." Although his words had no inflection and seemed calmly spoken, Beth took them as they were meant to be—a warning.

Ozzy left through the front door, and as soon as the door closed, she was there to lock it. Beth took steadying breaths, her hands trembling as she pressed them to her mouth. She was overreacting.

Nothing bad was going to happen. Ozzy was hurt, but he'd get over it. Eventually, he'd become serious about someone else, and Beth would no longer hold any interest for him.

She worried about the time until then, though, a sense of fore-boding beating along with her heart.

SIX

AFTER STARING AT the computer screen for over an hour and producing a total of thirteen words, Beth decided it was time for a change of scenery. She had plenty of notes and thoughts, but she wasn't sure how to put them all together. The story wasn't close to being ready to be written, not even the first page. Beth needed more of Harrison, and that wasn't happening today. Part of her worried that he was sick and that that was why he'd told her not to come, but Beth told herself it wasn't any of her concern.

Telling herself that didn't make her worry any less. How could she care about him so quickly, so completely?

"Feelings cannot be decided by time," she told herself with a single nod, and then raced for pen and paper to jot it down before she forgot it. Somewhere, sometime, those words would be needed.

Bundling up in layers of clothes and stuffing herself into her winter outerwear, Beth left the warmth of her home to trek through the snow and cold. She felt disoriented from switching from Harrison's reality to her own. Hers seemed trivial in comparison. What did she have to worry about? Bills and an obsessed ex-boyfriend.

Darkness hovered around Harrison, murky and impenetrable.

Beth looked up at the fiery sun, wanting to break through Harrison's darkness. Like the sun. She smiled and took a right at the end of her driveway, heading toward her parents' home. Harrison would resent her trying. He would tell her that wasn't why he'd hired her. Beth shrugged to herself. She was beginning to wonder why he'd hired her at all. His reasoning didn't strike her as being entirely truthful. Her brain was full of unanswered questions, and it weighed on her.

She quickened her pace as she passed Ozzy's brother's house, knowing someone inside probably had their eyes on the window and were watching her. Beth contemplated flipping them off, but refrained. She swore Ozzy went there as often as he did with the hopes of catching her in one of her many walks. Too many coincidental interactions with her ex made Beth think they were premeditated.

Her steps lightened as she turned down another street and the house disappeared from view. Harrison's intense eyes flashed through her head, and Beth stumbled as her pulse went into hiatus. The way he'd looked at her last night, the words he'd spoken. The heat, the tension. It made her stomach swirl and her hands shake. Harrison might be surrounded by obscurity, but there was passion in him as well. She was crazy to let herself think of him in any capacity other than as her employer.

She closed her eyes and took a calming breath before focusing on the houses around her. A lot of them were small to medium in size, some rundown and in need of repair, but there were a few that boasted of their owner's wealth. Splashes of color peeked out from beneath white, and as she watched, a chunk of snow slid off a roof to crash to the ground below. It moved like a frozen wave and sounded like thunder.

Houses were odd. People built them, lived in them for a while, and then they sold them. Another family moved in, moved out. Houses were recycled. Redecorated. Remodeled. Made into homes and then abandoned for another. It always struck her as strange that a home of one family could turn into a home for another. Their lives were imprinted in the walls, layers and layers of hopes and dreams and fears. Loss and love.

It was interesting how barren the town seemed in the winter, especially on the colder days. The houses appeared deserted, as did the cars parked in driveways and along the streets. People didn't go outside unless it was necessary—except for Beth, who was asking to get sick. The heat of the sun helped to keep her somewhat unfrozen, but as she finished the two-mile walk, Beth's cheeks and ears ached.

The Lambert house was white with black shutters and shingles. In the warmer months, yellow and red flowers bloomed in rock-edged beds while more were set out in pots. Beth had grown up helping her mom with her flowers and gardens in the spring and summer, a task she used to grumble about, but one she appreciated more as she got older. Being kept busy was a good thing, and having tasks and chores taught values not otherwise known. Of course, being responsible and practical never could dampen Beth's imagination.

She always wanted to tell stories; do things that could be retold as great stories.

Beth's eyes found the leafless tree she used to climb with Ozzy and then jump from, much to her mom's consternation. Beth was a princess, trying to save her prince. Or an explorer searching for lost

117

treasure. Jane looking for Tarzan. She never realized it then, but she was usually saving Ozzy, even as they played.

Her mom would chase them around the yard until they ran off and found something else to do, telling Beth she didn't need her daughter to break any bones when she had two boys who did it often enough as kids.

It was a poignant memory—spun in sorrow and joy. Ozzy was a sweet boy, but as the years went, he changed. Gradually, but irrefutably. One day Beth looked at him and didn't know him anymore. She mourned that little boy. The hint of a smile dropped from her face, and she inhaled deeply, wondering how the man in her house earlier that morning could be the boy she grew up with.

"Beth!" Her mom waved from the open door. "What are you doing standing out in this cold?"

"Hi, Mom." She waved back and approached the house. "Just remembering things."

"You can remember them inside, where it's warmer."

Sandy Lambert had blonde hair a shade darker than her daughter's. She kept hers short, saying she didn't want to mess with it when she had more important things to do. Her frame, once muscular and fit, had softened with age. She was still a formidable force, someone Beth strived to be like. Dressed in ragged purple shorts, pink slippers, and a gray tee shirt, she should be cold, but appeared to be too hearty to give in to it.

The look she leveled at Beth as she passed was penetrating and mixed with a dab of concern. "How are things with you? You look tired."

"Good. I got up early, that's all," she explained as her mom closed the front door after her. "I wasn't sure if you had the day off or not."

The living room, with its pale paneled walls and brown carpet, hadn't changed much since she'd graduated from high school, a small detail she appreciated. Her dad's brown recliner had been replaced with a dark blue one when the first one went kaput, and there were more recent family pictures on the walls, but otherwise, it looked much the same as it always had. No matter where life took her, inside the white house with the black shutters would always be her first home, and how she would base all future ones.

"I have the morning off, but we're getting a shipment of tools in later this morning, and your dad will need help sorting through it all. You know how he is—gets frazzled over everything. I'm heading over to the hardware store after lunch. You hungry?"

Her mom marched from the room without waiting for a response. Beth's parents had owned and run Lambert Hardware for the past thirty years. Her dad was always working on some project, and her mom was there with him, looking over his shoulder and rolling her eyes.

Beth removed her boots and coat, sweating now that she was no longer outside. It smelled like fresh baked bread in the house, a scent that grew as she stepped into the kitchen. The pale green room was small and cluttered, only a sliver of the refrigerator able to be seen under the photos and papers magnetized to it. Her mom liked to decorate with pigs, and there were little pink beings spread throughout the room.

She was handed a red bowl and a plate with an oversized slice of homemade bread with melting butter. Beth took them and sat at the square table in the center of the room, setting down the bowl before it further burned her fingers. "Thank you."

"How's the writing coming along? And the new project?"

Beth shifted in her seat, keeping her eyes down. "Slow, but okay. I haven't written much. It's only been a few days," she added.

Her mom didn't reply, stirring the soup around with her spoon.

"What's new with you?" she asked her mom, not keen on small talk but feeling anxious at the thought of silence.

"Benny and Jake are coming home Wednesday with their families and are staying for a few days. You'll be here for Thanksgiving next week?" It was asked like a question, but it wasn't. It was a confirmation of something already labeled as fact.

She dipped her spoon in the homemade tomato soup, blew on it before putting it in her mouth, and swallowed. Her mom believed in eating food personally made instead of in a factory as much as was feasible. The tomatoes used in the soup were from her garden. The soup was hot and filling, a blend of spices giving zip to the tomato base.

Benny and Jake were her older brothers, both smart enough to move from Crystal Lake as soon as they were able. Benny lived in Wisconsin and worked as a computer specialist, fixing problems that may arise with programming software. He was married with one daughter. Jake was the middle child, recently married with a baby on the way, and lived in a city three hours away. He was the manager of a sporting goods store.

"I miss Benny and Jake, and I haven't seen Benny in months. I will definitely be here. Where else would I be?" Harrison. She instinctively knew he would try to spend the holiday alone, like it was an ordinary day. Her stomach dipped, and she swallowed.

"Amanda Hensley stopped in at the store yesterday and said you and Ozzy had been spotted together at The Lucky Coin. I thought maybe it meant a reconciliation was in the works, and if so, you might be at his Thanksgiving instead of ours."

"So what if we were seen together there? We both work there. It doesn't mean anything."

Her mom tore off a chunk of bread and popped it in her mouth. "It was implied you were on a date."

Beth's face went hot, and she let the spoon drop from her hand. It made a small splash as it hit the soup. "We weren't on a date. He asked me to get a drink with him. Anyway, it was a mistake." She clenched her hands into fists. "This town needs to find better ways to spend their time than talking about the people in it."

"They do," her mom agreed. "But do you think they will?"

Beth thought of Harrison. She thought of what it would be like if the town found out about him. The talk that would follow, the judgment. How would he react to that? Not well, she was thinking. Beth's nails dug into her palms and she glared down at the bowl of soup.

"Beth? What is it? You're not getting back together with Ozzy, are you?" She tried to keep her tone even, but it wavered with an underlying layer of apprehension.

She looked up, shaking her head as she met her mom's blue eyes. "No. We're done. For good."

"Oh, thank God." Her mom placed a hand on her heart and closed her eyes.

A frown tugged at her mouth. "Really? I'm surprised. You love Ozzy."

"I do love Ozzy." She resumed eating her bread and soup. "But he isn't good for you. He never was. He's too needy. He held down your wings. You need to fly."

Stunned, she could only blink at her mother.

"You're my little bird. I want what's best for you, always." She smiled, reaching across the table to pat Beth's hand. Her hand was roughened by years of manual labor, but it felt like one of the best pieces of her childhood to Beth. "You know that."

Beth inhaled, held it, released it. "You never told me you thought that way about me and Ozzy."

"Of course not. You had to find out on your own that he wasn't right for you. But I'm glad you see things for how they are. Ozzy is a dreamer who only dreams, and you're a dreamer who goes after your dreams." She squeezed her hand. "I just want you to be happy, Beth."

"Thanks, Mom," Beth said in a faint voice.

Minutes passed before she spoke again, and when she did, it was with the voice of a child needing comfort from their mother. "Sometimes he scares me."

Their eyes clashed, her mom's sharp on her face. "Who, Ozzy?"

Beth looked down, nodding as she lifted her gaze.

Her features turned to granite. "Stay away from him, Beth. If he scares you, stay away from him."

"I'm trying."

"Don't try, do it."

Beth swallowed, her throat closing around the ferocity of her mom's tone. She examined her mom, saw the spark of a protective parent burning through her eyes and straightening her spine. She knew her mom would not be gentle with Ozzy if she found out he'd harmed Beth.

"I'll say something to Dan and Deb, tell them to make sure he leaves you alone. I'll say something to Ozzy too. What's he done?"

"Nothing, really. He just…makes me nervous. Says things he shouldn't, shows up where I don't want him to. All the time. It's okay, Mom. I shouldn't have said anything." Beth shifted on the chair and turned her eyes to her food.

Now that she'd voiced her concerns and seen her mother's reaction, Beth felt like she was overreacting. She felt like she was betraying him by speaking of him that way. It was Ozzy. He may be unstable at times, but at the center of him, there was goodness. He made mistakes, but it wasn't like he didn't feel bad about them. Beth's faith rang hollow.

She pointed her spoon in Beth's direction. "I better not hear about him harassing you, because if I do, me, your dad, and your two brothers *will* be having a talk with him."

Beth smiled at her mom's proclamation. Knowing she had her support made her feel better.

They finished their lunch with little talk, and once the dishes were washed and put away, Beth turned to her mom. "Dad still keeps all his sports magazines, right?"

"Yes." Her mom sighed and hung the dishtowel on the oven handlebar. "You know what a packrat he is. They're all in the den. Why?"

"I was just curious about how far back they go. Is it okay if I look around?"

She eyed Beth, her expression saying she was suspicious of her daughter's words. Everyone who knew Beth knew she didn't care about, or know anything about, sports. "Sure. Good luck making your way around the room. He has boxes and boxes of them. Shelves even. Everything is categorized by year and sport, if that helps."

Beth gave her mom a brief hug, smelling cleaning solution and hairspray on her. "Let me know when you're leaving if I'm still down there and I'll make sure I lock up when I go."

Her mom murmured acknowledgment, watching Beth with narrowed eyes as she walked the length of the carpeted hallway. Beth opened the door that went down to the basement and her dad's sanctuary in a house that was otherwise designated as her mom's. Turning on the light, she started down the steps.

It was cooler in the basement, the main room dreary with its cement floor and half-finished walls. The downstairs smelled of dust and staleness, the chill in the air weaving its way through her. Finishing the basement was one of her father's never-ending projects. He complained that he'd finally get it the way he wanted, and then he'd die. Which could explain his procrastination.

Die.

Death.

Harrison.

The words echoed through her mind, growing in volume and urgency. As far as she knew, his death was not coming anytime soon, and yet it felt like there was a shadow of it hovering just the same. Beth went still, forcing thoughts away from Harrison. Again. And then they went right back to him anyway. Her brain seemed to be hardwired to him.

Everything reminded her of him or made her think of something that pertained to him. There he was, alone in his house in the country, surviving. Enduring. He acted like he wanted it that way. Beth didn't accept that. What did he do for fun? What did he do to keep the insanity of his illness at bay? Did he allow himself to hope, to wonder, to dream? What brought him joy?

No one should live without some kind of happiness.

How many times had he smiled?

Not enough.

How many times had he laughed?

Not enough.

The walls shrank on all sides of her as she moved around boxes, totes, and rarely used exercise equipment, squeezing in on her like a blackened organ with her standing in the center of it. It was a warning to distance herself from Harrison, but she didn't know if she was able to heed it. Beth sighed, deciding it was time to be honest with herself.

She didn't want to distance herself.

There. It was out. Unable to be ignored.

Admitting it to herself was opening a virtual gate to invite in other truths. Like how she admired the vibrant shade of his hair, that it reminded her of fire. How she liked to look into his dark eyes that saw too much, seemed too old, and were trying to hide from her. How her breaths couldn't function right and her palms turned damp as she thought about his lips and wondered how they would feel.

"Shit." Beth closed her eyes, not sure she was ready to admit quite that many things.

125

Something shot through her, pushed back her shoulders, added grimness to her lips and determination to her frame. Harrison thought he had to deal with HIV alone. That was his first mistake. He didn't. Beth could help him, be a friend. He needed a friend.

The den was through a doorway with no door, a large space that smelled faintly of cigars and her dad's cologne. It was a dark room, decorated in black and brown. A man cave, as her dad liked to proudly call it. Benny's and Jake's various athletic trophies were set up in a bookcase. A spattering of Beth's awards were among them, but hers were for Forensics, Solo Ensemble, dance competitions, and poetry contests.

She trailed her fingers over the frame of a picture taken of them all when she was thirteen, and smiled at the memory of that day. It was Jake's sixteenth birthday, and he took the family car without asking, thinking he was entitled to it since he had his driver's license. The picture was taken after he got back from the store, and his misery showed in the scowl on his face. He wasn't allowed to drive anywhere for a month after that. He acted like his world was over. It was nice having older siblings as role models on how to not behave.

Her hand fell away, and Beth turned, not sure where to start. Her mom was right—there were magazines and other sports paraphernalia covering just about every inch of the room. The task could easily overwhelm her if she let it. Taking a breath, she searched her dad's handwritten stickered labels and found the football section on one of the shelving units. It shouldn't be a big deal, but Beth couldn't shake the sense of urgency that she must find something on Harrison. She wanted to hold his history within her hands.

The magazines blurred into one another, and when she finally came to one that featured Harrison on the cover, Beth flinched and dropped it. Carefully lifting it like one wrong move would cause it to burst into flames, she took the magazine and sat down on the old and lumpy loveseat, her back twinging when she moved wrong. The journal was cold against her fingertips.

Wrapping an old blue, musty smelling blanket around her shoulders, Beth stared at his face with its cut cheekbones and firm mouth. Harrison's red and gold hair was styled with the top in orderly disarray, and short sideburns lined the edges of his face. His jaw was hard with determination, his dark eyes alive and confident. The image exuded power and strength. A choked sound left her, and she traced a trembling finger down the side of his face. Beth hugged the magazine to her chest and focused on the television across the room, trying to calm an unstoppable need.

I'm too interested in him. I care too much. This isn't good.

It was of no consequence.

"Feelings cannot be decided by time," she whispered to herself.

She opened the publication to the right page, and she read about Harrison Caldwell. He studied forest management in college and hoped to work in an outdoor capacity once he retired from playing professional football. His hobbies included hiking, canoeing, and camping. A dream of his was to hike the Appalachian Trail. Long-term goals included having land in the country with his family and spending as much time outside as he was able.

"Beth? What's got you so upset?"

Her head shot up, and Beth looked at her mom, unaware that she was crying until one warm tear slid down her cheek. "Nothing. I'm fine." She closed the magazine and set it on the couch beside her.

"Are you sure?" Her mom had exchanged her raggedy clothes for jeans and a light blue sweater. She walked to the couch and sat down, picking up the magazine as she did so.

"I just...I was thinking of Ozzy." The lie felt thick on her tongue, and Beth's stomach roiled in response.

"Don't waste any more of your tears on that boy," she quietly chastised, putting an arm around Beth.

"I'm working on it." That much was true.

Her mom flipped the magazine to the front and frowned. "Such a tragedy. Your father and I saw him play once, when he was just starting out."

Beth looked over her arm, pretending to not recognize the man on the cover. The pounding of her heart said she did. "Harrison Caldwell."

"You know I'm a fan of sports as much as your dad and brothers. I never saw someone before him play with such spirit. He was an amazing football player. He moved across the field like smooth water. Hardly anyone ever caught him, or took him down." Her mom stood and put the magazine back in its spot among the others. "Why are you interested in Harrison Caldwell?"

"I'm not," Beth quickly told her, getting to her feet.

The look she gave her daughter said she was smarter than Beth thought she was.

"I saw something about him online, and...it made me curious." She shrugged, looking down at the thick gray carpet.

"I see." She waited, but when Beth said no more, she walked toward the doorway. "Well, I'm off to the shop. We'll see you next week? Come by Wednesday night if you can, just to say hi to your brothers and their families."

"Yeah. I will." Beth paused, looking at the place where a small part of Harrison was forever entombed. Would she come back here one day, and only have a magazine photograph and article to remind her of the man? A fresh set of sorrow flowed to the surface of her eyes.

"Are you coming, Beth?" her mom called from the other room.

"I'll be right up," she whispered, wiping at her eyes.

SEVEN

THE NEXT TWO days began with a text from Harrison, AKA Butt-monkey, as his contact was designated in her phone, telling her to take the day off. Thursday she was irritated and didn't respond, but by Friday she was worried. He had to be fairly okay; since he was able to text her, but what if he was sick from being out in the cold so much Wednesday? Why didn't he want her to come over? Why was she letting it get to her?

Beth paced around her bedroom with her cell phone in hand, torn between ignoring him again and driving over to his place. She settled for plopping down on the bed and sending back a text message.

> What's going on? Why do you keep telling me to
> not come over?
>
> *I do not owe you an explanation.*

"Pompous assed Butt-monkey," she muttered, texting back another message.

> You sort of do; I'm being paid to write your book.
>
> *You'll get paid.*

Beth angrily pressed on the keys, sighing heavily as she waited.

That's not the point.

She hit the send button and typed out another text.

Are you okay? At least tell me that. Please.

It was a long, nerve-wracking minute until he responded.

Yes.

Beth blew out a shallow breath of air and let herself fall back onto the unmade bed. The cell phone dropped from her hand and thumped to the carpet. She closed her eyes and rubbed her face, exasperation and concern making her skin flushed and her stomach sick. Her world was presently lopsided. She shouldn't be at her house—she should be at his. Beth liked spending time with Harrison. She liked leaving her world to be a portion of his. Part of her wanted to push him, part of her wanted to nurture him. All parts of her wanted to see him happy.

"So you'll take the day to try to write. Again. And maybe you'll have better results than the past two days," she told herself.

Beth was on the work schedule at The Lucky Coin tomorrow and Sunday, therefore, if she wanted enough time to construct the words necessary to make a story, today was the day. It was a good thing Harrison wasn't paying her by word count.

But before she could write, she had to get rid of some of her pent up energy.

Putting on a pair of black yoga pants she'd had for years and a yellow racerback tank top, Beth twisted up her hair in a messy bun and turned on loud, angry music in the living room. From watching her parents playfully sing and dance on a daily basis as far back as she could recall, music and dancing were ingrained in her at an early age, and Beth needed it. Watching them made her happy as a child, and she wanted to embrace that joy. Bestow it upon others. Songs broke her, healed her. Gave her meaning.

Music was power. Music was life.

She stood still and let the song wrap around her, tightening her muscles until she either had to move or combust. The bass and drums throbbed in her ears, woke up the dormant side of her that was spontaneous and carefree—the side she'd repressed for so long she'd forgotten it was there. The side of her Ozzy never understood, and so she hid it. Beth felt it stirring while in Harrison's presence, and she unleashed it in the solitude of her home. She spun around, arms overhead, head flung back. She turned in a circle until she was dizzy, and her throat was parched.

Beth felt invincible.

Certain areas of the one-bedroom home were drafty, but as she bounced around and bobbed her head up and down, Beth quickly worked up a sweat. She was ablaze. Her pulse moved with the tempo, her heart jumpstarted to fuel the gasoline of her motions. She was reborn in the music, laughing at the thought of someone seeing her head banging and doing air kicks. Beth closed her eyes and sang with System of a Down, grabbing her face and sinking to her knees.

She *was* the music.

The song ended, and out of breath and feeling less troubled than she had in months, Beth stretched out on the floor and waited for her body to calm. Her heartbeat was in her ears, her pulse streaming through her veins. She missed dancing. She missed herself. *You have her back. Now do something with her*, she told herself, and Beth laughed again.

Beth showered and dressed in purple leggings and a white long-sleeved top. With an apple and a cup of coffee sitting beside her on the end table, she opened up her laptop from where she sat on the couch and let inspiration take her away. It was a new, undiscovered world. Barren. Cold and empty. But as she wrote, it turned into something. Still dark, still mostly unknown, but alight with shards of loveliness. They glistened like mammoth-sized icicles in a frozen cave, twinkles of color in a white surrounding. It was Harrison's world, and it was strikingly wonderful, simple as it was.

Images and thoughts of Harrison swirled around her as she typed. The hours blurred, time was irrelevant, indistinct in the face of the pages as they grew. Darkness came, and still she composed. At one point, she made toast with honey. Another time, she put on a sweatshirt to block out the chill running through her.

She wrote of his dark eyes, and of the weight they seemed to carry. How his voice was deadly, even while not cruel, because it spoke plainly, honestly. It was unforgiving. It did not apologize; it meant everything it said. His inner strength that told his body to suck it up, that he was not going to be told what he could or could not do. Beth noted his rapture with music, how the melody pulled and swayed him. He thrummed with song, even when there was none. It was in his walk, in his voice, in his eyes.

Harrison was ill, but when she looked at him, she saw a man who acted as if he was immortal.

It was past midnight when she stopped writing, and as Beth shut down the laptop, her eyes and limbs were heavy. Her breaths left her, fast and shaky, and she raised her hands to her face, watching how they trembled. Beth squeezed them into fists, the appendages stiff and cold. She was already too close to Harrison, and she wanted to be closer. She wanted to be flush with him, her heartbeats in sync with his.

She went to bed with his black fire eyes licking at her brain and heart. Harrison was in her head. He governed there. She fell asleep to his scent wrapped around her in a suffocating embrace, smoky and thick. Beth dreamed of Harrison, pale and harsh and intense. His mouth was pure heat as it scorched her skin. Dark with a sickness he couldn't outrun. It wanted to control him, and he effortlessly controlled her. Beth was swimming in black, and she inhaled it, knowing it would burn. Wanting to feel it anyway.

ဆ ◆ ၣ

WHEN SHE AWOKE the next morning to singing birds, Beth opened her eyes and focused on the ceiling. The birds sounded like they were in her room, or in her mind. Fluttering through her thoughts with their small but strong wings. She wasn't entirely sure what she'd dreamed the night before, but she felt drained. Full. Harrison had invaded her existence while she slumbered and fixed himself deep in her soul.

Something monumental altered in her thoughts during the hours from night to morning. Beth had unknowingly made a decision, and she felt it in her bones as she sat up and took in the sunlit room. Beth was changed. It was a dangerous path, one she should avoid, if for no other reason than self-preservation. It couldn't end well. It wouldn't end in her favor. If she was thinking right, it wouldn't even start to *have* an ending.

But maybe she wasn't thinking right. Then again, maybe she was.

Beth spent the hours until it was time to work at The Lucky Coin researching what she could on HIV and if an HIV-positive person could safely have a sexual relationship with someone who did not have it. Most sites had the same information, but some went more in depth than others. She didn't think about the reasoning behind her quest to find out all she could, only the logistics. Was it possible? What did it involve?

HIV was transmitted through direct bodily fluids, like blood. Blood contained the highest concentration of it, followed by semen, vaginal fluids, and breast milk. Though rare, a pregnant woman could transmit the disease to her baby, but it was also possible for an HIV-positive person and an HIV-negative person to have healthy, uninfected children.

Saliva, tears, sweat, feces, and urine did not transfer the disease.

Beth swallowed, shame once more prickling her scalp at her actions and reactions of Harrison since finding out about his diagnosis. Sharing needles was a high-risk activity. She blinked and looked away from the computer screen, needing a moment to collect herself. She hated the woman who had so carelessly put a grenade on her own life, not to mention Harrison's. Who knew if Harrison was the only one she'd infected?

There were ways to control it now, where there hadn't been when it was first discovered. Antiretroviral therapy, or ART, was encouraged for the HIV-positive person. Harrison had mentioned that he took medicine called that. It was a mixture of medicines that slowed the rate at which HIV multiplied itself. A combination of three or more medicines was most effective, and it allowed the immune system to stay healthy. The goal of the antiretroviral therapy was to reduce the amount of virus in the body to a level no longer detectable with blood tests.

It wasn't a cure, but it was a stabilizer. A handful of hope.

Condoms, of course, were necessary for sexual intercourse. It was less likely to contract the disease through oral sex than vaginal, and anal was the most hazardous way to contract HIV. The HIV-negative person should take pre-exposure prophylaxis, which consisted of two pills that were to be ingested daily. It was suggested that the HIV-negative person be tested yearly for HIV and other STDs.

Beth closed the laptop, angry for Harrison, and a small part of her angry at herself and Harrison. She was biased—something she never would have thought of herself as being, and he had subjected himself to an isolation that wasn't required. *Except for you. You were allowed into his emptiness. He chose you. Harrison offered you something of him when he wouldn't anyone else.* It felt like a gift, how ever twisted that seemed.

More than anything, what struck her the most was the notion that she wasn't afraid. There was no fear in her bones, no doubts. Already she could sense a transformation in her from learning the little she had about him, from witnessing him in motion. Harrison had an unconquerable attitude. He wasn't scared of life, or death. What right did she have to be?

She stood, took a deep breath, and shoved everything she'd learned to a far corner of her brain. Beth couldn't dwell on any of that now. She had to go to work, and the thought of not getting a moment to herself to be able to determine what she was thinking, and what it all meant, had appeal.

ॐ ♦ ॐ

THE BAR WAS full of people, drinking and cavorting set on a course to a memorable night for many in attendance—or a forgotten one. Beth was glad she was behind the bar instead of trying to navigate through the human maze of old and young, men and women. It was the kind of place people came to hang out with their buddies, and if they were lucky, find someone to flirt with. She felt bad for the two waitresses taking and filling food orders at the few tables set up in the establishment. Food stopped being served at eight, and it was quarter to that. The waitresses didn't have far to go.

With the dim lighting, flowing beer, and rowdy patrons, the scene was set for mayhem. Within the last hour, the place got swarmed. Sweat covered Beth's body from bustling around the small space next to Jennifer Travis as they filled drink orders. It was a collage of mismatched bodies and scents inside the bar. On the weekends they had a DJ were always the busiest. The younger crowds liked to dance—so did the drunk people.

"Hey, Blondie! I need a refill." Beth glanced up at Wally Loomas and nodded as he waved an empty beer bottle in the air. Wally was a sixty-something-year-old farmer with a mane of wild gray hair who thought bathing and dressing in clean clothes were optional. He looked especially grimy tonight.

"We both have blonde hair. Is he talking to you or me?" Jennifer asked, reaching across Beth to grab a can of beer. She handed it to a middle-aged man and took his money.

"Whoever serves him first, I guess. I'll get it," she told her friend.

"Beware of the animal feces clinging to his skin." Jennifer's plum-shaded mouth twisted.

"I won't touch his hands," Beth promised, reaching into the cooler for a beer to replace Wally's empty one.

"It's a circus in here," the other bartender muttered, swiping long blonde bangs from her eyes. The rest of her hair was cut in jagged locks with the lengthiest ones ending below her jawline.

"Just wait until later," Beth said, smiling.

Jennifer groaned and tugged at her tight red top that showcased her tanned and toned midriff. "I know. I'm not looking forward to it, especially when the DJ starts. I'm dragging ass today." She waited on two women before turning to Beth. "Want to come over and eat a pizza with me afterward so I don't eat it all myself? I had a cherry sucker for dinner, and I'm starving."

Beth laughed and handed Wally his beer. "Yeah. Sure. If I'm still functioning halfway decent by closing time."

Jennifer was in her early thirties and, after divorcing her husband of three years, moved to Crystal Lake just over a year ago. She had no children, but she wanted them. She had no significant other at the moment, and she seemed to like it that way. Beth instantly liked Jennifer when she said she caught her husband with her best friend, and instead of going after the friend, like so many women did, she went after her husband. With a baseball bat. Minor harm came to him, but his car was a different story.

"I don't know," Jennifer said with a feigned look of concern on her face. "If Ozzy's spies find out about you being at my place so late at night, the next rumor will be that you're dating me."

Beth rolled her eyes as she made a rum and cola for Eric Johnson, a brown-haired man who worked at a car mechanic shop and came in only on the days and nights when Jennifer worked. He had a nice, shy smile, and as far as she knew, he was one of the decent guys in town. But Beth wasn't saying anything to Jennifer. If Eric was interested, he needed to speak up. Beth had learned early in life it was best to worry about herself and no one else. Too bad the majority of the town hadn't learned the same.

She thanked him when he said to keep the change, and looked at Jennifer. "I'm tempted to start that rumor myself just to shut everyone up."

Jennifer laughed and squeezed Beth's shoulder as she swept by, her sugary fruit-scented perfume coming and going with her. "Most—or all, really—of the men would secretly like that a little too much. Can you imagine the business The Lucky Coin would get then? Think of all the men who'd come in hopes of catching a show," she called as she walked backward to the ice machine.

Beth grinned and took a drink order.

The DJ started at eight on the dot, and the area was flooded with sound. The bass vibrated through the walls and Beth's body, and she danced along as she waited on customers. 'Unsteady' by X Ambassadors came on after three fast-paced songs, and she was blasted by thoughts of Harrison, the one person she was desperately trying not to think about. Beth almost dropped a bottle of flavored beer and set it down with a thump before a frowning woman. She muttered an apology and wiped her clammy hands on the backs of her jeans.

"Should we tell the DJ no one likes slow music until they're really good and drunk?" Jennifer commented as she nodded to the one couple who were making a halfhearted attempt at slow dancing. Other than them, the floor was empty.

"They do," Beth stated, jerking her chin at the couple.

Jennifer snorted. "They probably started earlier than everyone else. What time is Deb coming in?"

"She said by eleven," Beth answered, pushing loose strands of hair behind her ears.

"Eleven needs to get here, like, an hour ago. It's crazy in here." Jennifer chugged a bottle of water and handed a full one to Beth.

She thanked her for the water. Beth didn't mind the chaos. It kept her mind preoccupied.

As the hour neared ten, Ozzy showed up with Kelly Burbach, the woman who'd watched them when they'd attempted to have a drink together earlier in the week. Beth paused as she took in his unkempt good looks. The overhead lights, even dimmed, haloed his pale brown hair and added a golden sheen to it. He looked around the room with unhurried confidence, taking in his domain with the cool calmness of someone who belonged, and knew it.

She remembered how it used to physically hurt to look at him—because he was bright, as beautiful as a sun-kissed day. Beth didn't see that beauty anymore. She saw something pretending to be bright and lovely.

As if honed to the pace of her heartbeat, his eyes found hers. Ozzy kept his face neutral as he pulled Kelly closer, and before Beth could look away, he kissed her. It was deep and endless, telling Beth he was done with her, not the other way around. The kiss told her he was in control, not her. She waited for an emotion to hit her, but there was nothing, other than minor sadness. She turned away, her ponytail bouncing against her back as she strode to the opposite end of the bar.

"What can I get you, Sally?" she asked the loan officer who worked at one of the two banks in town. The gray satin blouse matched her eyes, and her black bob was side-parted, the dark locks hugging either side of her angular face.

"Orange juice and vodka, please, Beth." The woman smiled politely.

Her hands working like lightning as she prepared the cocktail, Beth handed her the drink and took the offered money. "How is Henry doing?"

Sally's husband was the high school principal and had a minor heart attack a month or so ago. Beth handed Sally her change.

"He's doing well, but he isn't one to sit still for long. He's a cantankerous patient."

"I bet. I remember him pacing the hallways during school." Beth smiled.

Sally's lips pulled into a real smile. "Restless man." She stood with her drink in hand. "I have some ladies waiting for me at a table. They dragged me out tonight, claiming I wasn't doing Henry any good by hovering. Henry agreed."

"Have fun. Be sure to dance."

The middle-aged woman chuckled, her gray eyes shining. "I might, if they play a song I like."

"In that case, you might have to request something," Beth told her, waving as Sally turned to meet her friends.

Finding a lull in drink orders, Beth went about restocking condiments and relishes.

"Do you want me to beat him up? Or her. I'm not picky."

Beth glanced at the pair as she cut up lemons and refilled the container of them. Ozzy had his hands all over Kelly, his front pressed to hers, a corner of his mouth hitched in that dazzling way of his. His expression said that Kelly was special, and that for the moment, he adored her. Not even a sliver of space was between the couple.

"It's okay," she told her friend. "It doesn't bother me."

Ozzy shifted his attention to the bar, and Beth. Everything about him oozed vengeance.

She looked away.

Jennifer's jaw shifted to the side as she stared at the pair, the scent of menace strong on her. "Well, it should. He only came in here because he knew you were working, and he's trying to hurt you. What a dick move to pull on someone you supposedly love, or even used to love. He mopes around in here during the day like you broke his heart, and now look at him. And how stupid is she? She should know what he's doing. Guys aren't all that original. If she has even half a brain, she could figure it out."

"Not if she doesn't want to," Beth said quietly, part of her feeling bad for Kelly. Once embedded in the heart, it was hard to remove Ozzy from it.

"God, this town pisses me off. Bunch of hillbilly fucks," Jennifer muttered, swiping bangs from her eyes.

Beth smiled, unable to take offense. Besides, she knew Jennifer didn't consider her part of the community, even though she'd lived in Crystal Lake her whole life. Jennifer told her once it was because she didn't act inbred like the majority of the town.

"He's acting like this because he knows we're done. For good. It's his form of retaliation," Beth explained, grabbing a dishcloth and wiping wet spots from the counter.

"Childish prick."

Beth laughed and patted Jennifer's tense forearm with her free hand. "You're a good friend, and I appreciate your support. I can handle him."

Jennifer turned narrowed eyes on Beth. "You shouldn't have to."

She shrugged and slung the damp dishcloth over her shoulder. The water held within the rag seeped through her shirt and onto her skin. "Lots of people deal with things they shouldn't have to." Her thoughts turned to Harrison and Beth's skin prickled.

"Incoming," Jennifer warned, setting herself in front of Beth and blocking her from Ozzy.

"I got this." She placed a hand on her arm. "It's okay. Really."

With a scowl twisting her features, Jennifer stepped to the side. "If you need me, I'll be right over here." She pointed to the other end of the cramped bar and marched in that direction.

"Hi, Beth." Ozzy's eyes glittered with golden intensity.

143

"Did you need something, Ozzy?" Beth made sure to keep her gaze averted.

"Just wanted to say hi."

"You said it," she said, finally looking at him.

Ozzy drummed his long fingers on the countertop, looking down and up. His eyebrows lowered, giving him a contrite appearance. "Listen, Kelly and I—"

"I don't need to know. Whatever you do is none of my business, just like whatever I do is none of yours." It was a reminder to him, and Beth knew he caught it when his mouth fell into a thin line. "If you don't need anything, I have other people to wait on."

She moved to turn away, but his hand clamped around her wrist, halting her. "You're wearing the shirt I got you for Christmas last year."

Beth glanced down at the emerald green top with silver thread along the collar, jerking back her wrist to try to get it out of his grasp. Ozzy held it a beat, letting her know he was only releasing her because he decided to. Beth swallowed, something like fear clenching her stomach. She told herself that wasn't it, and that it was silly to be scared of Ozzy.

But when Beth looked into his eyes, she didn't see Ozzy. She saw a man, and a reminder, and someone who could hurt when he chose.

"It wasn't on purpose."

"Maybe not consciously." He smiled, but there was nothing beautiful about it.

"Not even subconsciously."

"Sure. Whatever you need to tell yourself."

Beth studied his features, seeing hardness in the lines and hollows she didn't remember being there. His lips hinted at cruelty, and his eyes gleamed with hostile fire. With shallow breaths and a chaotic pulse, she moved down the bar, away from Ozzy. He watched her with a clenched jaw and fire in his eyes. He didn't say anything, but he also didn't take his eyes off her for a good, long while.

By midnight, a large portion of the patrons were intoxicated; others were headed in that direction. From what she'd seen, Ozzy was close to there as well. Before his mom showed up, he'd walked around the bar and restocked drinks for him and Kelly more times than Beth could keep track of. She was careful to stay out of his way after the first time he purposely slid his front across her back. After Deb got there, he stayed on the other side of the bar.

The music volume stayed the same, but the voices got louder. The once empty area in front of the DJ was full of dancing bodies. There were lines of people around the counter and more waiting behind them. Alcohol made people act how they normally wouldn't, and seeing it in motion as often as she did with bartending, Beth didn't drink much. If something could alter her actions and thoughts like that, she wanted to stay away from it.

Deb, Ozzy's mom and co-owner of the bar, pulled Beth aside and pointed to where Ozzy and Kelly were making out on the dance floor. "What is going on with my son and Kelly Burbach?"

Beth appreciated how Dan and Deb looked at both sides of every story, and didn't pass judgment. They didn't blame her for her and Ozzy's breakup, but they did let her know they were saddened by it. They didn't try to make her feel bad about choosing to move on from Ozzy, and she respected them for it. But they also couldn't accept that she was no longer a part of his life.

She looked at the short and wiry woman whose eyes Ozzy inherited. "I think they're dating, but I don't know. They showed up together."

Her sharp features hardened as she watched her son. "I always hope he'll decide to grow up and make good decisions, but I don't see that day coming anytime soon." Deb turned to Beth. "Kelly Burbach is a tramp. She's fooled around with just about every guy in this town within five years of her age."

Beth blinked. "Oh?"

Deb gave her a look. "Don't act like you don't know."

"Well, I..." she trailed off, shrugging. "Too often people in this town talk about things that don't directly involve them." Like Ozzy's gaggle of friends and family who kept tabs on her for him. As far as she knew, his parents were not part of that group.

"Hmm," was all Deb said before turning to yell at a customer who loudly remarked that she wasn't moving fast enough with his beer.

The lights flipped on full force at closing time, signaling the end of the night. With a few protests, the remaining people trickled out the door, some of them stumbling and needing help to get there. Deb, Jennifer, and Beth worked to get the place in order before taking off. Beth was aware of Ozzy sitting at a table across the room and the way he watched her with dark, hooded eyes. Kelly was nowhere in sight.

"I don't know how you aren't creeped out by him, because I am, and he's not even staring at me," Jennifer said as they washed up and dried the last of the bar glasses.

"He's drunk. I'm sure he's just waiting for his mom to give him a ride home." She outwardly brushed off Jennifer's concern even as apprehension pulsed through her.

"We leave together." Jennifer held her gaze until Beth nodded.

Ozzy staggered to his feet as Beth and Jennifer approached the front door, reaching out a hand and ensnaring Beth by the arm when they passed him. "Hey. I want to talk to you," he said in slow fragments. He smelled like beer and swayed on his feet, his eyes half closed and out of focus.

"Not now, Ozzy." Beth pushed at his hand, and it slid away. Her anxiety grew. A drunken Ozzy was one to avoid.

"You don't need to touch her to talk to her," Jennifer informed him, moving closer to Beth.

Lifting his head like it weighed a hundred pounds, Ozzy fought to keep Jennifer in his line of vision. "You." He pointed a finger at her. She slapped it down. "You stay out of it. This is between me, and Beth."

"Go home, Ozzy. You're drunk." Beth took the sleeve of Jennifer's brown jacket. "Ready?" she asked her friend, tightening her grip on the fabric like Jennifer was the kite that would take her away from the ground and Ozzy.

"Yeah. I'm ready. Pizza, followed by ten hours of sleep, is calling my name."

"Beth, don't walk away from me," Ozzy yelled after her, sounding broken. "Beth!"

"Ignore him." Jennifer steered Beth forward when she faltered. "He knows how to weaken your resolve, and all he has to do is act helpless."

"I feel bad for him," she whispered.

"I know that, and so does he."

"Beth, I need you. Please talk to me. I'm sorry, all right? I'm sorry for everything."

Beth's footsteps were leaden, making it harder to step from him. He was hurting, and it scratched at her heart. She briefly closed her eyes and took a deep breath, continuing forward. He wasn't hers to worry over anymore. Beth needed to worry about herself, and what she needed. And it wasn't Ozzy Peck.

The sound of something heavy falling to the floor hit Beth's ears, and she whirled around, ignoring Jennifer's words to keep moving. Ozzy knelt on the floor, his head lowered with his arms wrapped around it. His shoulders shook, and at first she thought he was crying, but it soon became apparent he was laughing. Beth stayed where she was.

"Sweet little Beth Lambert. Predictable Beth," he said in a shaky voice. "I never thought you'd be the one to end it. Since when does Beth Lambert have a backbone? Fuck my life." Ozzy laughed louder and flipped to his back, his eyes trained on the ceiling.

Heat bloomed in her cheeks, and Beth gritted her teeth. That was her, easily and wrongly pegged by everyone who thought they knew her.

"He is loco," Jennifer muttered. "Can we go now?"

"Yes," she hissed. "Let's go."

"What the hell is going on out here?" Deb demanded, jogging from the back office.

"Ozzy fell." Beth met Deb's gaze as she made her way to her son. "He needs a ride home."

With a frown twisting her mouth, Deb hunkered down by Ozzy, placing an arm around his shoulders as she looked at Beth. "Go home, Beth. I'll take care of my son."

Rooted in place by the shock of the blame she saw in Deb's eyes, it took a moment for Beth's feet to work. She numbly followed Jennifer from the bar, Ozzy's laughter following them. *Parents always choose their kids over others*, her mother once told her. She'd meant it to be encouraging, but it seemed like a barbed torch to Beth. Turned the wrong way and it burned, turned another and it stabbed.

What if the child did something unforgivable to someone else? What then?

Beth blinked and walked into a dark, chilly night.

EIGHT

BETH KNEW SHE must be wearing remnants of the weekend when she stepped into the reading room Monday afternoon and the first words out of Harrison's mouth were, "You look awful. I take it you had an inspiring weekend."

He stood near the windows as he so often did, reminding her of a self-caged bird. Without replying, she studied the dark coloring beneath his eyes, wondering at the strict line of his mouth. He held himself stiffly, and Beth searched his expression for an answer to his behavior last week. Harrison looked worse than her, worse than the last time she'd seen him. It wasn't anything startlingly obvious, but something was off.

"That good, huh?" he continued, his eyes trained on hers.

She could already tell the two of them were different from last week. While she was researching and thinking and coming to a decision, maybe he was doing the same. Beth was more emboldened, and he seemed more open, watching her in a way he hadn't previously allowed himself. There was a deeper hitch to his mouth, a stronger light in his eyes. She lifted her chin, refusing to look away when their gazes collided.

"My ex-boyfriend doesn't understand what the 'ex' part means," was the only answer she supplied. "And you?"

Harrison's mouth twisted and he replied dryly, "My parents decided an impromptu visit was in order."

"Your parents were here?" Beth's frown flipped into a faint smile. She'd been worried for nothing. Harrison had been in good hands, although from the way he was acting, it hadn't been an enjoyable experience for him. "That's great. I didn't think you saw them much."

"I don't."

"Oh." Beth trained her gaze on the melting snow outside the window. Her parents were everything, and without them, she'd be lost. They were the rocks that would shatter her free when she was locked inside a glass-built room of her own insecurities. "Why don't you?"

"They don't treat me the same as they used to, and it bothers me. I'm an invalid in their minds."

She nodded, her fingers tightening on the manuscript she carried. Beth looked at Harrison. "I understand."

Harrison tilted his head. "Do you?"

Beth swallowed. "I think so."

"I'm not sure you can."

In the silence that trailed his words, she shifted her feet and moved the stack of papers from under one arm to the other.

"What's that?" His eyes flicked down.

Feeling self-conscious and second guessing the great idea that came upon her yesterday, Beth felt her face go red. "Oh. Well. This…" She paused as his dark eyes drilled into hers in that impatient way of his. "This is the first story I wrote. You wanted me to read a book to get to know you. I thought maybe you'd be interested in reading something of mine to get to know me. Keep in mind, it isn't any good," Beth added when his expression went blank.

"Why would I want to get to know you?" he asked quietly, without malice.

"Maybe you don't. But if you do." Beth set down the papers on the couch and crossed her arms in the fire of Harrison's gaze. A glint of humor shone in the depths, made her senses spring to attention.

When Beth was with Ozzy, she felt weaker. Meek. Unsure of herself and what she wanted. In Harrison's presence, it was the opposite. He expected strength from her, and that made her want to be strong. His attention on her was heavy with the unknown. What was he thinking? What was he feeling? Was it anything like what she was? Each time she looked away, something brought her eyes back to him. Beth stopped fighting it and unabashedly watched him.

"I have questions for you." When a single eyebrow quirked, she continued. "For the book." Beth inhaled. "It's not bad out today—the snow is melting, and the temperature is in the forties. The sun is shining. Would you be okay with going for a walk and talking?"

His shoulders relaxed, and after a short pause, he nodded. "Yes. I'm okay with that."

"Oh. Okay. Good."

"You sound surprised."

She gathered up her hair and swept it over one shoulder, her fingers needing a task. "I always think you're going to tell me no."

His eyes watched the gesture, seemed intrigued by it. "Yet you ask anyway."

Beth looked away from his piercing eyes, feeling a smile curve her lips. "Yes. I do."

They didn't speak as they put on their coats and boots. Harrison's stocking cap fell from the pocket of his jacket and Beth reached down to retrieve it before he could. He outstretched a hand for it, and she tugged it down over his head, leaving a wave of reddish-blond hair visible on his forehead. Beth pushed the locks back from his face, her fingers tingling from the contact. His cheek muscles flexed as his eyes bored into hers. The shared look spiraled through her, bringing fire through her frame.

She waited for him to reprimand her for touching him, but he only turned toward the door and stepped outside. Beth let out a deep breath and caught up to him near the side of the house. A smile, small and triumphant, claimed her face. That was huge—that he let her touch him and that he didn't say anything about it.

Snow melted and dripped from the roof to form piles of slush on the ground. The sun reflected off the white pathway, blinding and dazzling. Harrison took them on a manmade trail through the snow that led behind the house and in the opposite direction of the hill they'd ascended the previous week. Beth hopped over a puddle of melted snow and landed in Harrison's path. He paused, his head cocked, and then stepped around her.

"I have the beginning of your story ready for you to read," Beth said after a moment of arguing with herself over whether or not she should say anything about it.

A slash of dark brown eyes cut open her senses before moving away.

Fighting the beat of her hyper pulse, she went on to say, "It's all of ten pages, but it's a start. It's in my vehicle. I'll get it when we go back."

Harrison didn't respond.

"Aren't you at all curious about what I wrote?"

His shoulders lifted and lowered.

"What if it's completely inaccurate, or..." Beth's eyes narrowed, and she felt the curve of a wicked grin take over her mouth. "What if I call you Butt-monkey in it?"

Harrison stumbled to a stop, his eyebrows shooting straight up as he looked at her. "Butt-monkey?"

Beth laughed, nodding vehemently. "Yes. Butt-monkey."

"What the hell is a butt-monkey?"

Head cocked, she squinted her eyes and tapped an index finger to her chin as she pretended to think about it. Beth dropped her hand and met Harrison's bemused gaze. "I guess it's someone irritating, like you."

"*I'm* irritating?" Incredulity put emotion and volume to his voice.

Beth was enjoying his reactions, feeling light and happy as she teased him. She'd surprised Harrison, and he couldn't get the walls up fast enough to shield himself from her. Unpredictability, Beth decided, was a perfect tool to use against an unsuspecting man.

"Especially when you're all—" Beth lowered her face, twisted her expression into a scowl, and said in a deep, sandpaper voice, "—don't do this, don't do that. Don't stand there. Don't say that. Do read this book. Don't look at me like that. Do call me a butt-monkey." She skipped forward, away from a shocked Harrison, who stood motionless, only his eyes moving, and only to blink.

Beth laughed, and she laughed harder when he blasted a glare in her direction as he shot past her. "I do not sound like that," he said stiffly, his long legs widening the space between them.

"You might even be listed under 'Butt-monkey' in my phone!"

His shoulders tensed, but he kept moving.

"How am I supposed to ask you questions when I can't keep up?" she called after him.

"I guess you'll have to keep up with the butt-monkey," he replied.

With a smile stamped to her face, Beth attempted to match her pace with his long strides, but she had to jog to do that. It didn't take long for her to get tired and lag behind, watching as he got smaller and closer to a forest of gigantic, spindly trees. Frustrated, she flung her arms out wide and let herself fall back into the snow. She hit the cushioned ground with a soft thump. It was oddly refreshing, watching air leave her mouth and nose in bursts of white, the sun above, trees in the distance, and Beth resting in her cold bed.

She closed her eyes and patted the powdery floor, counting off two minutes before talking. "Sorry about calling you stupid the other night."

"Did you do that?"

155

Beth's eyes popped open, and Harrison came into focus above her. "The snow…I called the snow—never mind."

"Here I thought maybe you'd added a 'stupid' to the 'butt-monkey'." He sat down beside her and set his arms on his knees, his face dipped in somberness. "My dad used to take me for walks in the woods all the time."

She went still, not even the coolness of the snow deterring her from hearing what Harrison had to say. The light moment was gone, replaced with a deeper ring of clarity.

"He'd point out the different kinds of trees and which leaves belonged to them. We'd collect rocks and anything else that was interesting to me. Find water, wade in it. Try to catch fish with our hands. Sometimes we'd see a deer, and we'd just stand there and watch it until it took off." Harrison's pale throat waved as he swallowed.

"We'd spend hours and hours out there. We didn't talk a lot of the time. We just walked, and looked around. Enjoyed the moment. Ate turkey sandwiches and drank apple juice. It was simple. My friends were going on trips and playing video games and getting all this expensive stuff, and my dad and I walked in the woods."

Harrison packed snow with his large hands, his head down. "I didn't know it at the time, but my dad was teaching me something great then."

"What?" she exhaled, carefully sitting up. Beth had to remember this conversation. This was important.

He tossed the snowball in the air, caught it. "To have solitude is a blessing, always rely on yourself before anyone else, and appreciate the beauty around you."

156

"And that's what you're doing."

Beth held out her hands, and he dropped the misshapen snow-ball into her bare palms. It stung her skin, melting from the heat of her hands. She watched as it got smaller and smaller until it was a tiny pool of water within her palms. Beth opened her hands, and it splattered to the snow.

"Yes." He got to his feet and offered her a hand, the significance of the motion one most people would overlook.

Beth took it before he changed his mind, feeling the strength of his fingers as they gripped hers and helped pull her to her feet. When he went to withdraw, she held on tighter. Harrison lowered his eyebrows, an unspoken warning on his lips. His hand was touched by snow, the skin dry and calloused. He was strong-willed, but even the most self-sufficient of men needed to know someone unobligated to care, could. Beth didn't want to let him go, not ever.

At some point since she'd met him, she'd unconsciously claimed him as hers, and hers he would stay.

"Don't," he said, soft as a light breeze, but as fatal as a tornado.

"Don't what?"

His voice shook as he told her, "I don't want anyone in my life."

She squeezed his hand, refusing to let his gaze look away from hers. "Then why am I here?"

For one catastrophic instant, he looked at her in such a simple, raw way that it splintered her heart and flooded it with feeling. He was a man, and she was a woman, and when his camouflage eyes became unveiled, Beth saw something in them that she couldn't ignore. It was the look of a man who saw what he craved, longed for, needed. Harrison stared through her eyes like she was already his and she wanted to give herself to him. She would, if he asked. Beth didn't care about anything but making Harrison realize he could still have things like friendship, love, purpose, happiness.

Even if his time on this earth was already foretold by fate, he could be well loved for the remainder of it. No life should be regretted, or forsaken, not even a compromised one. Especially not a compromised one.

But then Harrison stepped back, and the enigma was once more in place. He was Harrison of the shadows, a man she didn't know. A man who didn't want anyone to know him. She let go of his hand, and felt the emptiness ricochet through her arm. Beth sensed him retreat into himself as they walked, aware of the distance he purposely put between them.

"The book you had me read," she hesitantly began. "Why that one? What makes it your favorite?"

He took a deep breath, his shoulders lowering with the exhalation. "The kid was afraid," he said in a low voice. "He didn't know his dad; his mom died. He ran from anyone who tried to help him, because he was scared to trust others. He was alone. Homeless. Penniless. He had nothing." Harrison glanced at her, his eyes throbbing with emotion. "He had every reason to give up, and he never did. He had the worst odds, and he still won."

A twisted ghost of a smile haunted his visage. "I want to be like that kid. He's a fictional character set in the eighteen hundreds, and I wish I could have the courage he does. Talk about messed up."

"Everyone's scared of something," she told him, looking ahead as they walked. Beth couldn't look into Harrison's eyes right now. It would break something in her.

"What are you afraid of?" he asked after a moment.

Beth pressed her lips together. So many things, too many things. She glanced at Harrison, her footsteps halting when she saw the intensity with which he watched her. "I'm afraid I'm not good enough," she confessed.

His head tilted. "At what?"

She shrugged, feeling nervous under the directness of his questions. "At writing, more than anything." Beth inhaled slowly, sick with the admission. "What are you afraid of?"

"Everything," he replied in a whisper. "But especially you."

Harrison picked up his pace, leaving her behind. Her? Harrison was afraid of her? Her heartbeats sputtered and Beth's surroundings darkened and lightened. It almost made her smile to think of him possibly being afraid of her, but the hint of a smile quickly fell from her face. Maybe he was right to be afraid. She wanted to tell him to not be, but maybe she was the foolish one out of them, daring to take chances he wasn't, to think of possibilities better left unformed. To have hope. To dream. Selfishly deigning to forget everything but the man beside her.

"Do you play any instruments?" she questioned to change the subject.

A fallen tree branch cracked under his boots. "No. I thought about taking piano lessons when I was younger, but I knew I wouldn't be able to commit to them like I'd need to. Sports were my life growing up, and I didn't have much time for anything else."

"Did you want sports to be your life?"

His jaw flexed. "They were, and it was that simple."

"Do you sing?"

He shot her a look. "Not well."

"What about dancing?"

Harrison set his hands on his hips and gave her his full attention. "Where are you going with this?"

"When you were in the music room last week," she explained. "It was obvious that you care a great deal for music. I wondered if that extended to anything else. I'm only asking for research purposes." Foremost, Beth was asking because she wanted to know, but it was something that should be in the book. He hadn't answered her about dancing. Which, in her mind, meant he liked to dance. She could work with that.

"Music heals what nothing else can," he allowed, turning his back to her and climbing over a pile of tree limbs.

"What does it heal?" Beth navigated through the brittle foliage, catching her jacket on a sharp piece of wood. She tugged at it until the earth released it, plowing forward and stopping abruptly in order to keep from running into Harrison.

"The soul."

Music heals the soul. His words echoed through her mind. Beautiful. They were words she would not forget.

Harrison turned and placed a finger to his lips, setting a hand on her shoulder and firmly pushing. She opened her mouth to ask what he was doing, and he shook his head. Crouched beside her, he pointed to a small body of churning water. Beth went still, listening to the soothing sound of water as it flowed over rocks. On the other side of it was a doe and its fawn. As Beth stared at the animals drinking from the stream, she understood how special the moment was.

It was a realm of cold and white, but she focused on the scene before her, and the sound of Harrison breathing next to her. In. And out. In. And out. It was hypnotic—staring at the deer, listening to Harrison. Harrison's father shared something similar with him, and he was sharing it with her. The fawn was gangly, its reddish-brown coat spotted with white. It backtracked and skipped around the doe, close to being trampled a few times. Beth smiled at its gaiety and innocence. It didn't understand that there was danger everywhere. It only knew that it was alive, and it rejoiced in that.

Her eyes slid to Harrison's and found his on her. A ring of olive green circled his irises, made his dark brown eyes that much more captivating. Beth's heartbeat formed its own cadence, and it played for Harrison. Strong and sturdy. She wanted to kiss him, and feel his breath on her lips, taste the bitterness of his disease and turn it into something sweet. Obliterate his loneliness. The need grew in her stomach, pooled there like warm, thick molasses.

She let a slow smile overtake her mouth, careful to keep her thoughts and desires hidden. Harrison studied her face, his eyes like a caress. His gaze was remembering her, inch by inch. In the sharp bones and design of his features, Beth saw severity relaxed with an unnamed emotion. She liked it, whatever it was.

"Thank you for showing me this," Beth whispered.

Light flickered in his eyes, and he lowered his gaze to the ground.

Beth turned her eyes back to the wildlife. The deer and its fawn galloped further into the forest, and the surreal moment was broken. She straightened, feeling the loss of it like a blanket ripped from a cold body.

"Tell me what you were like in school." She glanced at him, smiling at the question she was about to ask. "Was it like the movie

'Varsity Blues'? Drinking and partying and girls in whipped topping and nothing else?"

Harrison snorted. "Not quite."

"What were things like then?"

He turned his eyes to the forest. "I got good grades, didn't drink or party all that much. I had a goal of playing football in college, and I didn't want to screw it up. Worked part-time in the kitchen of a local restaurant. Had a steady girlfriend from freshman to junior year." She felt the shrug in his words. "I was pretty boring."

"I doubt that."

Harrison looked at her, interest lightening his eyes. "What about you? What were you like?"

"I was pretty boring too. I never once got in trouble for anything. I wrote poetry and short stories for fun. Dated Ozzy. Babysat for extra money. I took dance classes until I was sixteen. After that, I don't know, I lost interest." Ozzy told her they were silly, and like the insecure person she was, she believed him.

That isn't you anymore.

His eyes darkened at the mention of Ozzy, but he didn't say anything. Beth's inhalation was shaky, knowing that just because someone didn't say something, didn't mean they weren't thinking things. What did the mentioning of her ex-boyfriend mean to Harrison? Something? Nothing? Everything?

She stood along with Harrison, her knees stiff from being motionless for so long. "Will you dance with me?"

Harrison's head jerked up, the frown on his face a definitive no.

"Will you let me dance for you?" Beth tried.

"That is an odd request."

"It isn't. You'll see." Beth turned and tramped through the snow, a spring to her step. It made her think of the fawn and she laughed. A new life, a new day, a new start. She hadn't wanted to dance in so long, and now her body ached to do so.

"What does dancing have to do with the book?" he asked her back.

Grinning, she picked up her pace, swinging her arms. "I can write it into the story. 'Harrison wouldn't dance, but that didn't mean the music didn't move him. The lyrics swept through his eyes, and his rigid mouth softened with the song. His very existence hummed with the melody. It made him dance, though he claimed he wasn't a dancer. That was because Harrison didn't realize he could dance without moving a single part of his body.' What do you think?"

When he didn't respond, Beth looked over her shoulder. "Harrison?"

Harrison stared at her, pale and unmoving.

She took a step toward him. "Are you okay?" A trail of blood appeared on his face, trickling down from his nose like a solitary, deadly announcement of his mortality. She gasped, stunned and horrified. "Harrison, you're bleeding."

His eyes didn't leave hers as a hand carefully went to his face, leaving a smear of red above his mouth. The blood dripped to the snow, red on white. It made the snow appear to be bleeding, uneven stains of it spreading and fading to pink, sinking into the soil. It was beautiful in a way, a splash of color on a pallid canvas. She watched it fall as she sprinted for him, her stomach rebelling at the wrongness of it. It didn't seem like a lot of blood, but its iron smell hit her hard.

Beth halted her footsteps and reached for his hand without thought.

"Don't touch me," he shouted, swinging away from her.

"You're bleeding. Let me help."

With his face turned away, he ground out, "If you get my blood on you and you have a cut on your skin, you could contract the disease. Stay back."

Beth inhaled icy air, feeling helpless and irrelevant. She was warm and she was frozen, flashes of horror controlling her body temperature. The facts of HIV couldn't be glossed over when she was witnessing the consequences of them in motion. This was minor compared to what she could be seeing. That didn't make her feel better. What happened to Harrison when no one was with him? What would happen to him as the disease progressed? Who would help him get through this until there was nothing left to get through?

She saw his future, and it was painted in streaks of black until that was all there was. And she hated it. Beth despised the disease taking over his body. How did one destroy the destroyer? She sniffed and fought the tears that wanted to come. To anyone else, it was a nosebleed. To Harrison, it was an enemy. To Beth, it was a threat.

"Is there someone I should call?" Her voice wavered.

Beth kept her hands stiff at her sides, and it felt like a betrayal. Her lack of movement was a lie. It wasn't her, it wasn't in her heart to stand by and do nothing. Her heart wanted to cocoon him, to hold him and lie about how everything would be okay. Lies weren't always bad. Sometimes they were all that could get a person through a day, a moment, a reality.

"Do you need to be seen by a doctor?" Beth briefly touched his shoulder when he continued to remain silent. "Tell me how to help you, Harrison."

Harrison pulled a glove from his jacket and pressed it to his face. His eyes slammed into hers, stealing the air from her lungs. "There's nothing to do for it."

He started toward the house. "If you really want to help me, you'll go."

Harrison refused to look at or speak to her once they were back to the house, locking himself in the bathroom before she could even try to talk to him. Beth didn't want to leave him, but she wouldn't stay where she wasn't wanted. Feeling helpless, she chewed on a fingernail as she came to the decision that she had no choice but to go. She decided to make her departure a positive experience and take the time to write more on his book.

It was madness, but part of Beth thought, if she just kept writing his story, then Harrison's life wouldn't be able to ever end. His story was left unfinished, and what kind of person would step out of their own tale before it was time?

Beth left as he instructed, but not before she retrieved the ten pages of the manuscript from the Blazer and set the beginning of his novel on Harrison's bed. She lingered in the room, feeling him like a mark upon her skin, smelling him in the air. Masculine, clean, erotic in his plainness. Her footsteps were heavy, lingering. Beth let the tips of her fingers slide across his dark bedspread before leaving the pristine, sparsely furnished room of a single dresser, one bed, and a solitary desk.

෩ ◆ ෫

THE FOLLOWING DAY, fear spiked her pulse as she entered the house. No text came telling her to stay away, but even if it had, Beth would have ignored it. Harrison could only avoid her if she allowed it. It wasn't about her writing his story anymore, although that was an important part of their association. It was about them—the thread that stitched her life to his.

Beth didn't announce her presence. She took off her jacket, hat, and boots, and marched to the laundry room. Opening the linen closet, she found cleaning supplies and a wood polishing agent. Logic wasn't necessarily a factor in what she had planned, but it didn't matter. Even as she understood why it was the way it was, the trophy room was no longer going to live in disharmony.

She knew that making a shrine out of his past wasn't the way to go. The awards he'd earned weren't him. They were a reminder of what he'd once been, who he'd been. Harrison wasn't that person anymore, and that person had never really been Harrison. He was more, deeper. He was all the stars, and all the galaxies, and everything beyond; held in the hand of all the worlds. Secret rooms, unknown floors, whispered passages. Beth wanted to discover them all.

Following that train of thought, he was more than the person he was being. He said he wasn't hiding, but he was. Harrison was hiding from himself. He gave the disease power over him, just as she gave Ozzy power over her. It wasn't the same, she knew, but power was power. And no one and nothing should have it over another.

As she entered the room, dust swirled around her like tiny dancers, and she blinked against it. Juggling in her arms the bottles of disinfectant and whatever else she'd grabbed, she moved to the center of the room and dropped everything on the floor. Beth closed the door and then moved to the window, unlocking it and pushing it open. Cool, new air wafted in, and she closed her eyes as she popped her head outside and inhaled deeply.

Beth tightened the ponytail on the top of her head as she turned from the window, tugged her pink tee shirt back into place, and eyed the overwhelming task before her. The room appeared unending, filled as it was, but in reality, it wasn't all that big. The task was daunting, but not unmanageable.

"Don't think about it," she told herself. "Just do it."

Sliding her cell phone from the pocket of her black leggings, Beth found a playlist of fast-paced music and turned the volume as high as it would go before she started moving all of the trophies and awards from shelves and desks to the floor. Beth coughed as she worked, sweat forming in the small of her back and in the hollow of her neck. Her fingers were covered in thick gray matter that made her nose wrinkle.

'The Sound of Silence'; remade by Disturbed, came on as she set the last trophy on the hardwood floor. Beth swept loose strands of damp hair from her face with the back of her hand and went still to better appreciate the music as she waited for her tired limbs to rejuvenate. As the singer's voice swelled and reverberated through the room and in her, Beth closed her eyes and did a lazy pirouette with a smile on her face. The music wasn't loud, but it didn't have to be to pulse with her heart. Ballet, tap, jazz, and hip-hop—she'd learned as many of the different forms of dancing as she could as a kid. This was a haunting song that deserved to be savored.

She sprayed wood polisher on a desk and wiped circles onto it as she shook her hips back and forth and bobbed her head to 'I Am' by AWOLNATION. The wood gleamed back at her and she moved to the wall shelves. Beth spun and dipped backward, her arms loose and flowing as she surged left and right, turning the cleaning into a performance. By the time she was done with the woodwork, it shone back at her like a shiny penny. Beth grinned and turned, her ponytail swinging with the motion, and reached for the first of the trophies.

The music shut off, the silence stinging in the wake of the song. Beth's head shot up, and she was met with the formidable being that was Harrison. The black of his shirt mirrored his expression. He stood in the doorway, one hand braced on the woodwork. The pose was casual, deceptive. Because his eyes leaked menace, as well as pain. Beth's hands unconsciously loosened and she dove for the trophy before it hit the floor, landing on the floor with it.

"Why are you always turning off music?" she grumbled, not knowing what else to say.

"What are you doing in here?" The measurement of his words was off, thicker.

Beth put down the trophy and stood, wiping her hands on the front of her pants. "Dancing. And cleaning."

"Why?"

She shrugged and twisted her hair around her hand, letting it go when her scalp stung. "Just because this part of your life is over, that doesn't mean you have to pretend it isn't there, or hide it away. You should be proud of what you've accomplished."

It took him a tense minute to respond, his eyes drilling into hers, taking her breath. "I am proud of it, but I also don't want to look at it."

"Fine. Don't." Her heart beat in her ears as Harrison stepped into the room and looked around. "But in case you ever decide you want to, it'll be here."

"It's a mirage. Looking at this reminds me of what I once was, and what I now am. My own body is fighting me, Beth." His eyebrows pinched together, and he lowered his eyes as his throat worked to swallow. There he was, the real Harrison. She was seeing more and more of him, and she'd give anything to keep him here, but not at the price of the hurt he was experiencing.

"Fight back," she whispered.

"I can't."

Anger lashed through her, and Beth slapped her hand on a desk, pain slamming through her palm and into her arm. "Fight back!"

"I can't!" Harrison shoved his face next to hers, his eyes black with death and fury. His mouth was nothing more than a slice of pink against white. "Look at me. *Look at me.*"

Beth looked into the tormented eyes of a man brought down by something no one ever should. She lifted her chin and straightened her shoulders. "I am looking at you."

Bloodshot eyes stared back. "I am a disease."

"No. You're not. Don't say that, don't think that," she told him, shaking her head. "You are not defined by this. You said it. You said it and you have to believe it."

"I try to. Sometimes I try to." Harrison swallowed, covering his eyes with his hands as if to stop seeing the reality awaiting him. He let his hands fall away, revealing the splintered pieces of his soul with his eyes glued to hers. "When I'm with you, I forget. But then, like yesterday, I am reminded. Again and again I am reminded."

"It's okay to have bad days, Harrison. You're having a bad day, that's all." Beth reached for him, and he stepped away.

"It's not okay to hope. It's not okay to pretend. It's not. It's not okay," Harrison muttered and showed her his stiff back.

He paced near the trophies and awards. He paused with his profile to her, and his hand trembled as he swiped it across his mouth. Harrison stared through the window to outside, looking at a freedom he couldn't feel. He glanced at her, his mouth contorted with anguish, and then he moved again. Back and forth. His steps jerky, his body wired with discontent.

"You don't have to lie to me, or to you." Beth followed the movement with her eyes, aware that Harrison's composure had cracked at some point during the time from yesterday to today. That look in his eyes, that desperation, it killed a tiny part of her. "You're right, you don't have to pretend. You don't have to act like you're okay when you're not. I'm here. Let me help you."

His footsteps halted, and he stood, bared and open—an unbeatable man struck down by the lightning of fate. The slope of his shoulders hinted at his hopelessness, and Harrison's eyes cried, though not a single tear appeared. "Every day I breathe is a lie."

Beth's eyes stung, her head shaking to deny his words. His life was not a lie, but a truth. Harrison's confession was not a weakness, like he believed. His breakdown was not something to feel shame over. It made him stronger to Beth, because even the strongest of individuals fell at times. What made them strong was that they got back up, every time.

"It's okay," she said in a choked voice. "It's okay to be scared, but it's not okay to let the fear take away everything good."

Craters of pain fell upon his being, demolishing the light. Creating holes that couldn't be filled. Pushing him back, and back. Back to the darkness. Back to the bleak world he didn't have to live in. Beth could see Harrison struggling against them, and she could see him wondering why he was. She was losing him. Beth couldn't let him go back there.

"I can't go forward, and I can't go back. You know what I do? I go through, straight ahead. I don't think about the past, because it hurts. And I can't think about the future, because that hurts too."

"Let me help you," she offered again, placing her hand, palm side up, in the space between them.

He lowered his eyes to her hand, stared at it like he didn't know what it was.

"Let me help you."

Harrison's throat bobbed, and he lifted crystalline eyes to hers—onyx awash in tears, glittering with beautiful tragedy. He extended his hand to hers, and his fingertips brushed across hers. Beth moved with the care of someone who approached a spooked and scared being, gradually closing the distance. She pressed her thumb to his hard cheek as a tear dropped from his eye. A single tear to symbolize a thousand.

He tried to wipe it away from her skin, and she retracted her hand, the warm wetness dissolving into her skin, becoming part of her. "Your tears can't hurt me, Harrison."

A broken sound left him, and he hung his head. Maybe he had to break to see that he could let her in through the cracks. Beth could fill the holes. She could patch him up with her light. She wanted to do that for him.

171

"I'm not here to write your book anymore," she whispered. Beth would write it; she needed to, and she thought Harrison needed it too, but it was second place to them, not first. "I don't think that's ever really why I was here. I'm here for you."

The truth was in his eyes when he raised them to hers.

Beth swallowed and looked away, unable to stare into that vortex for too long. If she did, she could see herself jumping headfirst into him. Drawing back her shoulders and attempting a brisk tone, she grabbed a spare cloth and tossed it at him. "Either help me clean this mess or get out. We're wasting daylight."

She picked up the nearest award, smiling to herself as Harrison slowly reached for another. Beth didn't look at him as they worked. His nearness heated up the room, filled it with tingles of energy, like little invisible sparks littered the air.

"I read the ten pages," Harrison said softly.

Beth went still and then forced herself to move. She grabbed another trophy and wiped the cloth around its edges and smoothness. "Oh?"

His eyes touched on hers and strayed. "You made me sound better than I am. My hair really isn't that nice of a shade of red, and my jawline is weaker than you described."

She smiled. "I only wrote what I believe. Besides," Beth added. "It's only the first draft. It's subject to change."

He snorted. "Does that mean there's a chance it will be less complimentary toward me when the final draft is ready?"

Her lips twitched. "I guess that depends on you."

A dozen minutes passed before either of them spoke again, and it was Harrison.

"Straight through," he murmured as he set a newly shining trophy on a shelf.

Beth nodded, her arm shooting forward. "Straight through. With me beside you."

NINE

THANKSGIVING WITH HER family was strained, because all the while she was interacting with her parents and siblings, she was thinking of Harrison. He'd assured her his mom and dad would be spending the day with him, but Beth had doubts. Each time someone had to repeat her name to get her attention, overwhelmingly hot shame colored her face. She should be enjoying her time with her family.

It was as the dishes were being cleared from the table that her oldest brother, Benny, tugged on a chunk of her hair. "What's going on with you?"

Beth picked up the large, ceramic bowl of mostly eaten mashed potatoes and walked with it to the counter. The heat of the kitchen, mixed with the other various food smells, including the melted butter and garlic scent of the mash potatoes, made Beth cringe. She'd eaten too much, and now her stomach was revolting.

"What do you mean?"

Blue eyes a tad darker than hers locked on her, telling her she couldn't fool him. Benny and Beth looked the most alike out of

174

the Lambert kids, favoring the same coloring and similar features. Seven years older than her, Benny acted more like a father figure than a big brother. He was a beast of a guy, tall and stocky with more muscles than Beth thought was necessary. Her oldest brother said he lifted weights so he could enjoy his beer in peace. Beth told him he was a disgrace to computer nerds everywhere.

Her brother set a clear square storage container on the counter and began emptying the mashed potatoes into it. "You barely said a word to Whitney, and anytime someone tries to talk to you, you're off in your own little world. And you look funny." At her frown, he added, "Like something is bothering you."

"I'm sorry. I just…I have a lot on my mind. I'll make it up to Whitney. Maybe I can steal her for a little bit on Saturday." Beth's eyes found her eight-year-old niece through the doorway that led to the living room. She looked like a mini-version of Beth, a fact she took great joy in. Whitney sat with her grandparents on the couch, telling them a story with loud sound effects and giggling.

Beth smiled faintly and looked at her brother. "I'm just distracted."

"Yeah." He snorted. "I did notice that." He paused. "Mom says you're writing a story for some old hermit who lives in another town and doesn't want anyone to know who they are."

She knelt down and rustled in the cupboard, finding the green lid that fit the container. "Something like that."

"How's that going?" Benny scraped the last of the potatoes into the container.

Beth avoided his piercing eyes as she stood. "Good. Really good. I'm a quarter of the way through the story."

"Everything normal with that? Your employer's decent?"

She tilted her head, trying to remain calm even as her pulse sped up. He didn't know anything. No one did. "Yes. Why?"

Benny shrugged his broad shoulders. "Why don't they want anyone to know who they are? Why the mystery? Seems weird."

"They're private, that's all."

Benny's broad features darkened and his eyes blazed, his large body taut and bristling with anger. "Mom also said Ozzy isn't taking no for an answer. I never liked him. Thought he could do whatever he wanted, and he could, because he always got away with shit. He was a punk as a kid, and he's still a punk, only now he's old enough that he should know better."

Beth handed her brother the lid. It was interesting how everyone had an opinion on her and Ozzy now that they were no longer together. "Ozzy just has to figure things out on his own. It takes him a while to accept things aren't always the way he wants them to be."

She hoped that was all it was. Beth's fingers curled. She'd talked with her landlord, and he'd assured her Ozzy wasn't given a key, and for now, Beth would trust that. She told herself she must have left the door to the garage unlocked, like Ozzy said, but a twinge in her conscience kept her from entirely believing it.

"That's the way a kid thinks, not a man," he stated.

There was no disagreeing with that.

"Benny, you need a beer?" Jake called from downstairs. He liked to whine that he was the neglected middle child who couldn't even share the same letter in his first name as them.

"Yeah. I'll be right down," he replied, his eyes unmoving from Beth's. "Something's going on with you, and you can deny it all you want, but I see it. You're unhappy about something."

Benny snapped the lid into place and handed her the container. "You don't have to do anything on your own. Whatever is going on, everyone in this house loves you and will support you. I got your back, Beth. We all do."

She wanted to confess it all—her fears over Ozzy, Harrison's identity and how she was overwhelmed by her feelings for him, and even more so, terrified of the disease living inside of him. The dream of writing a bestselling novel that seemed too far out of reach. The uncashed check from Harrison sitting on her dresser that was more money than she normally saw in half a year and that she didn't deserve—how being with Harrison made her sad at times but being away from him was worse, that she was also hopeful, and inspired, and strong in his presence.

But none of that could pass her lips.

Instead, Beth set the container down on the counter and hugged Benny, hard and tight, and when she inhaled the laundry detergent and cologne smell of her brother, she felt safe.

"Mom said something similar last week," she admitted as she pulled away.

"Who do you think taught me to be the way I am? Well, and Dad, but more Mom. She's tough as nails." Benny grinned, showing off a crooked canine. "And you—she taught you how to be too." He pointed a blunt finger at her collarbone. "Be it, little sister."

Beth good-naturedly slapped at his finger and put the mashed potatoes in the refrigerator. "I'm trying." She nodded to the doorway that went downstairs. "Go drink your beer with Jake and Dad. You're out of place up here."

She smiled as her brother jogged across the room and stomped down the stairs. Beth was lucky to have such a caring, supportive family. After cleaning the last of the few dishes and wiping off the counter and table, Beth hung out with her sisters-in-law, niece, and her mom for an hour. She laughed and talked about movies and music with Whitney, her eyes continually finding the clock on the wall. She didn't have plans to see Harrison; there was no reason for her to be anxious to leave.

But she was.

When Beth felt sufficient time had passed, she got to her feet and let them know she would be back Saturday. Her blood streamed through her veins, telling her to hurry to a destination she did not have. Beth didn't think she'd be at ease until she next saw Harrison. With a hug and a smile aimed at her family, Beth packed on her winter gear and headed out into the cold night.

Her breaths left her in wisps of white and Beth tipped her head back to admire the blanket of twinkling lights in the dark sky.

Instead of going home, she drove the Blazer out of town, slowing down as she passed the driveway that went to Harrison's. She told herself it was perfectly normal to check up on someone to make sure they weren't alone. Beth wanted to know he had someone. Trembles overtook her body and chattered her teeth in the cold interior of her vehicle. Lights shone from inside the house, and she could vaguely make out the form of a vehicle parked near the garage. Her heart unclenched just a bit, and she headed back to Crystal Lake.

Home wasn't where she wanted to be, and after she parked the car in the garage, Beth walked around the neighborhood. A few houses had Christmas lights up, but most remained bare. Every Christmas Eve her mom would take her and her two brothers for walks around town to look at all the different light and yard displays.

Eventually, as her brothers got older and left the house, it was only Beth and her mom. They'd stay up late and drink hot chocolate when they got back home, watch Christmas movies until Beth fell asleep beside her mom on the couch. Christmas Eve was one of her favorite memories because of that time spent with her mom. It made her think of Harrison exploring the countryside with his father.

Deciding it would be fun to walk around town and admire the lights with her family, and would help distract her from obsessing over Harrison, Beth grinned to herself as she headed back in the direction of her parents' home. She was sure her sisters-in-law, Whitney, and her mom would be up for it, even if the men weren't.

She didn't realize whose house she was near until a shadow separated from the night, revealing a tall, lanky figure. Beth went still, making out an all-too-familiar form. Ozzy looked at her with eyes that matched the darkness around them. He stepped from the lawn of his brother's house and stopped in front of her, directly beneath the light of a streetlamp. His hair was an unruly mop on his head, adding to his boyish looks, and he had on faded jeans and a long-sleeved white shirt.

"Did you have a good Thanksgiving?" His tone wasn't pleasant. It was accusatory, like the hardness of his features.

Beth took a step to the left, and he followed, sharp-eyed and stiff-jawed. "Get out of the way, Ozzy."

"Answer the question, Beth."

"I'm not doing this anymore. I'm tired of it. Please, just leave me alone." Beth stepped by him. "We are *done*."

Ozzy forcefully gripped her arm and swung her around to face him. "What are you doing at that house outside of town?"

"What?" she whispered, instant panic crumbling her anger. What did he know? Had he found out about Harrison? Beth attempted to pull her arm away, and he tightened his grasp until a sound of pain left her. "Let me go."

He put his face next to hers. Madness glowed in his eyes. "I know you've been hiding something. I followed you. You went there every day this past week and stayed for hours each time. That's where you were that night you couldn't come to work, isn't it? There is no job, is there?"

"Listen to how you sound. You're stalking me now? What happened to you? I don't even know who you are. You are disturbed, Ozzy," she ground out, more worried for Harrison than for herself.

For herself, she was enraged. Beyond fear. Beth's body trembled, and it wasn't from the cold. Fury, hot and thick, scorched along her flesh. She tried to wrench her wrist away from his grasp again, and again, it was to no avail.

"I don't know who *you* are. You aren't the girl I fell in love with," he spat out, clenching her wrist hard enough that she gasped.

"Let go of me now, or I'll scream."

Something in her expression or voice registered, and with a sneer on his face, he dropped her arm and stepped back. "Patty said you spent more money at the salon in one day than you used to spend there in a year. That's not you, not normally. Spreading your legs for some old geezer to make money? Is that what you're doing up at that house in the country?"

The crack of her palm on his cheek was as loud and menacing as thunder. Ozzy's face was imprinted with red, and her hand throbbed. Beth's voice shook as she told him, "Don't disrespect me like that again."

He lowered his head and glared into her eyes. "You're keeping secrets, and I'm going to find out what they are."

"My secrets are not for you to wonder about. This ends now. Don't talk to me, don't show up where I am, don't even think about me."

"Or what?"

"Or this won't stay between you and me."

"You're right," he agreed. "It won't. Not for much longer. Secrets only last for so long, Beth. Good luck trying to keep yours."

Beth shoved past him, his words freezing her insides.

"You were supposed to *be* with me, not leave me!"

She spun around and screamed, "You were supposed to love me, not *hurt* me!"

The door to his brother's house opened and closed. Steve Peck rested his back to the door, crossing his arms as he faced their way. "Let's go inside now, Ozzy."

Ozzy's chest heaved as he exhaled, the light going out from his eyes. Beth fought to breathe, but every time she inhaled, it burned. Ozzy looked at her, but she didn't know if he really saw her. Did he see their past, remember that night? The night when their love became twisted, dark. When it died a little, and died more and more as time went on. She thought Ozzy saw it, as clearly as she did every time she looked at him.

He nodded, slowly backing away, and turned.

Beth pressed her hands to her mouth and stumbled in the direction of her house. She'd hit him. She'd hit someone she used to love. How could she do that? After everything they'd once been to one another, they were less than nothing. Enemies. Beth dropped her hands, looking at them as she walked. Tears choked her throat, and she let them fall, wondering how her life had gotten so unrecognizable.

Maybe she should have stayed with Ozzy, pretended not to feel alone and neglected, pretended she loved him like she should. It would have been easier. At least one of them would be happy. Beth could have pretended he was enough. She could have talked herself into believing she didn't need to be her own person, and that being half of Ozzy was what she wanted.

Pretended that he loved her like he should, like she needed.

Pretended like she didn't know about his unfaithfulness.

Pretended that he never hurt her.

Her boots hit the curb to her yard wrong when she tried to step over it, and Beth's knees banged against it as she crumpled to the frozen ground. She sat like that, huddled up within herself. Broken. Scared. Angry. Sad. Fighting tears that were stronger than her. Beth cursed herself, and Harrison, and Ozzy, and her stupid, stupid heart that forgave too often, and felt guilt over moving on; and ached for a man that wasn't meant to be hers.

Come on, Beth. Put yourself back together. Feeling sorry for yourself doesn't help anyone. Get up. Get up and move.

When she was somewhat in control, she carefully picked herself off the ground, wiped snow from her, and with shaking fingers, the tears from her face. Beth straightened her lopsided ponytail and cleared her throat. Shoulders back, she strode past her Blazer and to the house, but at the last second, she continued back to the SUV.

ಏ ✦ ಐ

THE VEHICLE WAS gone from the driveway, but a single room in the house remained lit. The reading room. Beth wiped dampness from her face, but more followed. She didn't know exactly when they started up again, but she couldn't stop the tears. It was too much fear, too much grief, too much worry, all pent up and needing to be released. And Beth ached. All of her ached.

She used the doorbell for the first time since she'd initially approached the door over two weeks ago, and as she waited, she half-turned to go six times. She shouldn't be here. Harrison and she had gotten closer in the week since his meltdown, but there were still barriers between them. Unwritten rules. Even as her stomach dipped with anxiety and she told herself to leave, each time she turned to go, she turned back. Beth thought she always would with Harrison.

If he told her to run away, instead she would run to him.

The lock clicked, and the door opened to reveal dark eyes in a pale face framed with black. The dead space behind him seeped out to her. The emptiness that had no thought nor feeling, a void of nothingness, wrapped her in its somber grip. And Beth welcomed it. If Harrison had to live in the dark, she'd stay there with him.

Beth was partially convinced he'd shut the door in her face and tell her to come back Monday during her assigned working hours. But he didn't. He blinked at the sight of her, stepping back and allowing her room to enter. Harrison's hair was damp, and he wore a worn gray shirt and black pajama bottoms. The scent of soap drifted out to her. Beth walked into the foyer and faced him as he shut and relocked the door.

183

"Am I your prisoner?" she tried to joke.

His eyebrows lowered. "Of course not."

"Can I be?" That was more serious than she wanted to admit.

"Beth?" he questioned with confusion.

All he said was her name, and it was enough to wreck her. Her face crumpled when Harrison narrowed his eyes to better study her, and Beth inhaled a shaky breath. The tears were hot, and salty as they touched her lips. Uninvited. Her eyes burned, and her skin was swollen, and she was sure she looked quite unattractive. When her nose developed a drip, Beth's shoulders slumped.

"What's wrong? Why are you crying?" No question about her being at his house, like her unannounced arrival in the middle of the night on a holiday was a common thing to have happen.

"I wasn't—I'm not...not crying," she denied, swiping the tears from her face.

"Yes. I see that," he said dryly.

Harrison waited. When Beth didn't say any more, he moved closer. "Was it about your boyfriend?"

"Ex-boyfriend," she corrected, taking a deep breath against her chaotic pulse. "And why would you ask me that?"

"When women cry, it's usually about men."

What would Harrison think if he knew she cried more over him than Ozzy? Not with pain, but with sorrow, as if the reason would matter.

Harrison gestured for her to give him her jacket, and she did, watching as he hung it on the same hook she always did. It was a coincidence, but it struck her as noteworthy. She had a place here designated as hers, if only for her jacket. Beth kicked off her boots and wrapped her arms around herself as she met his inquiring gaze.

"Tell me about your boyfriend. What about him makes you cry?"

"Ex-boyfriend," she said through gritted teeth.

"Tell me about him," Harrison coaxed.

"Why?"

One shoulder lifted and fell. "Enlighten me as to the kind of man who could get Beth Lambert to love him, and then, break her heart enough to make her cry."

She took a hitched breath, not speaking until the urge to cry had passed. Beth knew what Harrison was doing, however awkwardly. He was trying to get her to talk about things in hopes that it would make her feel better. When he gestured for her to follow him, she did, not speaking until they reached the reading room.

"My heart isn't broken over him anymore," she said quietly, firmly.

A single raised eyebrow hinted at his doubt.

"It just—it's really messed up, remembering how things used to be. He acts so different now. It's hard to believe he's the same person I knew as a kid."

Harrison's expression was neutral.

Beth took in the room, feeling like she'd stepped into a sanctuary the moment she entered it. Just seeing Harrison, being in his presence, made some of the pain fade. He didn't touch her, but it felt like she was hugged by him just the same. A single lamp shone from behind his chair, the atmosphere calm and dim. It cast the room in shadows, but it was peaceful.

"Were you reading?"

His lips pressed together. "Yes."

185

"What?"

"What?"

Beth laughed shakily. "What were you reading?"

A glower sharpened his features, gave them an animalistic edge. He glanced at a stack of white papers resting on the coffee table, and she knew what he'd been reading, and why he looked like he wanted to take his time chewing her up. "Something we'll talk about later. For now, tell me about Ozzy."

"Ozzy," she mused, her guts churning. Beth shook her head, not sure where to begin, or how to explain. "Ozzy is almost too pretty to be a guy, but there's a ruggedness to him that makes it impossible to think of him as anything other than masculine. And he's charming, when he wants to be. He makes people feel important." Beth picked at her tee shirt, frowning at her old perception of him compared to this new one. She didn't see beauty in him anymore. She saw something that could be attractive corrupted by darkness.

"I didn't ask you to tell me how attractive and wonderful he is."

Beth smiled faintly. "Sorry, it just—let me explain and you'll understand why I brought up his looks."

Harrison gestured for her to continue.

"He's also vain, and fickle. Childish and selfish. When I was with him, he was supposed to be my world, and he was, for a long time. But then I realized there was more to the world than him, and he didn't like that." Beth looked up, touched eyes with Harrison and felt the exchange in her center.

Without saying a word, Harrison told Beth he understood.

She dropped her gaze. "Ozzy made me feel special. He was this beautiful man, and he wanted me. He talked about us traveling, marrying, having kids. He talked about the music he'd write, and the money he'd make from it. He talked about dreams, and our life, and all the time, he never asked me if it was the life I wanted.

"Ozzy told me I meant everything to him, but any time we disagreed, or fought, I became nothing. He would ignore me, act like I didn't matter. He would flirt with others, and worse. He would let women touch him, and he touched them. Right in front of me, like I wasn't there, like it didn't matter if I was. There were rumors of him with other women, but he always denied it."

Beth shrugged. "He wanted me, but it wasn't really *me* he wanted. And he would break my heart, again and again." She took a shallow breath, let it out.

"And you allowed it, because you loved him." There was no judgment in his tone, and for that, Beth was grateful.

"Yes." She nodded, her throat thick from reliving the ups and downs of her and Ozzy's relationship. "But when I told him I wanted to write, and he gave me no support, it was the start of the end. He didn't believe in me. I always believed in him, and it hurt, far more than I can ever properly explain, to learn he didn't have that same faith in me."

Beth straightened her shoulders, the heat of her conviction spiraling through her like lava. "I would rather be alone than be with someone who makes me feel like I'm alone."

Harrison leaned against the wall, crossing his arms as he studied her. "Are you sure you're over him?"

Sadness and resolution fell upon her like a heavy blanket, nauseating in their entirety. "I don't want to be with him, but there is a part of me that will always feel the loss of him. He was my best friend growing up, my first everything. Sometimes it's hard to see past that, to see what's there instead of what I want to be there. But I do; I see it. I know."

He lowered his head, almost immediately lifting it to lock her in place with the intensity of his gaze. "It's strange to me. To see someone cry over someone else," Harrison added at her confused look. "I don't understand it. At one point I did, but not anymore."

"Why is that?"

He raised a hand to his face, studied the veined skin. "What does it accomplish? Why do it? You cry and then you still feel bad."

"It's good to cry," Beth grumbled.

"You know what's good? Laughter." Harrison straightened from the wall. "I'd take laughter over tears any day. Find something to laugh about, Beth. Tears are selfish. Laughter gives."

The power of his words slammed into her, wrapped around her mind, and splintered her perception of why she chose to feel the way she did about certain things. She didn't have to be sad about the past. She didn't have to hold on to regret and guilt. Beth could let it go. She remembered a saying she hadn't thought of in years: *Everyone died one day, but every other day they lived.*

Beth sucked in air, felt the inhalation move her whole frame. She was living, Harrison was living. And because of that, they should laugh. It wasn't fair for her to expect things from Harrison she wasn't willing to do herself. It was time to believe in herself, fully, without the self-doubt that was always waiting in the dark. Beth would gather the light around her, and there it would stay.

"You're right," she told him.

"Was there any doubt?"

Beth narrowed her eyes at Harrison. "I don't see you laughing."

"I laugh on the inside every day." The brown of his eyes sparkled as if diamonds were trapped inside the irises. "I'm laughing right now."

"Tell me the last time you laughed, out loud." A challenge was in her tone.

"The night we shoveled snow. I laughed."

"Barely."

He studied her, humor taking some of the hardness from his mouth. "There was a distinct chuckle."

"That was one time." Beth crossed her arms, fighting a battle with a smile she knew she was about to lose. "When else?"

"The day you climbed the hill and fell three times. I laughed each time you fell."

"Great. Glad you found humor at my expense. Twice."

"What can I say? I enjoy your misfortune," Harrison deadpanned.

Beth tried to keep a scowl on her face, but it was no use. When Harrison met her eyes with his blazing with mirth, it completely vanished and was replaced with a grin. Needing movement, she brushed the hair from her face and shifted her feet. The dark melted away, taking her hurt with it. A slice of her soul was healed, a part of her heart stitched back up.

Harrison moved to his chair and sat, locking his fingers together and resting them on his abdomen. "There are times when we take more pain than we should from those we love, Beth, but don't think of that as a weakness."

"Don't think of fear as one either," she told him, unable to look from him as his body turned to stone and his eyes shot to hers. Quiet weaved around them as she sat on the couch. Beth crossed her arms and legs as she looked back.

"Fair enough," he finally allowed. Harrison set his chin on his fist. "Tell me more about Ozzy. Tell me what made you come here. Something happened."

"He has a temper." She took a choking breath of air into her lungs. "And he has a dark side."

"We all have a dark side."

"No." Her eyes flew to Harrison's. "Not like his."

Harrison stared at her, not only hearing her words but listening to them. "What did he do?"

"I saw him tonight." Beth's throat tightened. "I was walking to my parents'. His brother lives near me. Ozzy was there, outside, like he was waiting for me." She unconsciously rubbed her sore wrist, glancing down. Beth's eyes widened as she noticed the ring of fingermarks and jerked her arm back as if to hide the evidence of Ozzy's fury.

Harrison was to her before she could cover up her reaction to the sight of the small bruises. He crouched beside her, keeping space between them. Flints of steel held her gaze. "Show me."

Beth shook her head and gripped the wounded arm. "I told him to stay away. He won't bother me anymore. It won't happen again."

Conviction rang hollow in her words. Even she couldn't believe them anymore.

His mouth hardened into a thin line.

"The last time we broke up, I broke up with him." The bookshelf across the room held her gaze, and Beth gathered strength from all the many stories waiting for her to get found in them.

People talked about getting lost in books, and that was fine, but it was the opposite for her. They reminded her of who she was, and who she wanted to be. Books were nightlights in the darkest days. When she was lost, she could open up a book and feel the light of it, the life. It pulsed through the pages, brought words to her heart, and in doing so, gave her heart to the words. Beth could read on any day, and be better for it.

"It sounds horribly weak of me to admit, but all the things he'd done through our relationship—none of those things were bad enough for me to go. He always apologized. He always made me feel bad for being upset with him. And I always gave in." Her mouth went sour at the admission. *Not anymore. There is no more giving in.*

Parts of Harrison's face were obscured by the dark, others by his thoughts.

"But when I told him I was serious about pursuing a writing career, he laughed at me, like he thought I was joking. I spent my childhood and teenage years writing, and he knew how much it meant to me, that it was a dream of mine. For him to laugh…that was the end for me. He told me I was nothing without actually saying it. I didn't realize until then that that was possible—to make someone feel small without uttering a word." Beth's fingers worked at the hem of her shirt, tugging at it and releasing it, curling it up and smoothing it out.

"He went out with some friends that night, and when he came back, I had my clothes and most of my things packed. I told him I was leaving, and I wasn't coming back. That we were finished. I couldn't keep telling myself what we had was what I wanted when it wasn't. When I tried to leave, he stopped me."

Beth remembered the smell of alcohol on his breath, the feel of his fingers biting into her flesh. The fear, the disbelief. "He tried to take my bags from me, and we fought over them. I tried to get around him, but I couldn't. He grabbed the back of my neck and shoved my face to the floor, and when I tried to fight him, he went out of control. Furious. It was like looking at a monster. The things he said to me."

She inhaled. Exhaled. "He grabbed me by my ankles and dragged me across the floor of the house and to the door. He threw me out, and he tossed my stuff out after me." Beth went still and quiet as she relived the helplessness she felt. It was a surreal scene of black and sickness. It could have been worse. She knew that too. That didn't lessen what it was.

Harrison moved to recline on the couch beside her, close enough that she felt the heat of his body, but always physically out of reach. Ozzy left bruises on her collarbone and shoulders, proof of his maniacal love. The ones that hurt the most, that wouldn't fully heal, were the ones he'd left upon her mind and heart.

He'd broken her that night, just a little, enough to leave a tattoo.

"It wasn't long, maybe three or four days, and he was the old Ozzy again. Of course, he said he didn't mean it. Of course, he said he was sorry. Of course, he cried and promised it would never happen again, but it happened once, and it never should have happened at all. I stayed with my parents until I was able to get my own place. I never told anyone, and the bruises were hidden."

She took a sharp breath of air into her lungs and looked up. "I almost went back. He wouldn't leave me alone, and he kept wearing and wearing me down, and I started to minimize it in my head. I made excuses for him."

Beth met Harrison's fathomless eyes. "He knows I come here. He's followed me. I'm worried he'll find out who you are. It won't be good for you when he does."

He was shaking his head before she finished. "It doesn't matter. Don't think of it."

"You've done so much to keep your identity secret. How can you act like it's of no consequence if it's known?"

"Beth. It doesn't matter." His tone was even, inarguable.

She dropped her eyes to her marred skin, and Beth closed her eyes against the sight. *Stop being that girl who loved Ozzy Peck. Be the woman who told him goodbye.* She took a shuddering breath, told herself she couldn't be scared anymore, not of anything. When Harrison's fingers lightly trailed across the bracelet of discoloration on her wrist, Beth's breathing turned shallow. He thought he was poison, but he didn't realize how much he mended her.

"You're safe now," he said in a low voice, and Beth believed him.

"When I was with Ozzy, I felt...I felt like I lost myself. I was an extension of him, a possession." She opened her eyes and looked at Harrison. "But when I'm around you, it's like I'm finding me."

Beth smiled and shrugged, turning her eyes back to the books. The books that centered her, like Harrison.

His fingers dropped from her, and he moved farther down the couch, physically denying her words even as none passed his lips.

"We need to talk about that." He nodded his head toward the papers on the coffee table.

"Do we?"

"We do," he said firmly.

Beth set her shoulders back and clasped her hands together in her lap. "Okay. What is it?"

Black flashed at her from his eyes. "You mentioned an illness."

"Yes," she said evenly. Beth held his hard-eyed gaze. "Because there is an illness."

Harrison's jaw tightened, and he looked away.

"You're not letting me do what I need to do to give your story justice." Beth spoke sharply, her frustration coming out. "You told me to write your story, but then you have all these rules. You're only allowing me to write half of it."

He shifted his attention to her.

"It's there, Harrison," she told him gently. "And it doesn't have to be the focal point, but it is a layer. A necessary one."

Harrison rubbed his face, sighing as he cast bleary eyes her way. "What about you?"

Beth froze. "What about me?"

"Aren't you a part of the story?" he asked slowly.

She sat still, digesting his words. She inhaled deliberately, schooling her expression into calmness she didn't feel. "I'm a late addition."

A hitched eyebrow was the only response she got.

Beth jumped to her feet and stalked the room, wanting Harrison to understand. "Stories are made up of layers, right?" She turned to him, continuing before he had a chance to answer. "There's an outline, a first draft, second, maybe third, and a final. Each one adds another layer to the story. So there's you. You're the initial layer, the starting point, the main character. The reader has to feel like they know you. Add your features, your mannerisms, your thoughts, your feelings, and we sort of have Harrison."

"Sort of?"

She absently waved a hand at him, striding in the opposite direction. "Another layer could be your goals, something that happened to you in the past that made you the man you are. Some conflict. An illness," she emphasized.

Beth didn't have to look at Harrison to know he was frowning.

"Then there's how you deal with the conflict, or *illness*. That slaps another element to the story, helps shape and mold it. Gives it depth." Beth paused and fixed her eyes on him. "You aren't just some football player, or some man. You're a man who was told he has a disease that can kill him." Her chest squeezed, and Beth flinched around the pain. "But you're more than that, so much more. And I want to show that. I have to show that. Let me."

Harrison let his eyes drop to his clenched hands, his shoulders bowed against her words or his thoughts. "And what role do you have?"

Beth took a fortifying breath of air and squared her shoulders. "I'm the storyteller. I'm the best part."

He lifted his head and allowed a faint smile to crest his lips. "Think so?"

Beth shrugged and walked across the room. She grabbed a throw pillow from the bench and settled on the hardwood floor, knowing that before too long her back would regret her position. Until then, she would stay where she was. Harrison had to decide how he wanted his story to be told, but she thought it was an injustice to keep any aspect of his life out of it, even the harder parts.

"Okay, Beth."

She closed her eyes and breathed deeply, satisfaction hugging her. *Okay, Harrison.* Under the glow of the moon and no other light on this side of the room, she turned her head and looked out the window at the stars. "Be honest with me."

Harrison stepped over her and compacted his long body to fit on the bench beneath the window. He set his hands behind his head and aimed his face toward the ceiling. "What is it?"

The relaxed intimacy, coupled with the late hour and the deepness of Harrison's voice, made her bolder. "You didn't need anyone to write your book."

His answer was surprisingly fast. "No."

"Then why did I come here?"

"I looked up the residents of the town, did some research. I like to know the kind of people around me. You wrote an article," he said slowly. "I saw the potential in your writing, the passion for the subject you were discussing, and yes, I thought you were pretty. But that wasn't what caught my attention. It was your eyes. Innocent, hopeful. Haunted."

Harrison looked down toward her, his features black in the night. "I do want you to write my story, in your words. I think only you, with your heart and your openness, can write it as it should be. No one else."

Beth closed her eyes against the tripping of her pulse, breathing in his words and hugging them with her soul. "I figured you saw the article in the paper. The timing was accurate. You emailed me just a few days after it came out. The one about me graduating and the big writer dreams I had. You're paying me too much, by the way."

"It's not enough," he argued evenly.

"I have more at home ready for you to read," Beth admitted, popping open her eyes. "Do you want to read it?"

"No, not until it's done."

"How do you know it doesn't veer off into some fantasy land where you're dressed in a pink skirt and like to talk to peas?"

She caught the smile before he turned his head. "I trust you."

"You're paying a lot of money on trust."

"I don't need it."

Harrison scooted closer to the wall, and as soon as he did, Beth got up and filled the space, their bodies situated with his head near her feet and her head near his. He went motionless, and then he exhaled. Beth smiled to herself. She was tired, but content to talk to him until she either left, or fell asleep.

"What do you do all by yourself in the mornings and over the weekends?"

"Think."

"And what do you think about?"

"People, mostly."

"Oh?" She lifted her head and eyed him. "What about them?"

"Well, I find them interesting, for starters."

He said it so matter-of-factly that Beth laughed as she relaxed against the cushions. "Really?"

"Yes." Harrison shifted, either in nervousness or restlessness. "Do you ever think about all the different kinds of people there are?"

Beth tucked a lock of hair behind her ear and frowned. "I'm not sure I'm following." The rubber band against her scalp was making her head sore. She removed it and put it on her wrist, smoothing down the thick locks that had been held hostage by it for too long.

"Okay, well, let's say there is a room full of people." He paused. "Are you with me so far?"

Rolling her eyes, she clasped her hands together on her midsection and replied, "Yes. I'm somehow managing to hang on."

"You have all these people with all these different working brains. Some people are nervous being around so many people, some are enjoying it. Some are quiet, some talk. There are dreamers and scientists and know-it-alls. Observers, entertainers, shy people, loudmouths.

"There are people with empathy, sympathy, and apathy. There are some who don't know the dissimilarities between the three. Some who like broccoli, some who hate it. Some who have never even tried broccoli. Introverts and extroverts. We're all programmed in our own individual way. We all have a brain, and yet no two are alike. It's fascinating to me." Harrison stopped as if he realized he'd said too much, shown too much of himself to her.

"It is fascinating," she said.

Harrison's leg bent, and his foot bumped the outside of her thigh. "You sound fascinated."

Beth laughed. She liked this side of Harrison. He was actually talking to her instead of trying to push her away. "How was your Thanksgiving?"

"My parents cooked me dinner and refused to let me help in any way. When I went to wash the dishes, my mom shoved me back in my chair and told me to drink a cup of coffee. To be fair, it was delicious coffee. She wouldn't even let me take the pie from the oven." Annoyance sharpened his words.

"What kind of pie?"

"Pumpkin. My favorite."

"Your parents are ridiculously mean."

A short burst of laughter left him. "They're amazing. Overprotective. And amazing."

Beth sat up and rested her chin on her knees, studying what she could see of Harrison's face. "Can we do this all night?"

He pulled himself up to a sitting position. "Do what?"

She shrugged. "Talk. Not sleep. Research, you know."

Even though she couldn't see it, Beth felt his smile. "Ah, yes, research. I'd hate to stand in the way of that."

"Is that a yes?"

He reached out a hand, played with a lock of her hair. She felt his touch all the way to her scalp. "Yes."

They stayed up until the blackness outside turned to gray, and then pink. She laughed, and she heard the magic of Harrison's multiple times. Beth learned of his favorite sandwich—a BLT. His first kiss was at the age of thirteen, and he dated the girl for three months, even copping a feel before he was dumped for a guy with facial hair. Beth told him about the time she threw up at the roller rink one town over, and how she won her first dance competition at the age of seven.

"Sometimes," Beth whispered as dawn touched the sky in pinks and oranges. "I feel like everyone around me thinks I'm not strong. But I do, Harrison, I think I'm strong."

The silence filled the space between them, and as it grew, her elation dimmed.

And then Harrison spoke.

"I think you're strong, Beth."

Beth smiled as her eyes stung. "I think you're strong too—and lovely."

Harrison snorted, causing her to laugh.

"Keep talking, Beth. I like your stories," he whispered into the morning's hello.

She talked until her throat hurt, and her voice went hoarse. And at some point, his hand rested beside hers, close enough that their fingers periodically grazed one another's. It was a perfect moment in a collage of misfortune. A sick man and a wounded woman, both restored in the presence of one another's brokenness.

TEN

A S THE WEEKS went by, they formed their own rhythm. November crept into December, and with it, came more snow, more cold. Beth spent most of her days with Harrison, and some of her weekends. Nothing went past an unspoken point. They rarely touched. Sometimes they didn't talk at all. Beth observed, and Harrison lived, and it was as if they were in their own world of white. She knew what was happening, and she couldn't stop it. She didn't want to stop it.

Beth was falling.

Falling.

And falling.

Beth was falling for Harrison.

A glance of his eyes, the hint of a smile; his voice as it drifted along the air. Harrison's thoughts projected with a certain look that made her mind go blank and her words falter. The way her body sparked to life when he was near. How he echoed in her mind long after she left his presence. Beth was reborn in the eclipse of Harrison.

Ozzy became an afterthought, but he shouldn't have.

The smattering of Christmas lights and decorations around town had multiplied in twos and threes. Beth stopped on the busy sidewalk, one shivering form paused in motion while lives pulsed around her, their feet as fast as their heartbeats. It was negative ten degrees out with the wind chill, and frozen air left her mouth as she breathed, the tips of her ears stinging even under the cover of her thick hair and a stocking cap.

She tipped her head back and looked up at the lights strewn from streetlamp to streetlamp, white blinking in black. Beth felt something she hadn't in a long time. Confident. Shifting her gaze to the businesses with their doors and windows aglow, Beth pushed her hands in the pockets of her winter coat and crossed the street to The Lucky Coin.

It was her final shift as a bartender for The Lucky Coin, a fact that exhilarated her, and in the farthest setting of her heart, made it twinge, just a bit. Just enough to let her know it hadn't all been bad. It was a parting that should have taken place a while ago, but Beth had worked at the bar since she was eighteen. Eight years of her life were spent there. It wasn't easy to go. There were times when knowing the right thing to do, and actually doing it, were not necessarily a packaged deal.

With it being a Wednesday, most of the regulars were at the bowling alley across town for league night. Because of that, Beth was hoping for an uneventful night to end her employment with the Peck family. When she walked through the door and saw only a handful of people lined up at the bar, she hid a sigh of relief. There was an instant of a flyaway heartrate when she wondered if Ozzy would be at the bar, but it was clear he was not. She hadn't seen him since Thanksgiving night. That was good, but also suspicious.

Loving all fried foods, the smell of French fries that welcomed Beth was one she would miss. Beth hung up her jacket and hat in the hallway in the back of the building before meeting Deb behind the bar. Deb's greeting was cooler than Beth expected, but she pretended not to notice, effortlessly getting into her routine of serving customers, restocking what needed to be, and keeping the area clean.

"The bathrooms need paper toweling and toilet paper," Deb said in passing.

Beth set down the beer she'd gotten for one of the customers and frowned at Deb's taut back as she took the man's money and put it in the cash register. The shutting of the drawer was sharp, her hurt showing forth. The fall colors and homey atmosphere deadened somehow, turning from cheery to ominous. Beth was not welcome anymore. She felt the brittleness of exclusion in her bones. As she walked to the room that was loosely used as the owners' office, Beth wondered if Deb was upset that she was leaving, or if it was more—if Ozzy had said something. She didn't trust him to tell the truth. He couldn't even tell himself the truth.

It doesn't matter. You have four hours left, and then you don't ever have to step foot in this place again—or talk to any members of the Peck family, if you're lucky.

With toilet paper and paper towels in hand, Beth marched to the bathrooms. Her nose crinkled as she stepped into the men's. It smelled like urine and chemicals in the tan-walled room. She knew Deb cleaned them at least twice a week, but it appeared to be due. After she refilled the paper products, as a peace offering to whatever battle was unknowingly being waged between her and her employer, Beth asked Deb if she wanted her to take care of the restrooms.

Deb looked at Beth like she didn't know her, and didn't like what she saw. "You broke Ozzy's heart, Beth."

Beth felt her nerve-endings tauten. Golden eyes delved into blue, challenging her to deny it. Telling her not to bother. "He broke mine first."

Her stiff shoulders went limp, and Deb rubbed a hand against her short dark hair. "I understand how needy and controlling Ozzy can be. I know you can't be together, but I see how the breakup is hurting my son. I also know it's illogical to blame you, and I selfishly wish you were still together. For my benefit, and my son's."

You don't know your son, whispered across her lips, but she closed her mouth against it.

Deb sighed and wiped at the counter with a rag. "Maybe you quitting is the best thing that can happen. Yes. Please clean the bathrooms. It's a slow night. You can go home early. You'll still get paid for the hours you aren't here. Consider it a parting gift."

"Thank you," she said in a wooden voice, her limbs as stilted as her words as Beth left the bar area.

She blinked her eyes against the stinging burn as she went about sanitizing the bathrooms. Beth heard the door to the bar open, caught Ozzy's voice, and bristled. It wasn't her fault he couldn't move on, that he refused to let their relationship go. It wasn't her fault his mom didn't like that they'd broken up. So much guilt was shoved onto her, all because Beth made choices that others did not want her to make. The guilt was thick and heavy, an unwanted blanket. Her life didn't feel like hers.

Beth told herself it was.

She told herself to not let others make her feel bad, and when she strode out the door of The Lucky Coin for the last time, making sure to avoid Ozzy's stare, she told herself it was the best decision for her to make. One more shackle unlocked. One step closer to being who she wanted to be. She would prove to herself, and everyone else, that she could do whatever she wanted. She could decide to write, and she could decide to be happy, and she could decide to fall in love with a sick man.

Finally, Beth was seeing. Everything was up to her.

As she reached the Blazer, the air turned frigid, gusts of it snatching at her hair and pushing against her. The barely perceptible sound of boots moving over packed snow touched her ears. Beth would have missed it if she hadn't been listening for it. No one else was out, not even the headlights of vehicles shone on the street. The sudden temperature drop was an announcement, a signal of an unwanted guest, as if nature thought to caution Beth. She knew before she looked that she wasn't alone. She knew who was behind her without facing him, and she wasn't even surprised.

"Just tell me one thing."

Beth closed her eyes and counted three breaths. The quivering in her frame belied the calmness she fought to find. She wasn't scared of him, but Beth was wary. She set her shoulders to bravery and faced the dark stain that would not leave her white world. Thinking of Harrison helped, and she pictured his determined chin, his eyes as bottomless as a well.

Her voice was surprisingly firm as she told him, "I will get a restraining order against you if you put a single finger on me."

Ozzy held up his hands. "I'm not going to touch you."

"What do you want?"

Weariness had grooved creases beneath his eyes. With his faded jean jacket, red-tipped nose and cheeks, he looked cold, but his body remained immobile. His eyes were clear and bright, like a sunset on fire. When he took a step closer and Beth pushed her back hard into the vehicle, wishing she could sink through the metal and into it, Ozzy's brows pinched together. He dropped his hands. The vehicle was frozen, searing through her coat with icy heat.

"You're afraid of me."

This was the alternate Ozzy. The side that cared, and felt deeply, and had a childlike sweetness. The one who had big ideas and a disarming smile. The Ozzy who wouldn't hurt her. This Ozzy was fleeting, and she saw less of him more and more. His personalities were making her dizzy. How many minds could live inside one man?

"You say it like you can't understand how that could happen. I don't know you anymore. I don't know who you are, but you aren't Ozzy. How could I not be leery of you? You're a stranger." Beth clutched the keys inside one palm, careful to keep the sharp part pointed out, a small weapon that would buy her time if she needed it.

Ozzy gripped his shaggy hair and flexed his fingers. "I don't know—I've just, I've felt insane the last few months. You're gone. You're really gone, and I don't know how to deal with that. I don't know what's wrong with me," he mumbled, turning to the side and staring into the night. His arms fell to his sides.

"Harrison Caldwell."

That name passing his lips made her stomach fall, all the way to the ground. It pooled there, disbelief and dismay churnings its contents. Her fingers curled, wanting to scratch the name from his throat, his thoughts. One of her numb fingers scraped against the sharp edge of the key and pain pulsed there. It reminded her that she could feel even when she'd rather not.

"What?" She didn't understand how she was able to produce the word, or even the air that entered and left her lungs.

Ozzy turned to her, his eyes two golden ponds. They weaved and waved, a storm brewing from within. It would be destructive, and deadly, once it hit. "Harrison Caldwell. That's whose house you've been going to."

"How do you—why?" Beth wouldn't confirm his words, but denying them would do exactly that. She swallowed, felt her throat contract. Not saying anything was best. She turned her shocked eyes to the horizon, unconsciously looking in the direction of Harrison's house. Beth wanted to go there, and never come back to this town, this existence.

"That's who you've been seeing, that's the person who hired you. Are you even really working for him, or was that a lie too?"

Beth shifted her gaze to his, and stared.

"Beth."

She pressed her lips together, refusing to warrant his words with an answer. Beth owed him nothing. Placing a hand to the icy glass of the window, she steadied herself and put the key in the lock. "I'm going home. Don't try to stop me."

"Do you have any idea who he is, what he has?"

Her back stiffened, anger heating the cold from her body. Stealing the tremble from her voice. Disintegrating the trepidation from her eyes. Beth looked over her shoulder, met firestorm eyes with blue titanium ones, as indestructible as her faith in Harrison. She turned back to the Blazer. "I know everything."

"And you still chose him over me." His tone was derisive, disbelieving.

"I would choose him every time, over you and anyone else."

"He came to see me."

She froze with her back to him. Even the ice-covered landscape wasn't as motionless as her.

"Yeah. About a week ago. Showed up at my place in the middle of the night. He told me to stay away from you, said that if he ever heard I touched you again it would be the last time I touched anything."

Ozzy made a sound of incredulity. "At first, I couldn't believe who was talking to me, then what it meant sunk in. Harrison Caldwell wouldn't have warned me away from you unless he was involved with you in some way. After that, it all clicked into place."

A piece of snow skidded past her feet, and she knew Ozzy had kicked it. "So there you have it. I know your secret. It's sick, Beth. You're sick."

Her eyes glazed over with tears of fury. It wasn't sick. People would think that. They would criticize, and be disgusted. Because they didn't understand. And they couldn't. That was fine. That was life. But it wasn't her problem that others could discredit something they didn't comprehend.

"You say I've changed," he said from behind, his fading footsteps signaling his retreat. "Look at you. You've changed more."

"I have," she agreed, opening the car door. "And I like the changes."

She climbed in and slammed the door. Beth hit the locks, waiting until Ozzy left in his truck. She set her forehead on the cool steering wheel and tried to breathe. Beth had recently realized that she could miss something, but not want it back. She had been too busy looking behind her when she should have been looking ahead. That was the only way she'd allow herself to look from now on. Straight ahead. Like Harrison. With Harrison.

Harrison.

Chills swept over her body, up and down and crisscrossing over her. He'd confronted Ozzy. He'd stood up for her. He'd let his identity be known to someone, for her. Her hands shook with emotion for what he'd sacrificed. Harrison with his own nemesis living, growing, and inflicting havoc in his veins, fighting her battles. Overcome, she sat quietly in the cold as she breathed to steady her pulse before she attempted to go home.

Believing she was worth more than what Ozzy wanted to give her was the hardest thing she ever did.

Falling in love with Harrison was the easiest.

ೞ • ೲ

CONVULSIONS TOOK OVER her frame when she set eyes on Harrison the next day. He was the dark sun, fiery and consuming, and he lit her up. Burned her. She had to force her feet to stop, or Beth feared she never would. She'd walked right up to him, right into his arms, and she'd stay there, live there, breathe there. Beth would never go, not even when he told her to. Not even when he couldn't tell her to.

"How was your last day at The Lucky Coin? Did everything go okay?"

Beth inhaled.

Beth exhaled.

His copper eyebrows lowered over black, black eyes. He stood in the entryway, like he had been waiting for her. Like he was anxious to see her. Like he got up every morning hoping he would see her, that that was enough of a reason to meet another day, the same as it was for her. "What is it? Why are you looking at me like that?"

She curled the fingers of her free hand and shook her head, the erratic beat of her heart saying all the words she wouldn't.

"Beth. Tell me what's wrong."

Beth wanted to tell him so many things, but all she said was, "Thank you." Her voice was quiet and unsteady, and her fingers tightened around the handle of the laptop case.

"For?" He inclined his fire-kissed head of hair.

"You talked to Ozzy. Thank you. You didn't have to do that, but you did."

He gave a brief nod, looking away from her. "I did have to."

Her lips tugged down.

Harrison lifted his gaze to hers, the space from him to her disintegrated by the flames in his expression. So pale, so much strength overtaken by fragility. Harrison's body was imposingly tall, stiff with soreness. She knew he hurt, in his bones, in his muscles, in his soul. Her arms ached to hold him, to erase the pain, to take it away and into her.

"I did have to, because if I learned that he touched you again, I would have hurt him." His hands opened and closed, opened and closed. "I *wanted* to hurt him. Every time I think of him hurting you, I want to hurt him a million times worse."

Beth set down the laptop case and moved for him, stopping only when the time it took to take a breath was all that was between them. Harrison's lips were carved from rock, his jaw from the same. But his eyes were alive, and they felt. Sometimes sadness, sometimes grief and hopelessness, and other times, like now, they were ignited with emotion.

Swallowing around the beat of her heart, and the strumming of her pulse, and her tightly wound body that wanted to know the feel of his, Beth lifted her hand. Harrison turned her into music. And she wanted to dance within the song of his life. Feel him, kiss him, love him, burn with him, live in him. Be with him.

"Stop," he rasped when her fingers were an instant from touching the hard plane of his cheekbone. He closed his eyes, the emotion draining from them into his skin, straining his features. Harrison opened his eyes and showed her nothing. "This—this has to stop. Whatever this is, it can't end well. I need you to go, and not come back. This was a bad idea, and I'm ending it."

Beth's heart sputtered, faltered, thought about stopping altogether. She shook her head, denying his words, denying his right to tell her such a thing. "It's too late for that."

The skin around his eyes tightened. "This is an illusion, Beth."

"Why do you keep pushing me away?"

"I'm trying to protect you."

"Don't."

A muscle bunched in his jaw. "You don't know what you're saying."

"I do. I want you to stop. I know what can and can't be done. I know the risks. I know what it involves. Stop trying to protect me and just…just let us be." Beth touched the shell of his ear and he flinched, careful not to move. "I care for you. Don't make me feel bad about it, and you don't feel bad about it either."

"And in the end, should it come to that?" Harrison's voice sounded like broken glass, cutting her skin with his words. "When you have to watch my body and mind fail? When the disease grows, and I finally lose. When I'm covered in sores and my body is emaciated, and every breath hurts. When you can count the bones in my body through my skin. Do you think I want you to see that?"

Her eyes filled with tears. She didn't want to think about how the disease could ravage his mind and body before it was done with him. But she had. Over and over Beth forced herself to imagine all the possible scenarios. And none of it was enough to keep her away, or change her mind. Whatever decisions were made, whatever happened, Beth would know exactly what she was doing, as she was doing it.

"But if I choose to stay, if I want to be with you, let me. Please. Please, don't make me leave you."

"How can you say that?" Harrison's voice cracked.

"You inspire me. Everything about you inspires me. I wouldn't be able to write the way I have been without you." Beth looked into his eyes and saw emotions not put to names in them. "Your story thrums inside of me, in time with my heartbeats. I am better for knowing you, and I will not be the one to write the final word."

Harrison looked down. His voice was just a whisper as he asked, "Why would you choose this, choose me?"

"You make me want to dance." When he looked up with a furrowed brow, she added, "I haven't danced in years, not until recently."

Harrison blinked as if he didn't know how to process her words.

"And you make me want to write. There are so many things you bring out in me that were missing, that I didn't even know were missing until I got them back. I was lost. Learning about you helped me remember who I am.

"I'll never stop writing your story, Harrison. I'll write and write; until my fingers cramp up, and my heart overflows, and my mind goes numb, and I'll still write. I'll write you into every day of my life." It was a promise. An oath, and a confession.

He took a breath, and it divided halfway through. Beth wanted to take both halves and press them into one. Mend the fissures that constructed the man.

"I watched you dance, that day in the trophy room," he admitted. Harrison hesitated. "I'd like to watch you dance again."

Beth smiled. "And you shall." She offered a hand. Shook it when he stared at it. "Take my hand and let me dance for you."

The empty room with its bare walls and lack of life pulsed with Harrison's. He turned the lights and the walls and all the nothingness around them into a stage, and he was the performer. And who was Beth? Beth was the one Harrison let take his hand. It was warm and steady, and her fingers curved, never wanting to break contact. Just the feel of his hand on hers made her head dizzy, her mouth dry. Her core ache. Harrison's fingers electrocuted her, stung her skin with the sweetest shock.

They stepped into the soundproof room with its lonely chair. It didn't seem lonely anymore. It was a throne, and Harrison reigned there. Beth waited for him to sit, twisting her hair into a bun on the top of her head and holding it in place with the rubber band she removed from her wrist. She found the version of 'The Sound of Silence' by Disturbed on her phone and pushed play.

She stared into his dark eyes from across the room, his energy palpable around his form and in the air. His eyes narrowed a fraction as the music started, as she remained unmoving. The music reverberated through the room, echoed with beauty and sorrow. His index finger framed his jaw as he set his chin on his fist, his attention never leaving her.

And then Beth moved, sliding one leg back, arching her back and head as her arms swept overhead. She twisted in a low spin, contracting and releasing her body, flying. Soaring. Gliding. She dipped and turned, her neck loose, her face up. Faster and faster, until she was no longer a person and instead a piece of the music. Skin damp with perspiration, pulse speeding like it had a race to win, Beth danced. Her muscles cried, her heart sang, and Beth laughed, breathless and free.

She danced for herself; she danced for Harrison. The song changed to 'Save My Soul' by Rivvrs. Like a wave of motion, she swayed with the pull of the music. Beth turned and looked down at Harrison, needing him to dance with her. Needing that physical connection he continually denied. Her chest was in spasms with the force of her breathing, and as she gazed into dark eyes, she didn't recognize the man.

Eyes of desire, lips of passion; a face set with want and need.

He shot to his feet, and his hand shook as he covered his mouth with it. The hand she wanted on her bare skin. She imagined his fingers, long and strong, undulating over her like a waterfall, and her breaths came faster. Harrison would say he could never be hers, and she could never be his, but it was already so. She felt him upon her heart, a brand that would not fade. She saw her mark in his eyes, a glint that made them shine for her. The light that only recently came to his eyes.

Beth offered her hands, need sparking through her eyes to him and back like a live wire. *Touch me*, her skin whispered. *Love me*, her heart added. *Live for me*, her soul asked.

He tilted his head, his eyes moving from her hands to her face. She didn't imagine the crack in his voice as he asked, "What are you doing, Beth?"

"Dancing," she said breathlessly.

"You don't dance like anyone I've seen."

She smiled, and it was tipped in secrets. "Good."

Standing face to face, hands up, she pressed her palms to his and applied the smallest pressure. Beth kept their fingers unlocked. She stared into her own eyes through his, saw the building fire, the heat that couldn't be ignored for much longer. Lines grew around his eyes as Harrison stepped back. Beth nodded once, moving her right arm out in an arc, Harrison moving his arm with her. She turned, and he went with her, and they gradually swayed the length of the room. It was slow, awkward.

Harrison's smile was faint. Apologetic. "I'm not good at this," he told her.

"You're as good as you need to be," she told him back. Beth paused before telling him words that had nothing to do with their dancing. "You're as good as *I* need you to be. Focus on me, Harrison. I'm all that matters."

He missed a step, his eyes shooting to hers. The harshness was gone from his features, leaving them sweet and soft. He stared into her eyes like he was listening to her, like her words made sense to him. Hope—she saw a glimpse of it in his frame.

She carefully moved her hands to the back of his neck and loosely locked her fingers. His throat moved as he swallowed, and he hesitantly set his hands on her waist. She briefly closed her eyes against the thrill that tingled through her skin, exhaling slowly. Beth chased his gaze until she caught it, and held it, the smile on her lips reaching up to her eyes. His hair tickled her fingers, and she inched closer, her face next to where his heart worked at an astonishingly powerful rate.

Beth heard it, felt it, revered it.

"You smell good, like sunflowers and sunshine," he whispered as the song ended.

A small laugh left her as they stopped moving. She didn't want to be the first to pull away, and she wasn't. It was Harrison. She studied his back as he showed it to her, seeing the lines and hints of muscle and bone. Beth wanted to run her fingers up and down the bumps and crevices of it.

"What's happening between us?" When she didn't immediately answer, Harrison turned.

"We're getting to know each other's heart. I'm glad I was introduced to yours." Beth gingerly set her hand on his chest, felt the beat of his life against her palm. "I like your heart, Harrison." She looked up, her eyes clashing with his.

"I like your heart too," he told her falteringly.

Beth lightly touched the valley beneath his lower lip and above his chin. Harrison let her, closing his eyes and taking a deep, unstable breath. There was faint stubble that made the pad of her finger tingle. She studied his face as her hand fell away. His expression revealed things his mouth never would. He wanted to dream, like her. Beth's eyes watered. She wanted him to know it was okay to dream.

"I'll write you a world where no one ever dies, and there are no diseases, and everyone is good. I'll make one for you, and you can live there. Every day, every night. You can pick up the papers and live in the words," she said softly.

His eyes flew open, pain splitting his features. Harrison took a step back, unbalanced on his feet.

Beth made up for the distance he put between them, her legs weak and heavy. Her heart pounded, so hard, so fast, so loudly. How could he not hear it? How was it not resonating through the room? "Or I'll read them to you, each night, before you fall asleep. You can go to sleep dreaming of your world. Each time you close your eyes, it will be there for you. Waiting. I'll do that for you. I want to do that for you."

"You can do anything," he told her, his voice breathless and uneven. "You can write your worlds, and your stories, your books. You can do that, Beth. Never forget that you can do anything."

"What if…what if more than all of that, I want to be with you? What then?" As soon as the question was asked, Beth went still, as still as Harrison. She hadn't meant to ask it, but it had been there, in her thoughts, hovering, needing to be heard. *Let me do that for you. For me. Let me write our world and let us live inside it.*

All the light drained from his face. "That is impossible. You have to know that."

"I don't believe in impossibilities," she told him, her bravery growing now that she'd said the words she'd been harboring, locked deep inside her. "And you just told me I could do anything. I want to be with you."

"Beth. You don't understand what you're asking, what you would be welcoming into your life." Harrison's eyes tightened. "Heartache and misery."

"I do know. I researched it." She shook her head, a self-deprecating smile tugging at her mouth. "I researched it *over and over*. I know the risks. I know all I need to know, and I'm telling you, I'll do it. Whatever I have to, I'll do it. I'll take a pill, I'll get routine checkups. Whatever. I'm all in. All you have to do is say yes."

A sliver of hope touched his face, raw and real, and it broke a piece of her heart. He looked so sad, so unbelievably shattered a lot of the time. He was stiff and dark and silent, holding it all in. Fighting. Pretending. She was telling him he didn't have to. Beth was holding the invisible key to unlock all he was afraid to. He just had to take it.

"You talk about the bad things that could happen, but what about all the good? You feel it too—what I feel for you." Beth watched his features tighten. "I know you do. If you tell me you don't, I'll know you're lying."

"There could never be anything physical between us. I wouldn't let you risk it."

"There could, if we were careful."

"If we were careful." His lips twisted in a sneer. "What kind of a relationship is that? Every day I would carry fear that I was unintentionally harming you in some way. Nothing could be spontaneous. Everything would have to be planned out, tested. It would be sterile, lacking. I would never know the feel of you wrapped around me. There would always be something between us. Figuratively. Literally."

The room turned hollow, devoid of life and laughter. It went back to the emptiness she found in the house on her first day in Harrison's employ. A bitter scent entered the air, and it was that of her heart crushing. She felt the pieces of it crumble. Harrison told her she could dream, as long it didn't involve him. Harrison told her she could do anything she wanted, as long as she kept him out of it. Harrison was a hypocrite.

Harrison wasn't done twisting her insides.

"And what if something happened, things got out of hand, and we weren't careful? What then? You might be okay with putting your health at risk, but I'm not okay with allowing you to do so."

He put space between them, and he kept putting more, until he was at the door, and then he was in the hallway. He didn't have to move at all to reconstruct the wall. She felt it fall into place. He turned back once, to utter a single, catastrophic word.

"No."

ELEVEN

A WEEK PASSED. A week of awkward conversations, prolonged silences, and darted looks that turned into lingering ones when the recipient wasn't paying attention. She wanted more, and his slanted looks said the same. But Beth was willing to take a chance, a leap—*yes*, a risk, and Harrison was not. It was making her edgy, short-tempered. All she could think about was time, and how they were wasting it.

What would he say if she told him she'd already met with and discussed her options with a doctor? What would he say when he found out that she'd already gotten and started a regimen of prophylactic pills? Knowing what she'd done made her heart spin inside her chest, and her pulse shot up and down and side to side. Part in anxiety, part in anticipation. He would tell her she was crazy, that she was stepping into unknown territory she was not allowed to walk. Beth would tell him she was removing all the obstacles set before her, before them.

When Beth made her mind up about something, she couldn't be dissuaded. Her mom found that out when she was thirteen, and one of her friends got in a car accident and had to have their long hair cut off. Beth was adamant that her hair be cut in a similar way to keep Britney Zalinski from feeling bad about her unwanted short hair. When her mom said it wasn't necessary to cut her hair to let her friend know she was thinking of her, Beth cut it herself. Badly.

"Let's go for a drive," she suggested, keeping her eyes trained on the notepad on her lap. She didn't want to see Harrison's reaction—feared it, in actuality. He would tell her no, and Beth would feel small. It seemed to be one of his favorite words.

"Where?" Harrison sat in his customary spot, always with a book in hand.

She wondered if he'd already read through his collection of books and was rereading them. She wondered if he was really reading, or if he was staring at the words, like she was. So many letters, shoved together into words, into sentences, into paragraphs that were supposed to mean something. They were in her handwriting, written by her, and Beth looked at them and saw gibberish.

With a frown pinching the skin between her eyebrows, she looked up. It wasn't a direct no. "I don't know. Anywhere. I can show you the town."

"No," was the immediate answer, and she bristled at the sound of it.

"Have you actually ever been to Crystal Lake?"

"Yes. I had a meeting with Michael Peck, remember?"

Beth swallowed and dropped her eyes. Ozzy. He was suspiciously quiet lately. She didn't think it was because of Harrison's talk with him—she thought it was because he was up to something. It wasn't like him to step back, give up, let go until he said it was time. She didn't trust him to keep Harrison's secret. He had no reason to, and more reason to not. Every day she woke up waiting for Ozzy's next move.

"The fewer people who know who I am, the better," Harrison continued. "I want peace, and that leaves you once you're around civilization."

"Then how about we take a drive around the countryside?"

"No."

Beth's face burned, and her lips went into a line. "Why not?" she said through her teeth.

He shrugged one shoulder, looking unruffled by her irritation, even looking like he was glad for it.

She set down the notebook and stood. "You're always telling me no, and don't, and stop. Screw you, Harrison." She swiped the paper and pen from the couch cushion and stormed from the reading room, her feet loud and angry against the hardwood floor.

Yanking her coat from the hook, she shoved her arms through the sleeves and hopped around as she tugged on her boots. Beth grabbed the pen and notepad from where she'd tossed them on the floor and slammed the door after her. She was over halfway through his story. Soon there would be no reason for them to spend time together. Soon she would be gone from his life.

Blinking at the paper and pen like she didn't know what they were doing in her hand, she chucked them into the Blazer and shut the door.

Beth squinted her eyes against the fierce rays of the sun and turned toward the driveway, pretending her heart didn't lurch at the thought of no longer seeing Harrison. She shivered, more from her emotions than the chill in the air. Never hearing his voice, or feeling his presence, never seeing the glimpse of a smile he couldn't help. No. She refused.

They were getting somewhere, day by day. He was seeing possibilities where he'd only allowed himself to see nothing. Now... now he purposely closed off his eyes to her. He looked at her, but he didn't *see* her. He said he was going straight ahead, but somehow in recent days he'd bypassed her, taken a different path. One that didn't make sense, one that went nowhere. Because Beth was right before him, and he abandoned her.

Beth inhaled raggedly, shoving hair from her mouth and eyes as she aimed her feet in the direction of the road that steeply swooped down. She braced herself against the dip in the earth and carefully stepped on the packed snow and ice.

"Beth. Beth!"

Tightness formed in her jaw, and she kept going, not really having a destination in mind. That Harrison went after her meant something, but it was paltry in comparison to what she wanted of him.

"*Beth.*" He caught up with her, out of breath. Fingers brushed along the back of her jacket, a touch she shouldn't be able to feel through the fabric. Her nerves were heightened with every aspect of Harrison. "Where are you going?"

She spun around, angry and frustrated. "Time is something you could lose, at any second. Right now, there are so many better things we should be doing than...than *nothing*. Than this." Beth gestured to the space separating them. It was invisible, merely air, and it felt like a hundred steel walls. "Time is a gift, and it's being wasted on us. I don't want to waste any more."

Harrison took a step back at the look on her face, his eyebrows slamming together. His cheeks were two patches of color on a pale face. A face she had memorized, a face she saw in her dreams. A face Beth never wanted to stop seeing.

"If you don't want to be together, then all of this is pointless. I shouldn't even *be* here. It just makes it harder. I should go. I can write your book from my home. Being here with you, but not really being with you, hurts, Harrison." Saying that hurt her, and the thought of Harrison agreeing hurt her more. Breathing hurt her, and waiting for him to respond hurt her too. Everything *hurt*.

Harrison swallowed, the motion seemingly painful to him. Maybe he hurt as much as she did.

"I can deal with your illness. I can deal with the days of hopelessness and sadness and anger. I can deal with it all, if I know you won't shut me out. I know you want to be with me too. I see it in your eyes." Beth clasped her hands together, her eyes telling him to believe her. To have faith—if not in him, then in her. "You're allowed to be happy."

Shards of pain, like sharp daggers of glass, filled his eyes. Cut the light from his eyes. Deadened them. But he didn't say anything. Harrison looked at her, and said nothing.

Words spewed forth. Words she hadn't been aware she thought, until they were leaving her mouth. "You're not the only one in the world with HIV, you know? And it could stay HIV. You don't even know that it will progress to AIDS. And you're just out here, pretending not to exist, and for what? So people talk, and people look at you funny, and people write stupid articles about you. People talk about *everyone*! People talk about me getting my hair done! People talk about *everything*. So what?" She threw her arms up over her head.

"You could be doing something good with your knowledge of this disease, and instead you're doing *nothing*. You're a public figure. People listen to public figures. You could be helping people, helping people who are struggling to understand what's going on with their bodies, their lives, their futures. Suicidal people, angry people, depressed people."

She stood in the driveway, a small figure with a loud voice, and Beth forgot about Harrison's feelings, and his anger. She forgot about everything except what she needed to say, and he needed to hear. He looked back, a tall, voiceless figure made of granite. He didn't try to talk, or move, or look away.

"You could be talking to kids, explaining how important it is to use caution, and condoms, and how even when you think you know someone, you still need to be smart about things. Explain to them the danger of needles, and drugs, and how one seemingly unimportant moment can be life-changing. What about the kids born with it? The ones who are even less blameless than you? They need someone to look up to, someone who understands what they're going through."

Beth sucked in a ragged breath, her body shaking with emotion. "Who are you helping right now? *No one*. You say it doesn't bother you, and I know it does. You say you want this isolated life, and I know you don't. You're scared, but you don't have to be. *Do something about it*."

"You don't," he began in a voice that shook. "Get to tell me how to feel." His eyes were cold, filled with deadly resentment. "You have no idea, *none*, what I'm going through, or how I feel, or what I'm thinking." Harrison's voice grew, lashed out in quiet destruction.

"Then tell me," she beseeched, wrapping her arms around herself in a desperate attempt to get warmer; to feel not quite as lonely as she did right now.

His jaw hardened.

Harrison drove her to create, to be something better. And what did he do? He kept himself in a prison of his own making, cut off from a million beautiful moments. It didn't have to be this way. It could be different. Not perfect, but who really needed perfection? She didn't want perfection; she wanted Harrison. That was all. That was it. A simple request with all kinds of ramifications. The unfairness of it stung her eyes with the promise of tears and Beth looked away from his form, the sight of him painful to her.

"You gave up," Beth choked out. "You said you didn't, but you did."

His reaction was instantaneous, and explosive.

"I didn't give up," he roared, flinging his arms in the air.

Harrison cursed as he watched her, as she felt the color leave her face. Snarling, he tugged the stocking cap from his head and flung it across the snow. Harrison's chest heaved and his face twisted with fury as his control snapped.

"I didn't give up, Beth. The world gave up on me. *Me.*" He slammed a hand to his heart. "What was I supposed to do after that? Huh? *What?*"

Beth blinked, all of her crumpling inward under the haze of his pain, and rage, and injustice.

"They judged, and they ridiculed, and they made me feel like a *piece of shit*." Harrison turned and stalked away, whipping around to face her. His eyes were lightning and his face was the storm. "I didn't give up. I didn't choose this. All right? I just—I couldn't stand it anymore. I couldn't be around my friends, knowing they couldn't understand. I couldn't be around my family, seeing the fucking sadness in their eyes, *every day*, like I was already dead."

Harrison took a shuddering inhalation and looked at the ground. Bleak and quiet, he said, "They put me in the ground before they ever knew if it would come to that."

Beth took a breath, and her heart rejected the motion, squeezing, squeezing. Until she couldn't breathe anymore, and her chest ached, and she feared it would never stop aching. She didn't understand. He was right. Beth didn't know what he went through, what he was still going through.

She couldn't imagine having everything figured out, and then being told there were no more certainties. She placed a hand on her heart and pressed down, trying to alleviate the pain it throbbed for Harrison. And then she stopped, her hand falling away. It was okay for it to hurt. It should hurt. Harrison needed it to hurt for him.

Cracks lined his face, heartache oozing out of them. Harrison stood like he was being attacked on all sides, outwardly, inwardly, his body curved in around itself. He should never stand in such a way, never feel so beat down for being who he was. "I thought I'd make it easier on everyone and just be alone."

"But you're not alone," she whispered in a wobbly voice. "I'm here. You have me."

Harrison stared at the ground, looking up with eyes brightened by tears to ask, "What should I do then? Since you seem to have all the right answers. What do I do?"

Beth shook her head. "I don't have the *right* answers. There are no right answers. But I have hope, and you don't even allow yourself to have that."

"And you? What are you going to do, Beth?" He took a step closer, snow crunching beneath his boots.

"What do you mean?" Her throat burned from all the words that earlier catapulted from it, and in the absence of anger, came apprehension of the unknown. Where would she and Harrison go from here?

Harrison's eyes took on the sun, captured it inside the irises, and annihilated it. His expression mocked, demanded. "All these things you tell me I should be doing, you see yourself standing by my side as I do them, right? You, with your big heart, and your big dreams—what are you going to do? Live in the castle with the moat full of alligators with me?"

"Are you telling me I can't?"

"I'm telling you it would be reckless, but no, I'm not telling you, you can't."

She said the words on an exhale. "You make me want to be reckless. You make me want to be everything I never knew I could be."

His jaw shifted forward, and his eyes took on their own life. Shadows and light whispered through them. Happiness, fear, shock, doubt. His forehead wrinkled, and smoothed. Harrison's expression went so blank she swore she imagined it ever holding any kind of emotion.

"One day at a time, Harrison," Beth told him shakily. "Each one a chance to make it brilliant. That's the only goal either of us should be thinking about."

He blinked, a flash of sorrow hit his eyes, and then it was gone. "I'm going for a walk. I need to think. I can't think when I'm near you."

She watched him swoop down to retrieve his hat, slap the snow from it before slamming it on his head, and then he strode away. She turned to look at the road that angled down. Beth took a deep breath, feeling her chest expand. She let it out. The more times she did that, the calmer she became. Minutes passed, and she let her mind wander, go as unpainted as a bare wall, and it helped. The cold didn't touch her; she was an inferno of conviction.

Beth walked up the short incline to the Blazer, took back the notepad and pen, and followed the trail of Harrison's footsteps. She thought she knew him. Partly, she was right. Mostly, she was wrong. Beth didn't have a clue how Harrison really felt, but she didn't have to, to know she cared.

Finding a spot far enough away where she could observe him, but also wouldn't disrupt Harrison from his thoughts, Beth sat on the winter ground and set her notepad on her knees. The snow seeped through the bottom of her jeans, a shockwave of cold that got her brain working. Beth's eyes bored into the figure in the distance.

Suddenly Beth felt unworthy to try to put all he was into words. She dropped her gaze to the pen in her hand. She wasn't talented enough, smart enough, she didn't know enough. Harrison couldn't be explained in a book. She chewed on the inside of her lower lip as she thought. *Simplify your goal. Show the world how you see him.* That she could do. And maybe it wasn't enough, and maybe it would be found lacking, but she would do her best. Beth would pen Harrison in thoughts and feelings and color and life, full and light.

She forced her eyes back to him as he strolled through the melting snow, his hands shoved in the pockets of his orange jacket, the black cap tight against his skull. His head was angled to the side, the cut of his cheekbone and brow visible to her. Harrison looked reflective, lost in thought as he gazed toward the creek. Beth jotted down notes, her hand struggling to work as quickly as her mind.

The sun found him, shone through and around him as if he was the show and it was the spotlight. *What will he do next?* an invisible audience wondered, hushed and expectant. As she observed Harrison, she realized she was the audience. Beth was the one waiting, enthralled by the physically unwell man who exuded his own form of life. His frame was slight, gaunt with disease, and yet he stood tall, defiant against the thing that strove to defeat him.

Beth blinked her eyes and wrote about how the proud tilt of his chin told a tale of unconquerable spirit. He stood alone, nothing but trees and hills around him, and he was *vibrant.* A painting of red and black and brown with white skin. He wasn't classically handsome, but Harrison was large, overtaking space from his mere presence. Undeniable. Intimidating. Intense. A force that, knowing he would fall, would go down fighting.

"You fight, Harrison," she said softly. "Don't stop fighting."

She didn't write about the man before, the man he'd been, as Harrison had requested. Beth couldn't. She didn't know that man. She wrote about him as she knew him. He'd said his life wasn't about the disease, and that was true, and in keeping with that frame of mind, writing about him before it became a part of his existence would be wrong. It would separate him, turn him into a story of before, and a story of after. Beth only wanted to write of Harrison. And she did.

Music and nature, walks and reading. Cold eyes, heated eyes. A face carved from the toughest of stones. A man with a disease, a man who packed all of his pieces tightly inside, and tried to make them invisible. Dark fire, black fire, blazing fire. A warrior who only had to decide to not give up. And he hadn't. Beth knew that now.

ഌ • ര

THE SKY WAS black and starry, peaceful for someone other than her. She let out a slow, uneven breath, and used the spare key Harrison had given her to unlock the front door. Beth didn't really know what she was doing. But the hours spent at home forced her to admit that she didn't want to be at home, and she didn't want to be alone. What she wanted was simple. Singular.

Harrison.

Her heartrate was fast, chaotic. It pounded with anxiety and need, with fear and anticipation. In the daylight hours, she gathered up her things and went home as soon as he came back from his walk. An afternoon of eyes that never quite touched and soundless voices did not appeal to her. Beth didn't say goodbye, and neither did he. Maybe it was madness to come back. Maybe Beth was asking to be hurt again. But she needed an answer, something, and then she would know what to do.

He would tell her to go, or he would ask her to stay.

The lock clicking open sounded abnormally loud, and she wondered if all of the countryside heard it. Beth tiptoed inside, locking the door behind her. She took off her boots and coat in the darkness and headed for the stairs. She didn't pause or take a moment to reconsider, because if she did, she might leave.

His bedroom door was open. She stood in the doorway for a moment, listening to his steady breathing. It was lyrical in its symbolism. It meant he lived. Beth tiptoed to the bed, watching his chest lift and lower, seeing the puckered line between his eyebrows. What thoughts haunted his dreams? She smoothed it with her finger and leaned down to press a kiss there.

A hand, surprisingly strong and hard, clamped around her wrist. "What are you doing here, Beth?"

Harrison smelled like cotton and life, clean. Strong.

"I wanted to see you." Her voice was soft, and it wavered. Harrison wouldn't like that. It would let him know she was upset about something, and if he thought it was over him, he would tell her to stop. Like she could just turn off her feelings.

"You saw me once today. If you recall, it wasn't all that good of a time. Go home. Get some sleep."

"No. I needed to see you. Now. And I'm not going, not yet." Beth reached for him, her hands touching his jaw, her blood singing with a bittersweet ache. She wanted him to stop telling her no, and instead tell himself yes.

He shot up to a sitting position so fast his forehead banged against hers, and she fell partially onto his lap. His grip tightened on her wrist. It didn't hurt, but it was firm, an unspoken warning for her to stop whatever she planned to do. Beth's free hand braced his chest, feeling the thundering of his heart beneath her palm. His skin was warm, and taut; it didn't seem real that he could be anything other than eternal. Harrison felt like everything she ever wanted wrapped up in one man.

"We can't, Beth. We can't do this," he warned, his voice vibrating with heat. But the tone of his words brought her closer. He didn't mean them.

"We can. I want you, Harrison. All of you. I'm not letting you push me away anymore."

"Don't think I don't want you. I do. I want you," he panted, grabbing her hand and squeezing.

Harrison moved her hand to his erection, pressed it there. He groaned, guttural and deep. His chest heaved, and his breaths came quicker, a shield splintered by the touch of a woman. She went still, fascinated, all of her flooding with warmth. Liquid desire mixed with adrenaline. That sound, she wanted to hear that sound pass his lips again and again, more and more. Beth's core throbbed, her fingers wanting to wrap around him and make him lose his mind with pleasure. Her pinky twitched, and Harrison's hand pressed harder to still the movement.

His skin burned through the boxer briefs, hard with want. "I want you so bad, bad enough that I could die tomorrow if I was guaranteed all of tonight with you. Any night. All the nights," Harrison whispered. He gently pushed her hand from him. "I'd sell my soul for it. You drive me mad with your scent, and your eyes, and your words. And your heart, always your heart, staring at me from your big blue eyes. You think I'm strong, you think so many things I don't have the heart to tell you aren't true. I want to give you what you want, Beth. I want to give you everything, all of me. But I can't."

"I love you," she blurted, snapping her teeth together at the unintended confession.

Harrison turned to stone, a dark shadow crisscrossed with light from the moon outside the window. "Then I feel sorry for you."

Beth's mouth trembled, her hand reaching for the man who never allowed her comfort. "You don't mean that. I know you don't. Harrison—"

He jumped from the bed. Back and forth, he paced, his shoulders hunched forward, the pads of his bare feet slapping across the hardwood floor as he moved, an angry beast caged inside four walls. Four walls he chose to build. Four walls he could destroy.

"No. You're right; I don't. I feel sorry for me. I'm so fucking stupid," Harrison muttered. "So fucking stupid!"

He spun toward the wall and punched a fist against it. He stood like that, his back waving as he breathed, his hands splayed against the wall with his head bowed. "You are not allowed to love me," he said raggedly, pleadingly.

Beth scrambled from the bed, hovering behind him. So near, and so far. She lightly rested a palm to his shoulder, and he jerked in response. Harrison went still, and when he didn't push her away, Beth touched her mouth to the place near her hand. She couldn't understand how her heart pounded the way it did without stopping. It was too much.

"It's too late. I already do."

"I came here to be alone." The words were low, without emotion.

She nodded behind him, both hands touching his back, each on one shoulder blade. Beth slowly turned her head and set her cheek to the smooth, hot, unblemished skin. She closed her eyes as she loosely barricaded him in, not to trap him, but to let him know he had her strength as well. She stood with him, and she would fall with him. Beth would pick him up when he couldn't stand on his own. And if he couldn't stand with her, then she would lie down beside him.

"I accepted it. The plan was almost beautiful, really. I was going to eat and drink whatever the hell I wanted, or whatever my body would allow, and I was going to read. Reflect on things. Listen to music. Go for walks. Enjoy my time. I simplified my world so that it was easier to one day leave it."

Beth trailed her palms down and around his torso, her arms meeting at the center of his stomach. Too skinny. He was too skinny. She inhaled, exhaled, held him. Harrison's hands slid down the wall and stopped on her arms. She tensed, expecting him to remove them, but he didn't. He cocooned them, hugged her arms as her arms hugged him.

"What you said today—you were right. All of it. You're right."

Beth held him tighter. "I won't give up on you, Harrison."

He took a shaking breath, his head further lowering.

"I haven't let anyone touch me in years," he said quietly, his voice rough. "And then you showed up, and all I've wanted since is for you to touch me."

She brushed her lips across the hollow of his spine, felt him tremble in response.

"I did this. I brought you into my life."

She smiled faintly against his back. "You didn't make me fall in love with you. It just…happened. I want to be in your life. I want to be a part of it."

"No one will look at you the same. They'll stare, and they'll talk, and your life will be harder than it has to be. They'll say you have the disease, they'll call you terrible things. They'll leave stores when you enter them. If you're linked to me, Beth, then you might as well have HIV. You'll be treated like you do. There will be nothing quiet, nothing peaceful, about being with me.

"They'll look at you funny when you eat at restaurants. If you use a public restroom, they won't use it after you. They'll look at you like just being in your presence is enough to guarantee them catching it. Or even worse than all that, they'll look at you with pity."

"I don't care," she said in a wobbly voice, and she meant it.

"Are you listening to this, Beth?" Harrison flung her arms away and turned, pinning her with his tormented black eyes. "Your life won't be anything like you're used to."

"I want to be with you. I don't care about anything but that."

"You can't be with me," he said shortly.

Anger at Harrison, at the unfairness of life and death, bristled through her like spiked bones of determination. Beth felt her face twist, the corners of her mouth fall. "You wanted me here. You asked for me."

"I didn't—"

"Don't lie to me." She crossed her arms and stared at the pale features facing her. "You were lonely, that's why you hired me. You didn't need a book written, you needed someone in your life to make you feel not so lonely."

"If you think that's true, then why did you keep coming back?"

"Because I needed you too, and I still do." Beth swallowed and dropped her eyes. "We need each other."

Harrison's reply was long in coming, and quietly spoken. "I wasn't lonely. I was intrigued."

Somewhere in the room, a clock ticked off the seconds. Beth went still, letting his words settle around her heart. Realizing what they meant. They were not here because of pity, because of unwanted isolation. They were not together in this room by default. She was here because she wanted to be, and Harrison wanted her to be. The blackness weaved around them, but it wasn't cold, and it wasn't fearsome. It was alive, dark, consuming.

"I do need you," Harrison whispered finally, brokenly, reaching for her. His arms, threaded with muscle, went around her and Beth gasped at the feel of them, immediately hugging him back in case he decided he changed his mind. For so long, for so long she'd wanted this physical connection with him.

Harrison breathed in, forcefully. He breathed out, erratically but sure. "Tell me what you want."

"I want you."

She felt his sad smile in his voice. "You already have me, Beth."

"I want all of you," she whispered, her voice cracking and tears filling her eyes.

Harrison touched his forehead to hers. "You do. I'm yours." His fingers gripped her shoulders, squeezing her and he was still not close enough. Beth wanted all of him to mesh with her, she wanted them to be as one. She wanted all of him, even the sick parts.

Never enough, it would never be enough.

She didn't realize she'd said the words out loud until Harrison's grip tightened and released, until he said, "It might not be enough, but it's the most I can give you."

Beth shook her head. "No. You can give me more. You can let me sleep with you, and you can hold me. And…you can kiss me."

I'm yours, I'm yours, I'm yours. The words repeated in her mind, pulling a smile to her lips, adding lightness to her being.

She walked to the bed and laid down, wondering if Harrison would follow. The sheets were still warm from his body, and it was like being embraced by Harrison's arms. Twelve ticks of the clock sounded before he walked to her. He stared down at her, his body lined with moonlight and shade, a medley of dark and light to make up a conflicted man. Guilt and desire fought, hopelessness and hope warred, and at the center, was Harrison. Being tugged in a million directions, never sure of himself, never sure of anything. He could be sure of Beth.

"Beth."

She focused on his eyes, twin beams of life in a white face. "Yes?"

He went to his knees beside the bed and lassoed her in his arms before resting his cheek on her stomach. Beth held her breath, let it out slowly. He was holding her. Harrison was touching her of his own volition. His skin was hot against hers, his exhalations a wisp of seduction in the form of air.

His arms tightened. "I love you."

Harrison whispered it, and she was glad. It didn't mean she heard any less emotion in it, it didn't mean it meant any less.

The truth was more likely to be whispered than shouted.

Already her limbs shook, and her heart paused. Already she felt the monumental cocoon of those three words around her being. Beth moved her hand from the bed to the crown of his head, letting her fingers sink into the softness. Her smile deepened. His hair was as silken, and as coarse, as she'd imagined. She trailed her fingers down the curve of his ear, and went back to caressing his hair.

Beth had known he was falling as assuredly as she was.

"I'm sorry I tried not to." He pressed his face to her ribcage.

She partially sat up, bringing her arms to his back and her face to his hair. "Thank you for finally inviting me in. Please don't feel guilty about it."

He took a sharp breath, his body relaxing as he released it. "You say I inspire you, but you don't know that you do the same for me."

Wrapped around one another, they sat in the dark. Still. Quiet. Just breathing. Just feeling.

When a crick formed in Beth's neck and her arms went numb, as if sensing her discomfort, he moved from the floor to the bed, his chin held up by a fist as he watched her. Beth stared back, wanting the moment to never pass. Wanting time to stand still, to keep them locked in this span of discovery. His hand trembled as he touched her lips; his fingers were little pulses of sensation as they swept across her cheekbone. Harrison touched her face like he was afraid she would disappear if he pressed too hard.

Beth's chest hitched with each inhalation, and the air that left her lungs was raspy and loud. He'd barely touched her and she was ignited. Her lips swelled, aching to know his. She felt like she'd been waiting her whole life for something, and this was it. Anything she'd ever wanted lessened when compared to Harrison.

He leaned down, and with nothing but his lips touching hers, Harrison kissed her. It was slow, and full of tenderness. Yearning. He tasted sweet, and warm. He kissed her like it would be the last. He kissed her with reverence. Harrison's mouth was shaped to accommodate hers, and the kiss tugged at her stomach, liquid heat swimming through her veins and womb.

When memories faded, and the years were too many to count, when a thousand books had been read and a thousand walks taken— when instances of beauty and life were melded into one smile to signify them all—Beth would remember the night Harrison Caldwell decided to let himself love her. It would shine among a million stars of amazing moments, and it would gleam the brightest. And she would smile, a secret smile that held all of her love for him in the bend of it.

Beth pulled him to her, and he caught himself with a hand on either side of her shoulders, his face all she could see. His palms pressed into the mattress, creating fissures around Beth. Glinting eyes, lips heavy with desire. Beth held his face in her hands and his eyelids shut, his cheeks fanned with pale eyelashes.

"You cleaned the trophy room," he muttered.

A frown formed between her eyebrows and she laughed quietly, her fingers dropping to his wrists. "What?"

Harrison's arms convulsed with the strength it took to keep himself from melting into her. He looked down at her, his features hard with emotion. "That's when I knew—that I was—that I love you. That I am in love with you. You did that for me. You forced me to remember something I was trying to forget, something good, something I shouldn't have wanted to forget.

"And when you write—you frown, and shift around, and play with your hair—sometimes you even smile…" He took a deep breath. "I could watch you write for eternity."

Beth gripped his wrists and gave them a sharp pull. Harrison landed on her, stealing her breath with the motion and feel of him. He went still, even as his heartrate escalated to a dizzying beat, pounding against her chest. Her teeth sank into her lip as she shifted and felt him respond. Harrison dropped his head to her shoulder. Sweat covered him, sending a shockwave of possessiveness through her.

He was hers, all of him. The good, and everything else.

Beth flexed her hips and he moaned. He went up on his elbows and thrust his body up, and Beth closed her eyes at the feel of him through their clothes, hard and ready.

"We can't—" he started.

"Don't tell me what we can't do. Just show me what we can," she commanded, her voice throaty and raw.

Harrison brushed his lips across hers. A feather of a touch. "Beth," he hesitated.

"I went to the doctor," she said before she lost her courage.

He jerked back.

"I just—I wanted to be prepared, just in case. I wanted it to be one less thing for you to worry about. I'm healthy, and I'm taking medicine."

The stare he aimed at her was heavy, and long. Beth shifted her eyes away and back as she waited. Harrison finally blinked, calm settling over his features. He nodded, once. Hesitated again. "But if—I mean—are you sure?"

"I am so sure." Seeing Harrison nervous made her heart smile. She shook her head, shook his denials and fears away. "I trust you to know. I trust you. You're in charge. I'll follow your lead."

His throat shifted as he swallowed. "I don't have any co—"

"I do. In the pocket of my jeans." Beth smiled at the look he gave her. "I'm prepared, Harrison. I told you."

"Anxious, even." Wryness entered his eyes.

"You have no idea."

Hunger shot across his face.

When he placed his mouth to hers again, and applied light pressure, she opened hers. Beth's fingers curled at her sides, then moved to his back. Her grip gently molded to the hard muscle, holding him to her. His hips moved forward and back, and Beth moved with him. Harrison's mouth was firm, in control, and he tasted like ardor and mint. His mouth was a tool of seduction.

Beth struggled to breathe, to articulate thoughts. But she couldn't. She could only hang on, and feel.

He efficiently stripped Beth of her clothes, not taking any time to watch what he was unraveling until there was nothing but air on her skin. Harrison didn't move, frozen in place as his eyes tripped over her body. He said her name. That was all. But he said it in prayer, or maybe as a plea. Her smile told him it was too late. His lips on her neck said he knew.

"I'm going to give you everything, everything I can," he told her, his voice shattered with rawness.

"I want everything."

She arched her back as his breath whispered across her skin, her hands gathering the sheets around her, fisting them. Beth breathed in as his lips brushed across her abdomen, breathed out as his fingers ran along the inside of her thigh. Her body thrummed, trembled. Eyes closed, thoughts were swept away by the way he made her feel. Harrison pressed a kiss on her hip bone and her muscles tensed.

Beth tugged at his boxers, needing his skin on hers. Harrison froze, his head lowered. The air that left him was ragged, fragmented. He knelt on a precipice, scared to stay, scared to fall.

Fall with me.

"I'm sure," she reassured him when he looked up, not even the hint of a tremble in her voice.

He knelt between her legs, removing the last article of clothing that separated them. Dizzy with the sight of him, not sure she wasn't going to pass out from the power of her feelings mixed with the agonizingly sweet torture her body was enduring, Beth went to her knees. He was beautiful—lean alabaster sinew and muscle. And then her eyes dropped. Beth took him in her hand, watched as his head dropped back, baring his neck. Air hissing through his teeth.

Harrison was on fire and Beth stoked the flames more.

"This is going to be embarrassingly short," he muttered when she put her face to his stomach.

Beth smiled against his torso, and then she licked his skin. He tasted like salt and man, her control slipping when she moved her mouth toward his center and Harrison moaned, gripping her head and tightening fists around her hair. She barely touched him before she was on her back and he was above her, glaring down at her like an insatiable, starving animal. Like she was the only thing that could assuage his hunger.

Straddling her, he moved his palms up the fronts of her legs and stomach, his face following until his mouth met hers, slowly, languidly. Almost chastely. And then more forcefully, telling her with his mouth what she was doing to him. Harrison's fingers shook and the breaths he exhaled sounded constricted, choked. Beth didn't even try to talk. It was useless. His hands and fingers touched her in ways that made her body tense and her mouth beg incoherently.

Beth retrieved a condom, heard the tear of the wrapper and then felt Harrison's heat between her legs. When he entered her, the pleasure was intense, so much that it almost hurt. They both went still, hearts pounding against each other's skin, lips locked. Flesh on flesh, body to body, they were one. Harrison cradled her head and Beth anchored him to her with her legs. She moved, and he tensed. She moved again, and he slowly responded. They found their tempo, and it escalated, grew faster. More intense. Harder. It was wild, and gentle. Slow and hard. Beth didn't want it to stop, didn't want to ever be separated from Harrison. He was her heart.

In the dark, it was Beth, and Harrison, and that was it. That was all that mattered.

TWELVE

IT WAS BETH'S favorite kind of winter day. The sun was out, the temperature was bearable, and Harrison was by her side. Beth cherished all her days spent with him. Days that were never long enough and passed too quickly. Her boots seemed to find every possible slush spot, but that was okay. Everything was okay. Better than okay. Being a late morning on a Tuesday, there weren't a lot of people out, but there were some. Enough. They were around *people*.

She looked at him out of the corner of her eye and smiled.

He tightened his grip on her hand. "What?"

"This is nice. Unusual. And nice."

"Walking with me is unusual? We walk all the time."

"Where anyone can see us?" Beth widened her eyes and waved a hand in front of them and toward the rectangular buildings to the right of them. "This is unusual."

"If I look at each day instead of all the weeks and months, then it isn't overwhelming. This is just a day. One day. I can make it through one day. Where anyone can see us," he quietly added.

They were in Logansville, Minnesota, a city of thirty thousand people that was an eighteen-minute drive from Crystal Lake. Anywhere they went, there was a chance someone would recognize him. The plan was to do some Christmas shopping and have lunch. It had been an uneventful morning so far, just the way Beth and Harrison wanted. Eventually, everything Harrison had tried to keep private would be public knowledge, including her. That last part bothered him more than it did her. He was troubled over how she would be treated. Beth wasn't concerned; she didn't care what others thought, not in this.

"Do you feel okay?" Beth stopped him with a hand on his arm. "Are you worried? Nervous?"

Harrison dropped his gaze to where her skin touched his, a faint smile on his face. Beth's hand fell to her side as he cupped her face, looking into her eyes with ones that danced with contentment. Harrison was happy. She loved seeing that look on his face, knowing she helped put it there. She'd never thought herself capable of making another person feel how he did. Beth didn't know she could make someone feel important, special. Harrison brushed his lips across hers once, twice, before straightening, a light kiss that plummeted her stomach to her toes.

"I feel like everyone is looking at me," he admitted as they crossed the street.

"If they are, it's because of the scowl on your face, and not because they know who are you."

"I'm not—" He looked up, caught the frown on his face in the reflection of a window as they passed.

Beth laughed and pointed to a store on the corner. "That's the one I wanted to check out."

They were almost to the peach-colored shop when Harrison asked, "Have you told anyone about us?"

Her pulse quickened. "No. I didn't know if it was okay to." She took in the straight line of his mouth. "Have you?" Hope lifted her voice.

Harrison tried to look nonchalant, but the way he wouldn't meet her eyes ruined it. "I may have mentioned you to my parents," he told her.

"Really?" Her face beamed with a wide smile. "What did you tell them?"

He laughed and swiped a hand over his mouth, the gesture alluding to his nervousness over the topic. "I told them you're stubborn, that your heart is as big as the world, and that you make me want to dance, even though I'm terrible at it. Please don't cry," he quickly added when her lower lip wobbled. "You know it makes me feel bad when you cry."

Beth took a steadying breath and wiped her damp eyes. "At least they're happy tears."

"They want to meet you—my parents." He inhaled, not releasing it for a beat. "They want us to have Christmas together."

She placed her palm to the sharp bone of his cheek, and smiled. "I would love that. I want to spend all the holidays with you."

He let out a breath, shadows she hadn't noticed were there dispelling from his frame. "This is…this is different for me. I don't want to assume anything. You have to understand that I didn't see myself in any kind of relationship, ever again. I had everything mapped out. And then you showed up, eight minutes late, and destroyed all of my plans."

"They were terrible plans."

Half of Harrison's mouth hitched up.

"And…" Beth grabbed his large hand. "Technically, I was at your house on time."

"You were right on time, Beth, eight minutes late and all."

With the sun to Harrison's back, it haloed him, turned his hair to fire and added a shimmer to his porcelain skin. Looking at him made her heart pound in a way it normally did not. It made her want his bare skin on hers. Beth was a mess, and it was all because of Harrison, and it was the best kind of mess. He made her body hum and her mind work in triple time and her soul flourish.

Her mom had commented on it, saying she looked happier than she had in years. Jennifer had asked her who she was sleeping with. Beth had smiled, not answering.

"What are you thinking?" Harrison asked, his head cocked as his eyes drilled into hers in a way that made her pulse escalate.

"I'm thinking I need coffee." *And your mouth and hands on my body. But first—coffee.*

People passed by, and they were inconsequential. Unnoticeable. It was Harrison with his dark chocolate eyes that could see all of her dreams, and her, and demanded her to reach them. Beth opened her mouth to say something, and paused. She glanced behind her, a mark on her back saying eyes were there, staring into her, but Beth saw nothing, no one. She shook off the unease and smiled at Harrison, pulling him into the coffee shop that also had a small supply of unique gifts available for purchase.

A bell above the door signaled their entrance. Beth and her mom liked to stop in for coffee whenever they were in Logansville, which wasn't more than a half-dozen times a year. The room was divided in half, the left part set up as a quaint coffee shop and the other part filled with books, knickknacks, tee shirts, purses, and other goods. What could be seen of the walls showed that they were pale yellow in color.

Not a lot of light shone through the row of small windows that lined the tops of two walls, making it darker in the building. The floor creaked as they walked. A robust scent of coffee wrapped around them and Beth sighed with bliss, briefly closing her eyes. When she opened them, Harrison was there, studying her with rapt attention. He looked at her like he wasn't sure what he was looking at, but whatever it was, he liked looking at it.

She self-consciously rubbed her nose and shifted her feet. "What? What is it?"

He wordlessly pulled her behind a rack of books, tugged off her stocking cap, and with his cold fingers framing her face, Harrison kissed her. Beth's body immediately responded, sparked to life with the fire of his touch. Her thoughts mirrored her heartbeat, proclaiming: *I love you I love you I love you I love you.* Beth didn't allow sadness into their union. Like Harrison said, it was one day at a time. Today was only one day, one good day.

Someone nearby cleared their throat, and they broke away. With stars in her eyes, Beth smiled at Harrison. He grinned back, looking younger than his years. Looking free of his worries and fears. She didn't know how her love alone wouldn't be enough to keep him with her until her last breath was taken. Beth almost thought it could.

The woman cleared her throat again. "Would you like to try a latte sample? It's pumpkin spice."

249

Beth looked around Harrison, meeting the amused eyes of Midge, the owner of Coffee and Trinkets. She was shorter than Beth and about thirty years older, on the heavy side, and whenever Beth had seen her, she was in a dress. Today it was a long-sleeved purple one with white snowflakes along the hem. The dark-haired woman held out a small Styrofoam cup to Beth and Harrison, who each took it with a thank you.

They spent the next hour drinking cups of coffee as they scanned the display of items for sale. Beth bought a shirt that read 'No talkie before coffee' for her dad and an ornament in the shape of a desktop computer for her brother Jake. Harrison procured a stack of books and journals. They thanked Midge and stepped outside.

She felt the shift in the atmosphere as soon as they left the shop.

Something was wrong, different. The air was energized, and it was coming from the group of people standing on the corner next to them. It wasn't a pleasant sensation. It felt like nails being dragged down her skin. Beth looked at Harrison, watched the color drain from his face, how all the muscles and bones of his face went sharper, vengeful. Tight-lipped, his eyes blazed with black fire.

"What's going on?" she stupidly asked, even though it was obvious.

"They know who I am." His head jerked once toward the mass of suited men and women.

"How?" It was a whisper, and she wasn't sure Harrison even heard her.

Soon they were surrounded by people. Eager, hungry people. People who didn't see Harrison Caldwell as a person, but as a story. Harrison's hand tightened on hers and he moved in front of her, as if to keep her safe. It was too late. She knew that as soon as she caught sight of the news van parked along the street across from where they stood. His body was taut next to her, living armor against a horde of teeth and eyes, and voices, so many voices.

The coldness in the air sank into Beth, froze her. She was numb, unmoving. Stunned.

"Harrison," she said in a choked voice, clutching his arm.

Harrison partially turned and spoke closer to her ear. "It's okay, Beth. Don't say anything."

They were swarmed, people thrusting microphones toward Harrison and voices shouting over others.

"Mr. Caldwell, is this your first public appearance since being diagnosed with HIV?"

"What's it like to live with HIV?"

"Is there a chance you'll come out of retirement?"

"Harrison, is this your girlfriend?"

"How does having HIV affect intimacy with one another?"

"Mr. Caldwell, have you made Logansville, Minnesota your home?"

"Were you aware that Nina Hollister, the woman from whom you contracted the disease, died less than a week ago? How does that make you feel? Does that make you more worried over your own health?"

Harrison stopped breathing. The air left his lungs, but did not return. He turned to stone. The fingers around her hand went limp. Beth felt him sway, and she set her arm around his waist, anchoring him to her, holding him up if she had to.

"Harrison," she whispered against his arm. "We have to go. Let's go."

"What does your girlfriend think of the fact that you're putting her at risk?"

"What's in the future for you, Harrison?"

"Come on, man, you've been hiding away for years. Give us something," an especially belligerent reporter demanded.

They were turning something good into something ugly. Each question chipped away at her, each one brought her pain, but it was all for Harrison. They were hurting him. Beating him down. Morphing him into something bad instead of the man he was. She wanted to scream at them to shut up, she wanted to clap her hands over Harrison's ears so he couldn't hear them.

He straightened and looked at her. There was nothing on his face. It was empty. Empty face, empty mouth, empty eyes. It was like staring into a void. "Go to the truck, Beth. I'll come as soon as I can."

"No." She shook her head, her jaw taut with resolution. "I'm not leaving you. I refuse."

"Go to the truck." He pressed the keys into her palm. "Please. For me. I'll be there shortly."

She stared into his eyes. They were the mountains, and the valleys, the earth, and the sky. They were everything in the world that meant anything, and they were crying. Bleeding black. Sobbing sorrow. Fading into nothingness. Beth's body trembled and she turned her gaze to the swarm of vipers, hating them all, wanting them all to be crushed with guilt for what they were doing to this man. He was better than them, better than all of them.

Beth focused on Harrison, and spoke clearly. Firmly. "I love you."

Emotion flickered in his eyes, brought a twitch of life to his visage. Harrison's face softened. He nodded, once.

When she broke away from him and headed in the direction of his truck, a newscaster made a beeline for her. Harrison blocked him, stating, "Follow her and things are going to go bad for you real quick."

Beth saw the man's face blanch before she turned the corner and lost sight of them. She tried to walk fast, but her legs were leaden. Hurrying made time slow. What was happening? What were they saying to him? What was he saying back? What was he feeling? Her hands were fisted tight, her fingernails digging into her palms.

A pinpoint in the distance was her destination, and Beth aimed her eyes and feet for Harrison's black truck. She was cold—so cold; her body was shaking from it. Worry stroked her hair, whispered in her ear that everything would be different now. Held her in its arms and cooed that she was a silly girl, with silly dreams, and silly hopes, and that the world was laughing at her.

As she passed an alley between two buildings, a figure shifted, breaking through the motions of her shocked brain. Beth paused, catching sight of Ozzy lurking in the gloom of dirty snow and brick. She had to blink a few times to believe what she was seeing. Him in his jean jacket and his disrupted hair and his golden eyes. The depth of her repulsion was startling.

She hated the sight of him.

Her limbs turned to stone, along with her heart, and she glared all of the loathing she felt for him through her eyes. She looked at him and saw something small, something weak. Ozzy stared back, not speaking, not explaining. Not even lying. Because Beth already knew. He did this. He followed them, and he let the news stations know where they were. He ruined any chance of Harrison's continued peace, and all to spite her. To think that she'd loved him once, a boy masquerading as a man.

"I will never forgive you for this," she told him in a voice that shook.

The coldness in his gaze melted for an instant, and she saw the phantom of regret line his mouth. Beth blinked her eyes, and it was gone. Not that it mattered. This was unjustifiable, no matter how bad Ozzy felt about it as time went on. He slunk back into the shadows, where he belonged. Beth left him there, like she should have a long time ago. Some mistakes couldn't be undone, some wrongs could not be mended.

⁎ ◆ ⁏

THE RIDE BACK was quiet. Harrison didn't try to talk, and Beth's throat ached with the need to question and reassure. And comfort. She wanted to comfort him. Her mouth felt heavy, unable to function. Thoughts raced through her mind, powerful enough to freeze her, to stab through her heart. She saw herself and Harrison, held together, high above, in the palm of their surroundings, and she saw them crushed by the fingers of judgment. Effortlessly. Without remorse.

What if he gave up on her, on them? Had he already?

She told herself that wasn't an option, but doubt was there, telling her it was, especially when he remained quiet. Guilt sat in the middle of them, and it was hers. Harrison would tell her she was wrong, that she didn't have anything to do with what happened today. But it was Beth's fault, however indirectly. Part of him had to think it was. As much as it killed her to not shout to everyone what Harrison was to her, she hadn't spoken a word about him, not to anyone. And still, because of her, he'd been sent into the water with the piranhas.

A wall was between them, and it was one Harrison wordlessly told her not to climb. He seemed lifeless, a robot man driving a truck. He wouldn't look at her, and even as her chest squeezed and squeezed, taut enough to paralyze her, she was glad. Beth feared what she would find in his eyes. Anger, hopelessness, or worse—nothing at all.

His ex-girlfriend was dead. It made it real; it shouted that a similar fate might be in store for Harrison. He couldn't ignore it. Beth couldn't pretend there wasn't a chance it would happen with Harrison. She closed her eyes, inhaling deeply. She clenched her teeth to keep a sob unleashed. If she started crying, she wouldn't stop, and Harrison would feel her tears deep in his soul. The thought of bringing him any more pain than he was already feeling made her want to dig out her own heart and bind it to his to fortify its resistance to hurt.

Someone he'd known and loved was gone, and even if he only had the lingering *sliver* of affection yet in his heart for her, Harrison still felt the loss. Loss she could one day share.

The loss of him.

Their perfect winter day was ruined.

The sky was as blue as any ocean, and as tumultuous. As far out of reach as it could possibly be from where she was. The trees

255

were dead and dark weapons masquerading as silent sentinels. Even the snow was lethal, glittering like glass, and quick to cut her skin should she touch it.

Beth's vision blurred, but she would not cry. She would not cry. She would not—a tear slipped from the corner of her eye, traveled down her cold cheek, pooled on her chin, and dropped to her jacket.

Dusk had cast the town in gray by the time Harrison pulled the truck up to her little house. The streets were barren, not a person in sight. She didn't know what she expected, but it wasn't the emptiness that greeted her. The multi-colored lights Jennifer helped her string along the roof a few days ago turned on, added a garish spotlight to their goodbye. Beth was in a different reality, one she didn't recognize. The earth was numb, spinning backward. Upside down. It was all warped, wrong.

"Harrison, please talk to me," she whispered, staring straight ahead, seeing nothing.

He didn't.

Swallowing around a dry mouth and throat, Beth reached for the door handle, and when she was about to open it, his hand touched her arm, staying the motion. She looked into tormented eyes, the pain of his heart splashed across his features like unseen blood. "Tell me, no matter what, you still want me."

Her eyes filled with tears. Beth's heart thawed. She took a choked breath of air. And another. "I still want you. I'll always want you. That isn't going to change."

Harrison looked like he wanted to say more, but no words came. His grip tightened, as if the thought of letting go appalled him, and then he did, abruptly, with finality. "I have something to do. I'll be back," was all he told her.

When will you be back?

Her eyes asked, her mouth refused.

Beth nodded, her head heavy on her neck, and stepped from the truck with legs that felt like noodles. She watched a tight-jawed Harrison drive down the street. Conflicted eyes, torn man. She entered the house, not bothering with lights, her coat sliding from her arms to pool on the floor. Beth kicked off her boots and sat down on the couch.

She closed her eyes, her body stilled; her ears strained to listen. The sound of an engine, tires as they plowed through slush on the road. The ticking of the clock in the kitchen, the faint hum of the refrigerator. The low rumble and fanning sound as the furnace kicked on. A car door shutting somewhere outside. Where the quiet used to bother her, this time it offered serenity. Beth understood why Harrison chose to live the way he did. Too late, but she understood.

Beth wanted to live in that silent, solitary world with him.

She waited for him to call, email, text, or even come to her house, but as the minutes fell into an hour, and evening descended, Beth knew she wouldn't be hearing from Harrison. Feeling like she should be doing something and not knowing what, Beth turned on the television. It didn't take long to find her and Harrison. Images of them were splashed across the television, giving a tainted feel to their relationship, all while sugarcoated with best wishes and eyes of sympathy.

They speculated on her—who she was and what she wanted from Harrison, why she was in the picture and what it meant, on their possible relationship, on his health and career. On too many things they had no right to. Beth watched with dry eyes as something sacred was shredded. That was what he'd gone through, every day for years, only it had to be a hundred times worse for him. That was why he'd chosen isolation.

He made himself invisible so that no one could hurt him more than he already was.

Anger ripped through her, hot and savage, and Beth's face twisted. A scary calm waved over her as she left her house and drove to Ozzy's. It was a four-minute drive, the house located on the other side of the small town. Four minutes of feeling and thinking nothing. But the anger stayed, churning, building, wanting to erupt. She'd never felt destructive, not like this. Like she could ransack his place, ruin everything he loved, burn the house down around him.

Beth didn't see a brown house that once symbolized a separation of her heart. She saw a structure that stood between her and what she wanted to destroy—destroy the thing that had harmed what she loved most. The wind picked up, swirled her unbound hair around her face. She felt like a warrior on a twisted quest of vengeance. Beth's breath left her in gasps of white air. She'd never felt so protective, so possessive. It made her feel faint, and insane, and powerful.

She pounded on the door of Ozzy's house; hit the door with her fist until her hand ached and her knuckles were swollen. Until the skin cracked and her hand went numb. She hit it until she couldn't feel it anymore. All the helplessness she felt, all the rage, she pounded it into the edifice like she could smash the emotions into nothingness. Beth punched the door until it opened.

Dressed in brown jogging pants and a threadbare white shirt, Ozzy didn't look surprised to see her. He didn't look anything. He looked at her like he was bored, indifferent. He looked at her like she, and what he had done, meant nothing. Her body convulsed from the cold she couldn't feel, with rage she couldn't stop feeling.

In a low, too-even voice, he asked, "What do you want?"

"This is all your fault," she spat. "You did this."

Silhouetted by the light from inside, his features were kept in shade, but she caught the glint in his eyes, the shifting of his jaw. She wanted to hit him. Beth's hands twitched with the urge. She wanted to hit him and hit him and hit him and never stop. Ozzy, with his forever dreams and his angry heart. She wanted to hit him for Harrison. Beth wanted to hit him for being selfish, and for not being able to let her go, and for all she couldn't put into thoughts or words.

"You ruined any chance of him having peace here," she choked out. "And for what? To get back at me? To hurt me for moving on from you? That wasn't supposed to happen, right? I was supposed to love you forever, and pine after you, and take you back, always take you back. No matter what you did, no matter how you hurt me."

She sneered at him, feeling the ugliness of the expression in the pit of her soul. "And you say I'm sick."

He remained mute, calm. Only a faint tick under his eye showed that he felt anything at all. The door clicked shut behind him, locking the light inside the house and leaving them both in the dark. It was fitting. That's where the memory of her and Ozzy lived now, in the dark.

The words were volcanic, a scream of pain and hatred, as they left her. "Say something!"

A crack showed in his flawless exterior; it grew as she watched. Anger roughened Ozzy's voice, turned his features into sharp knives, blades that sliced and cut. "What do you want me to say? You picked a corpse over me."

His words stabbed her, broke through the skin, twisted. And twisted. Her body shook, and it wouldn't stop. She didn't think it would ever stop. It shook with grief, with unfairness, with pain. With fury.

Pain.

And fury.

The two emotions rotated through her, wounding her heart on repeat.

"I chose not to be with you long before I knew Harrison. I picked *myself* over you. I couldn't be with you anymore." Beth shook enough that her words trembled from the force of it. "I couldn't. I couldn't do it anymore. I couldn't live in your world, Ozzy."

She trained her eyes on him, wondering how he got so lost. "And because of that, you sought to hurt mine."

His nostrils flared, and he took a step closer. "You never should have left me, Beth. We were supposed to be together, work through our problems, *love each other*, and instead you left me. You left me for some—some *diseased* guy. How do you think that makes me feel?"

Beth gasped, feeling the blade of his words deep in her being. Entitled Ozzy. Always the victim Ozzy. Manipulating Ozzy. He gathered guilt in a basket of righteousness, distributing it as he saw fit, but never to himself.

"This isn't about you," she hissed, holding a hand to her heart, as if she could shield it from his words.

"No. You're right." He nodded. "This isn't about me. This is about you deciding to ruin everything we've ever been to one another by choosing to be with some guy who probably has less than five years to live, instead of choosing to be with me, someone you grew up with, someone you've known your whole life. You just tossed me aside for *Harrison Caldwell*." He said the name like it was bitter, and filled his mouth with sourness.

"We were over before I ever knew Harrison!" Madness shouted through her words, shouted that she was falling, and she didn't know how to stop. Beth was falling into the darkness, and she wasn't sure if she could survive. She didn't know if she cared.

They had to be making a scene. There had to be neighbors listening, watching. Spying. Let them. Let all the world see the moment Beth Lambert fractured. It was overdue.

"No, we weren't!" Ozzy slammed a hand to the side of the house, causing her to jump. He looked at her over his hunched shoulder, more animal than man. His eyes glowed in the partial dark. "We weren't over yet. I could have gotten you back. We could have worked things out. We always did. We could have again."

He straightened, ran a shaking hand through his unruly hair. "What is it? Is it his money? Is that what's keeping you with him?"

She laughed. It was harsh, and giddy. It was the kind of laughter no one hoped to hear, because it rang with the promise of a meltdown.

"It was a mistake to come here. I can't talk to you. It's like talking to a wall." Beth swung away, marching toward the Blazer on legs stiffened by cold.

"Because you know I'm right."

Wrath tightened her hands into fists, and she spun around. She could feel the imprint of her own hands on her throat, squeezing, choking. "I can't talk to you, because all I can think about is how pointless everything is that comes out of your mouth. There is a man, a good man, a man who doesn't deserve what's happening to him, alone, in a house, with—with no one, no one but—"

Beth broke off, her throat scraped raw by invisible blades. "This was our first day out, as a couple, and it blew up. It was perfect, and then it was ugly. Because of your vindictiveness. Because you can't see past yourself. You can't understand, not any of it. How I feel...how he feels. I'm trying to let him know it's okay to dream, to smile, to think beyond what he knows."

She went quiet, staring at the sidewalk streaked with snow.

"I knew it wouldn't last, this box he shoved himself inside of. He knew too. I know he did. But...we weren't ready. He wasn't ready. I'll never be ready." Her thoughts changed, went from Harrison's life being altered to the possibility of it being erased. "He might...he might just be gone one day. How does that happen?" Beth's voice ended on a whisper, so quiet it was shrill, piercing her eardrums and reverberating through her body.

She sank to her knees on the pavement, the ice and snow numbing her knees and legs, and she bent her head. Beth inhaled slowly, fighting tears. She didn't want to cry, not in front of Ozzy. The only thing that registered was her pain, and how much it hurt. It felt like every part of her was torn apart. Waves and waves of agony swept through her, closed her throat, burned her eyes and mouth.

"I'm sorry." His voice broke through the grief, his hand heavy and warm on her shoulder.

262

Beth scrambled away from his touch, stumbling to her feet and closer to the Blazer. "Don't touch me."

"Beth. I'm sorry." Ozzy's eyes were entreating, and he almost seemed genuine.

"You're not sorry," she denied, shaking her head. "You're never sorry for anyone but yourself."

"I'm sorry you're hurting like you are. I mean that." Ozzy pulled in a breath. "I didn't know." He stepped closer, his face broken up in pieces of emotion. Some she understood, others she never would.

"Didn't know what?" she demanded in an unsteady voice. Beth wanted to shrink away from him, but instead she went motionless, waited until he stopped walking to breathe.

"I didn't know you loved him."

Beth lifted her head.

"You know I didn't mean it." Night covered him as wholly as it covered her. "That night...I was messed up. When I...when I hurt you. I'm messed up, Beth. This whole thing has got me crazy. I just...when you told me you were leaving, I felt like I was trapped inside of a nightmare, and I haven't stopped feeling that way since. I don't know how to deal with you not being in my life anymore." His jaw jutted forward, a scowl taking over his expression to hide what he didn't want her to see. His shoulders shot up, as if to deflect whatever words she was about to say.

Beth said nothing.

Ozzy shifted his jaw back and forth, looking like the words he was about to say were ones he'd rather not. "I could have made different choices, better ones. I could have thought about you more and me less. I should have loved you like you deserved. I know you don't believe me, and you probably won't forgive me, but I am sorry."

He gave a short bark of laughter, shaking his head. "I wasn't thinking when I contacted the news. I saw you together, and you looked so happy, and I couldn't stand it. I wanted to hurt you, and I knew hurting him would do it. I am sorry. I'm a million times sorry. I thought I would feel better, seeing you like this, but all I feel is sick."

Her head pounded along with her heartbeat, and as she met Ozzy's unwavering gaze, she felt profound relief. It coursed through her veins with the power of a wave, cleaning away the dirt. Eradicating the black taint of their association. They could both start fresh, without the other to poison them with the past. Alone, as if strangers. They *would* be strangers.

"I have to go." Beth paused as she got to the Blazer. She looked up, met the eyes of the man who had once been everything to her, and she felt him drift away. Ozzy let her go, in that instant. She couldn't tell him it was okay, because it wasn't. She couldn't tell him she forgave him, because she didn't. Not yet. Maybe not ever.

They stared at each other, looking at ghosts from another time, a different set of people. Words seemed irrelevant, but so did the silence. He watched her, his eyes drifting over her features like he was saying a final, quiet farewell. They would see each around town. They might even talk once in a while. But Ozzy and Beth as a couple were done. They would not be again. Her heart was no longer his to bruise, to pick up only to put down.

She swallowed, opened her mouth, lingering and not sure why.

"Don't say anything else." A sheen of dampness covered his golden eyes, made them shine like broken gold. He swallowed and looked down. "I'm sorry I'm such an asshole. Be happy, Beth."

Friends, lovers, enemies, and now, nothing. It was funny how one person could be so many different things to another. Funnier still how they could go from everything to nothing. Her thoughts turned to Harrison as she left Ozzy's. And they could go from nothing to everything too.

THIRTEEN

THERE WAS A small support group waiting on Beth's lawn as she parked the Blazer near the curb. Her eyes swept over the trio huddled under the glow of the Christmas lights, looking for a fourth person who was not there. She turned the key, and the engine went quiet. Beth inhaled a breath of calm, told herself to bottle it. Her mom reached her before she fully got out of the vehicle, pulling her out and into a hug. A layer of icicles covering Beth's skin melted in her mom's arms.

"Well," she said as she straightened, staring into her daughter's eyes. "That explains a lot of things."

Beth wasn't sure if she was going to laugh or cry. She was grateful for her mom's undisputed acceptance. Even though the day was a mess, in a way, she was glad. The truth was out, and the relief of it made her legs weak. No more secrets, no more hiding. She hoped once Harrison had a chance to think things through, he would agree.

"Harrison Caldwell," her dad said, awe deepening his voice. Gray-haired and short, Glen Lambert was a soft-spoken man who loved all sports and his family—possibly in that order.

He drew Beth into an absent hug, bringing the scent of his peppery cologne with him as he placed a kiss on her forehead and patted her back. Not much taller than Beth, he craned his neck back to meet her eyes. "You know he used to play football, right?"

She laughed softly, meeting Jennifer's eyes over her dad's shoulder. Jennifer looked ready to burst with whatever she was keeping inside. "Yes. I am aware."

"My daughter's dating Harrison Caldwell. And he lives here. *Here*, in Crystal Lake, Minnesota." Her dad looked shell-shocked that she not only knew who Harrison Caldwell was, but that she knew him. He shook his head and stepped away. "This is amazing," he said to himself.

"It's a little more than that, Glen," his wife told him, motioning toward the house. "Can we go inside before my fingers decide I don't need them anymore and decide to freeze right off?"

Beth's eyes stung. Not a single word from either of her parents about the disease running rampant through Harrison's body. Not a single look, pitying or otherwise, to give Beth any reason to think they saw him as anything other than a man their daughter had chosen to be with.

"I brought pizzas." Jennifer nodded to the garage door where two frozen pizzas sat on the ground beside it. "Do you want to get the oven preheated, Sandy? We'll be right in."

Her mom nodded, and with her husband's arm in one hand and the pizzas in the other, she waited until Beth unlocked the door to sweep inside, firmly shutting it behind them after telling them to not stay out in the cold too long.

Beth jiggled her keys, pocketed them, and looked at her friend. Jennifer's blonde hair glowed in the dark, her eyes large and sparkling as they met Beth's. Jennifer embraced Beth hard, squeezing all of her love for Beth into the hug. Beth returned it, glad she had such good people in her life.

"I just want to know one thing," Jennifer began as she let go, sweeping wayward strands of jagged hair from her eyes.

She felt her lips curve. "What's that?"

"He has huge hands and feet." She paused, locking Beth in place with her gaze. "*Huge.*"

Beth laughed. "Yes. He does. What did you want to know?"

Jennifer's eyes danced. "That was it. I just needed verbal confirmation."

"Pervert," she teased.

Her friend shrugged. "I need to know everything, but when you're ready. Not now, but soon. Very soon."

She smiled faintly and looked at the dark house across the street, crossing her arms and shuffling her feet to keep warm. Patricia Mumm, a retired piano teacher, lived there. She went to bed as the sun went down, and she got out of bed as it came up. Never seeing the moon, never knowing the wonder of the night.

Beth let her head fall back, stared at the circular nightlight in the sky. It was full, whitish yellow, so big, so far away. She used to tell her dreams to the moon. She'd never known this one, the one that involved Harrison, and it was one of the most cherished. Life never went as she planned, but Beth had to appreciate that right now. If it had, she'd be a different person, living a different life, and not the one she should be. She would be like her neighbor, stuck inside a dark house with dreamless, moonless sleep.

"You love him."

Beth glanced at Jennifer, caught the knowing look. "I love him," she agreed.

"That's all that matters, Beth. This is a fucked up world. If you can find someone good to love, and they love you back, fuck everything else. Love them, let them love you back."

She took a breath into her lungs, slowly let it out. "Have you ever felt something, and you couldn't really explain how it happened or why, but it just felt *so right*?"

"Yeah. I think so."

"That's how I feel when I'm with Harrison. Everything makes sense when I'm around him, even the things I don't understand."

Jennifer kicked a patch of snow, bouncing on the heels of her snow boots. "Then why aren't you with him now?"

Beth blinked her eyes, a vague ache throbbing through her heart. "He left. He said he would be back."

She set her arm around Beth's shoulders and turned them toward the door. "Then he will be. Can we go inside now? My nose is numb."

Beth wasn't aware of how cold she was until she stepped into the warmth of the house and her skin began to thaw. She wiggled her frozen toes and rubbed her icicle hands on her jeans. The low hum of the television reached her ears and she spied her dad reclined in an overstuffed chair across the living room. The herb and garlic scent of melted cheese and red sauce hit her senses and Beth's stomach growled with hunger.

Her phone vibrated, and Beth fumbled in her coat pocket for it, anxious to see if it was Harrison. Her shoulders slumped as she read the name and number. It was her brother Jake. "Hey, Jake."

"Hey, you. I didn't realize my sister was famous."

Beth cringed and hung up her jacket. She walked into the kitchen where Jennifer and her mom were getting out plates and glasses. "She's not. Unless you count possible infamy."

"Close enough. How are you doing? Are you okay?"

"I'm okay," she told him, sitting down at the table. Beth immediately stood, needing movement. She walked the length of the kitchen, turned, and walked back.

"Okay. Good." Relief could be heard in his voice. "So...you think Harrison would ever want to throw a football around with me?"

Beth smiled as she heard Jake's wife scold him in the background.

"I mean...never mind. Sorry. You're tough. Hang in there. See you at Christmas."

They said goodbye, her phone alerting her to another incoming call.

Benny didn't give her a chance to say hello. "You picked a motherlode of a secret to harbor, didn't you?"

Beth laughed quietly and pushed hair behind her ears. Jennifer offered a plate with pizza on it, and she shook her head, turning from her friend's narrow-eyed look. "You could say that."

"You know what is important? If you're happy. Are you happy?"

"I'm happy," she said, her words clear and steady. Beth looked up and found her mom's eyes on her. Her eyes softened, and she turned back to the stove where she was dishing pizza onto plates.

"Turn on the news."

"What?" Beth frowned, her eyes shooting to the living room.

"Turn on the news," Benny repeated. "We'll talk soon."

"What was that all about?" her mom asked, walking toward the living room with a plate of pizza in each hand.

"Benny said to turn on the news," she told her, following with her pulse sprinting ahead of her.

"Glen."

"It's already on," he replied.

An image of Harrison was on the screen, determined stiffness to his jaw, eyes of impenetrable black aimed at the monitor. Beth recognized the pretty green siding of his house behind him. He looked powerful, invincible. An invisible breeze fluttered the longer locks of his hair and her fingers itched to smooth it from his face. She sank to the couch when her legs refused to hold her up any longer.

There were lights on him, but she could tell it wasn't full dark out, and she wondered if he'd had the press conference immediately after dropping her off. Was that the exchange he made earlier in Logansville? For them to give him time to get her home before agreeing to speak with them? Her heart squeezed.

The living room was quiet, filled with the sight of Harrison, and when he spoke, his voice was the only one permitted. Though harsh with discontent, the warmth of his timbre washed over her, made her scalp tingle. Jennifer grabbed Beth's clammy hand in hers and held it.

"To be quite frank, in instances like this, I view the media as savages." A titter of nervous laughter followed that. Harrison's hard face remained so, his eyes trained forward. Anyone who looked at his face knew he wasn't joking. "Because of my career, I realize the media feels as if I should expect to be in the spotlight, that it's part of the job, in a sense."

His jaw tightened. "Let me be clear about one thing: I don't owe anyone anything. I realized that soon after I was diagnosed with HIV. What I do in my personal life is my business, no one else's."

Harrison inhaled, his chest compressing and releasing as he let out the air. "But it's also wrong of me to hide away like I am ashamed of myself. I'm not." He stood taller, as if only now realizing he believed his words.

"Which is why I've decided to turn this affliction into something positive. Being ill sucks." The outline of a smile appeared. Uncomfortable laughter sounded, like people weren't sure if they should laugh or not. "But living shouldn't. In the near future, I'd like to talk to communities about necessary precautionary actions they can take to lessen the chances of contracting and spreading HIV, help others struggling with the illness. I'd like to be a mentor to those who need one. But my personal life, and those within it, are to be left alone."

He paused, his eyes narrowing like he might say more, and then he nodded. "Thank you for your time."

The screen went to a reporter. Beth stared at the television monitor, seeing blurry faces and hearing muted voices. Harrison's speech was less than two minutes in length. One hundred twenty seconds of words that took him from a statistic and spun him into a voice, a hero. Harrison ruled the screen, and seeing that, Beth knew he was the right man to be a spokesperson of HIV and how to prevent contracting it, and also on how to live with it. Not die. Live.

Beth's body hummed with pride.

"That's a strong man there," her dad said, nodding at the television. Admiration glowed from his face as he watched the clips of Harrison's life and career displayed across the screen. A narrator highlighted his accomplishments as the photographs shifted from one to another.

A knock at the front door had Beth frozen. She looked from Jennifer to her mom to her dad. They looked back expectantly, her dad with his eyes wide and mouth full of food.

Jennifer gave her a small shove when she continued to sit like an unmovable boulder. "Answer it."

Needing a moment to collect herself, Beth smoothed her green tee shirt and made her way to the door. She told herself it wouldn't be Harrison, even as her brain screamed that it was. It had to be. She wanted it to be. *Please.*

She opened the door and was met with dark chocolate eyes, and her heart. Her heart looked back at her. She'd missed it. Beth hadn't known, but it stopped beating when he left, and only now did she feel it start up once more. Fast, powerful, pure and sure. Beth swallowed, instinct telling her to get as close to him as she could as fast as she was able.

His eyebrows were lifted, a question in his eyes. Beth opened her mouth, and then she shook her head, reaching for him. Hand around the front of his jacket, she tugged him inside and grabbed his face, smiling all her love at him. Beth didn't know what to say. No words would suffice.

She settled on, "I'm proud of you."

Harrison opened his mouth to reply, and she kissed him, tasting coffee and something sweeter. His hands slid up the back of her neck, causing her skin to break out in tiny convulsions, and when his fingers found her hair, tightened against the locks, her breaths came more urgent. The kiss lasted a lifetime, and ended prematurely. He clutched her to him with arms wracked with tremors, his chest shifting against her, his heart racing for her.

"I love you," rumbled across the crown of her head.

Beth craned her neck to meet Harrison's gaze. It was dark, but full. Bottomless, but shining. It was so much it appeared to be nothing. "We're in this together, Harrison. All the way."

He frowned, his expression doubting her words. It passed, and when he nodded, she knew he believed her.

"I wanted it to be my decision, and I resented that that was taken away." Harrison swallowed and looked down. "I'm worried you think the only reason I decided to publicly talk about it was because I had no choice. It makes it seem like I was ashamed of us, that I was trying to keep you a secret along with everything else." He settled his gaze on her. "I want you to know that isn't true. You're the best part of my life, Beth."

"I would never think that, not in a million years. I know your heart." Beth grabbed his hand and threaded their fingers, bringing his hand between them and settling her other hand on it, clasping both of her hands around his. That was them. Two into one.

He studied their joined hands, and his mouth twisted with pain. "Hearing about Nina—it just made it all more real. I don't feel nothing anymore. I feel sad, really sad," he said quietly, not lifting his eyes. Harrison took a deep breath, his frame shuddering around it.

Beth pressed a kiss to his jawline.

He closed his eyes, his lips falling into a line. Harrison inhaled again and looked up. "Thank you for making me see what I couldn't on my own."

"Thank you for seeing me," she whispered back.

Half of his mouth lifted. "You're all I've seen since you showed up at my house."

A female sigh and a sharp intake of breath told Beth they had an audience. She'd forgotten her parents and Jennifer were at her house. She'd forgotten everything but the man next to her. The three of them were squeezed side by side into the hallway, waiting. Beth dropped his hand, and Harrison stepped back, looking unsure of himself in the face of her guests. She reached for the hand she'd abandoned, holding it tighter than she ever had before.

"Hey. This is Harrison Caldwell." It was a lame introduction, and Beth's face flamed at the shaky deliverance. She felt Harrison's amused smile without looking. It was obvious who he was.

"My boyfriend," she added firmly, feeling him tense in surprise beside her. His hand squeezed hers, and she smiled for him even as she looked straight ahead.

"That's my mom, Sandy. My dad, Glen. And my best friend, Jennifer."

Her dad worked his jaw, looking like he'd lost his voice but was still trying to talk. Her mom had the customary suspicious look of a parent when meeting their child's love interest for the first time. And Jennifer played with a lock of hair as she studied him, paying special attention to his hands and feet. Beth rolled her eyes, and Jennifer grinned.

"Hello," Harrison said politely. "It's nice to meet you."

"You too," her mom replied, the calculating gleam disappearing and friendliness replacing it. "Are you hungry? We made pizza. Come in, come in—don't just lollygag in the hallway. Beth, get him some food. We'll find a movie to watch."

Beth's mom reached for Harrison's hand and pulled him into the living room. He looked at Beth once over his shoulder, and she smiled reassuringly at the flash of panic in his eyes. Beth watched her mom with her boyfriend, warmth crashing over her at Harrison's allowance of her mom's touch, and her mom doing so without another thought. It wasn't a big deal unless someone turned it into one. To her mom, he was a boyfriend. To her dad, he was a football star. To Jennifer, well—

"Nice. Very nice," Jennifer commented. "Think he has any football friends he can introduce me to? Tall ones, with big hands and feet."

Beth laughed and shook her head. "You'll have to ask him."

"Oh, I will."

As she filled a plate up with pizza in the kitchen, Beth heard her dad ask Harrison, "Can I get your autograph?"

৪০ ◆ ൞

CHRISTMAS EVE WAS spent with Beth's family, and Harrison seemed to enjoy the time with them more than even Beth did. They played board games, laughing at her dad's star-struck expression each time Harrison addressed him. Her brothers took turns telling embarrassing stories about Beth as a child and teen. The highlight of the males' day was when Harrison agreed to play football outside with them. He was fluid and graceful, not missing a catch. Spiraling the football with each throw. Beth watched him, knowing her heart was shining in her eyes and not caring who saw it.

Beth's family adopted Harrison in a single day, strengthening his allies against whatever came his way.

Christmas Day was at Harrison's house, with his parents. Beth was nervous—more than nervous. She couldn't sit still. She'd changed her clothes ten times and tried three different hair styles. In the end, she chose gray slacks and a pink sweater, deciding to keep her hair down. All in all, she felt quite plain. She could have avoided hours of indecisiveness if she'd elected to not lose her head for a while.

"Unless you're willing to fix whatever grooves your incessant walking over the hardwood floor is going to produce, I suggest you stop. And sit."

It was so like the antagonistic Harrison from the first days of their association that Beth paused and blinked at him. He kept his head lowered as he looked at the weekly paper, but she saw the glimpse of a smile in the curve of his cheek. Dressed in black jeans and a forest green sweater, he looked casual and sharp. Beth marched over to him and snatched the paper from his hands. When he protested, she threw it behind her.

Harrison shot to his feet, towering over her as his firecracker eyes glared down at her. Her mouth went dry, her palms turned slick, and Beth eagerly met his harsh mouth as it descended, swooping down to steal her breath and any bit of her that wasn't yet his. It was all his, nothing but dust left to mark it as anything other.

His hands roved up the inside of her top, across her bare stomach and back. Harrison's fingers brushed over her breasts, teasingly, taunting her, maddening her pulse. Down her sides, sliding the length of the front of her pants, pausing with inches between his fingers and the place she throbbed. Harrison crept closer, and she gasped in anticipation, all of her numb and tense, shaking and out of control.

Hot and demanding, he latched his mouth once again to hers, slanting his head to deepen the kiss. Beth arched her back as she moaned, pressing closer to him, feeling him through his jeans as he bent his knees to fit against the juncture of her legs. Her fingers grabbed the short strands of his hair, pulled. He growled and hitched his body up, his lower half rubbing against hers.

"Harrison," she murmured, and he kissed her more fervently.

Where they were, the day of the week, even the imminent arrival of his parents—it all faded away in the heat of their want. He spun them around, and they fell onto the couch with Beth beneath him and their lower halves off the couch. It was an uncomfortable position and Beth didn't care. His hand went between them and Beth gasped at the feel of his fingers as they skimmed the waist of her pants, dipped down past her underwear, and into her.

Her head fell back and Beth closed her eyes, loving the feel of him, even his fingers, especially his fingers. Panting, dazed and a ball of excruciating sensation, Beth moved against his hand. She froze, hearing something, faint but real. Like tires on gravel.

"Harrison." Urgency entered her voice.

"Keep moving, Beth. Don't stop," he said against her neck.

"*Harrison.*" Beth shoved at him. His hand fell away, emptiness filling her at the loss of his touch.

He stared at her, his hair mussed, his eyes unfocused and throbbing with desire. "What's wrong?" His words were thick, and Harrison shook his head as if to clear it.

"I heard something."

"What?" He frowned. His eyes were sharper, some of the fog gone from the blackish brown depths.

"Hello? Harrison?" a woman's voice called, adding in a quieter tone, "Go see if you can find him and Beth. I'll start unloading the food in the kitchen."

They stared at each other for an instant, and then they propelled into action, Harrison adjusting himself as Beth tried to fix her hair and straighten her clothes. Color bloomed in his cheeks, and his eyes sparked with heat when they met hers. Beth shifted anxiously, wondering how things had gotten so out of hand at the worst possible moment. She took in Harrison's rumpled appearance and bit her lip to keep from laughing. He gave her a lopsided smile that shot yearning through her quicker than any kiss could.

"Well, it's good to know some things don't change," a brown-haired man said from the doorway, looking between the two of them.

Harrison's features turned sheepish. "Hey, Dad."

279

"Hello, Harrison." He studied his son, shifting his eyes to Beth before returning his gaze to Harrison. His eyes were dark brown like Harrison's; as warm as melted chocolate. "Why don't you go and get situated? I'll distract your mom for a few minutes."

They didn't need any more encouraging. Feeling like a teenager getting caught in her boyfriend's bedroom, Beth sprinted from the room and up the stairs. Harrison was right behind her. At the top of the stairs, she whirled around and planted a kiss on his lips, laughing as their heads clunked together. He chased her down the hallway to the bathroom, pinning her against the wall and stealing another kiss.

"That was awkward," Beth told him, his hands set against the wall on either side of her head.

"Just wait. It'll get better." The way he said it didn't comfort her in any way.

He kissed her again, a soft, lingering touch that tantalized her mouth and body.

"We have to stop." She didn't want to stop.

"Yes," he agreed. "For now."

Beth's stomach dipped at the promise.

"Not touching you is killing me, and I foresee an evening of torture, and it won't stop until I'm inside you."

"Harrison, don't talk like that when there is nothing we can do about it," she moaned, her body jerking at the thought of him and her in bed.

"Nothing we can do about it *now*." Harrison stroked willful strands of hair from her face. "Later."

Later was a boring word. One that indicated an interval sometime in the future. No specification designated to it. It was lazy. But when Harrison said it, later was the most beautiful of words, especially coupled with its intent. Later had never sounded so perfect. Later was presently her favorite word.

"Later," Beth confirmed, ducking under his arm and into the bathroom to douse her face with handfuls of cool water.

Somewhat composed, but no less nervous, ten minutes later Beth held Harrison's hand as he introduced her to his parents. They were in the kitchen, their backs to them as they worked around the kitchen, setting out a feast of rolls, baked ham, pasta salad, pies, and other delicious looking and smelling foods. Earlier in the week, Harrison let Beth know his mom insisted she bring all the food, and told them not to worry about preparing anything. Her one request was a hug in exchange for the meal, he told her grudgingly, looking apprehensive about her reaction.

Beth merely smiled.

And when his mom, tall and slim with large gray eyes and chin-length black hair, turned and opened her arms to Beth without a word, Beth smiled again. Mary Caldwell gave Beth the best kind of hug—one of pure warmth. She kissed her cheek as they separated, her eyes shining at her like Beth was one of her most favored people. "It's so, so good to meet you. You have no idea how good it is to meet you."

"T-thank you," she stuttered, surprised by the welcome. Beth's face was hot, and when she looked up, Harrison winked at her from where he stood next to his dad. They were imposing men, both tall and broad-shouldered with dominant presences. In some ways, Harrison took after Timothy Caldwell, and in other ways, he was solely his mother.

"Harrison talks of you fondly, and often," Timothy said as he shook Beth's hand, giving her back a few meaningful yet still awkward pats before stepping away.

"And you got a tree," his mom exclaimed, gesturing toward the entryway. "It's perfect."

"It was Beth's idea." The tree was fake, eight feet tall, and wrapped in white lights and deer ornaments. It added a spark of life to the otherwise empty foyer.

"Harrison, what do you say about going for a walk in the woods?"

Harrison looked at Beth. "Sure. Are you okay with that?"

Mary set back her shoulders and eyed her son. "Of course she's okay with that. She's with me."

She nodded, smiling at Mary. "I'll help your mom. Maybe you'll spot a deer or two."

Harrison lightly gripped her face between his large hands, pressed his mouth to the skin above her eyes, and left with his dad.

As soon as the front door shut, Mary narrowed her eyes at Beth and Beth instinctively took a step back. Cold with apprehension, she looked at the woman who gave Harrison life. How must she feel, knowing it could end before hers? Beth's heart stung and she shifted her feet, needing noise or movement instead of this silence.

His mother tilted her head, studying Beth like she wanted to see into her heart and know its truth. Beth would gladly show it to her, if she could.

"Harrison's changed," she stated, looking down to straighten the red with white snowflakes tablecloth she brought. Mary leveled her eyes on Beth. "He's better. He's living like he should be."

Beth's throat bobbed as she swallowed around the thickness of it.

Her eyes filled with tears, making them shine like glittery silver. "I don't think he could take it if he went back to that sham of an existence."

"He won't," Beth choked out, hating the thought of losing him to anything, even his own depressed mind. "I'll be with him." *Forever* was left unsaid, but it was implied.

Mary took a full minute to assess her, and then she nodded, redirecting her attention to the dinnerware. "Good. You're good for him. I can see he's happy." She took a calming breath and reached for a covered dish. "I brought homemade orange sweet rolls. Harrison loves them. Would you like to try one? And maybe we could have some coffee? Do you like coffee?"

"I love coffee," Beth said with enthusiasm, causing Mary to laugh.

The afternoon turned to dusk, and as Beth got to know Harrison's parents, she saw where his goodness came from. They were generous, and kindhearted, and they loved their son. That much was obvious.

After the meal was eaten, and the kitchen put back to order, Harrison's mom and dad hugged them goodbye and headed back to their home an hour away. They'd moved nearer to their son after he'd relocated here, but far enough away that he didn't feel smothered. His mom told Beth over dessert that they wanted him to have his own life, but they wanted to be close enough to help out when he needed it. Beth understood, and her heart made room for Harrison's parents.

With only the glow of the Christmas lights to guide her after shutting down the laptop in the reading room, Beth walked into the foyer. She reached around the back of the tree, the fake needles prickling her arms as she moved, and scooped up the long envelope that was hiding behind it. Harrison was reading his second story of hers in the bedroom, and with her feet softly padding along the cool hardwood floor, Beth set out for that room.

A lamp offered the only light, and it cast the room in fuzziness, adding a romantic element. Harrison was stretched out on the bed, looking sleek and tawny, like a resting tiger. At the sound of her footsteps, he set down the paper on the bed beside him and turned his head toward the doorway.

"Hi," she said, smiling.

"Hi." He sat up and patted the spot next to him. His hair was disheveled, and the sight of it made her want to run her fingers through it and mess it up more. "Done writing?"

"Yeah, sorry. I just—I had to get something down before I forgot."

He was shaking his head long before she stopped talking. "Don't apologize. Just come here."

Beth climbed up beside him, resting her back against his chest. At his nearness, her pulse spiraled down a dizzying track in response. She breathed in the scent of his skin, thinking if they could never have any more than this, she would be content. Harrison wrapped one arm around her and set his chin on the top of her head. Beth raised her arm and tapped him on the forehead with the slim white envelope.

"This is for you. It's nothing, really, but it is symbolic," she said vaguely, smiling encouragingly when he shifted around and frowned at her.

Harrison went to his stomach on the bed with his arms dangling over the edge, fingering the white parchment. Eyes trained down. Not talking. Nothing but his fingers moving. Impatient, Beth situated herself in a similar pose and tried not to rip the envelope from his hands to open it herself. When she was about to say something, Harrison carefully opened the envelope, removing the contents.

His body went still, but she could tell from his profile that his eyes skimmed over the lettering again and again. "What is this?"

"It's a brochure."

"I see that," he said evenly. "Why are you giving it to me?"

Beth moved to the floor and looked at Harrison, their eyes level with one another if he ever looked up. When it was clear that was not going to happen, Beth gently butted her head to his. He shifted his eyes to hers, and she smiled. "Because as soon as the weather is warm enough, you and I are going to hike the Appalachian Trail."

Harrison blinked at her, looked down. Looked up. Blinked some more. "How did you even know?" he asked in a low voice.

"I found an ancient article on you in one of my dad's old sports magazines. You said that hiking it was one of your dreams. You should get your dreams too, Harrison."

"No one—I mean, I didn't—I gave up on thinking I could ever do this." He took in a ragged breath of air. "You'll do it with me?"

Beth kissed his warm forehead, pushing hair back from his brow. "Of course. We're a team, remember?"

Harrison scooted from the bed and drew her into his arms and against his chest. "Thank you. I missed out on a lot of things I didn't have to." He went still, his held breath telling her there was something he was hesitant to say. "Promise me, Beth, that if this doesn't happen, you'll do something equally as great."

She dropped her eyes to her hands. "It will happen, Harrison."

"But if it doesn't," he insisted.

"Something great like what?" Beth asked in a voice that cracked.

"I don't know. You'll go on adventures, and write about them, and you'll dance. You'll be happy."

Throat thick, Beth nodded jerkily. "I promise."

He released her, a mischievous gleam to his eyes smoothing away the clouds. "I got you something too. Something small."

Harrison got up and stretched, the shirt lifting and exposing his torso. Beth studied the expanse of flesh, wanting her fingers and lips to replace her eyes. With a pop in his knees, he walked across the room to the closet, pulling a small box down from the shelf. He offered it to her as he knelt before her, his dark eyes dancing with light.

Beth smiled as she turned the box upside down and gently shook it. Laughing at the scowl Harrison gave her, she said, "I hope it isn't breakable."

"Kick it around a few times and see," he replied dryly.

She grinned and popped open the top, taking out box-shaped Styrofoam. Cringing at the sound of it shifting and contorting as she worked, Beth maneuvered the protective layer from around whatever was inside it and was rewarded with a white coffee mug with black lettering that read: *I am Writer. Hear me type.* She snorted and fondly touched the cup.

"I love it," she told Harrison, lifting her eyes to his. "Thank you."

His eyes darkened to ebony, and he outstretched a hand. "Beth."

"Yes?"

"It's later."

EPILOGUE

WEEKS TURNED INTO one month, and then another. On and on it went, until it was spring, and the snow melted, bringing new life to the earth. Why couldn't it bring new life to Harrison? That was Beth's first thought, and she knew Harrison would resent it, tell her everything had its time, and other stuff she knew but didn't want to hear.

Beth practically lived with Harrison, only going home when she had to. If it came to it, and every day she prayed it did not, she would be with Harrison until she could no longer do so, and then she would finally make a town other than Crystal Lake, Minnesota her home. Go on adventures, write about them, dance. Be happy.

She vowed it to Harrison, and he vowed to stay with her.

Harrison visited a handful of schools, and each time he did, he left with straighter shoulders, a burning light in his eyes. He had purpose, and it draped over him like a well-fit suit—or cape. To her, he was a conqueror. Beth went with him, at first staying in the background. Eventually, after urging from Harrison, she stood with him,

288

talking about her experience as an HIV-negative person involved with an HIV-positive person.

She began a website, sharing her thoughts and stories, and soon, she was asked to write articles for papers, and then magazines. Beth talked of the biases she once had, and how she overcame them. She talked of ignorance, and how that hurt the uneducated person more than anyone else. She talked of how having awareness was a choice more people should make.

Her dream of writing professionally happened, and it happened in a way she never would have believed.

And she loved Harrison—every day, every night, she loved him.

Every day he walked with a straight back and his head held high.

Every night his shoulders drooped, and fatigue ringed his eyes.

And she loved him.

Every day.

Every night.

It was after nine in the evening on a Saturday night when she typed the last word of a story she never wanted to end. In a way, it wouldn't. The story would live in her, in her thoughts, and her smile, and her words. And it would always live inside the pages.

Alone in the reading room, Beth printed off the three hundred pages of her thoughts and feelings, all for Harrison Caldwell. There were more, so many more she didn't know how to say. Other than the joy she received in creating, there would be no payment for this. Tearing up the checks he'd given her, Beth had told Harrison the money he'd meant to pay her for the book would be better used for another purpose. He told her to pick something, and she did. AVERT, one of the first HIV and AIDS based charities, received a large donation from Harrison Caldwell, in Beth Lambert's name.

She turned off the lights, her bare feet pattering on the hardwood floor, and checked the locks on the front door. In the dark, Beth ascended the stairs with a sheaf of papers clutched to her chest. There was finality to this, this that first brought them together. Something that bound them was about to be taken away. Beth didn't want any part of them gone, not even this story. Her pulse thrummed with the wrongness of it, her breaths shaky. She didn't want to say goodbye to anything that gave her Harrison.

Harrison stood in the middle of his bedroom, his back to her. His head was tilted back, hands on his hips. The soft brown pajama pants were looser around his hips than they were months ago, and there was added length to the long-sleeved gray shirt that hinted at the loss of weight.

The virus was getting tougher, and Harrison was getting frailer. His last checkup hadn't been what they'd hoped for—the virus was mutating. The doctors were trying different medications, but in the meantime, Harrison was feeling the effects. He was tired all the time, and his skin had an unhealthy tinge. He was sick off and on, and he wasn't eating enough. She told herself they would find something that worked, soon they would find something that worked.

Soon. All of her hopes rested on *soon*.

She would give anything to have met him earlier, not even before he had the disease, just before she had. Months, weeks. Days, even. Just a little more time. Beth swallowed, blinding herself to the shadows of destiny, but it refused to be ignored. The disease crept through the cracks of the walls, spread along the plaster, in wait. Watching. She briefly closed her eyes, gathered her strength. No. It couldn't have him. Not yet. Hopefully, not for a long, long while.

"What are you doing?" she asked softly.

"We're going, Beth," he said without turning to face her.

Beth frowned, stepping closer. "Going where?"

"To the Appalachian Trail. In two days. We're going."

"Harrison," she began, the words frozen on her lips as he looked at her.

Determination, fierce and grave, slanted across his face like an unapproachable vow.

Beth let out a slow breath, nodding. "Yes. We're going."

"In two days," he reiterated, one fiery eyebrow cocked.

"In two days." There was a lesson in every decision, and Harrison had just taught her one. He was still here, and he could do what he wanted while he was, and he should. He should do it all, every damn thing he'd ever dreamed of.

His bottomless eyes lightened, clouds were wiped from his visage, and the smile he gave her, though exhausted, was blinding. His facial bones were more prominent, the grooves beneath his eyes and below his cheekbones deeper. "I was thinking something else too."

"About?" Beth prodded, moving for him.

The smile expanded. "You."

She returned the smile, setting the papers down on the bed to wrap her arms around his body. Thinner, but still Harrison. "What about me?"

Harrison's scent of laundry detergent and him trickled over her senses, weaved serenity around her as his arms met across her back and he squeezed her to him. "I love you."

Beth nuzzled the side of her face against his chest. "I love you too. That's what you were thinking? That you love me?"

"Yes." Harrison dropped his arms and stepped back. "I think it all the time. It's my mantra."

Before he got too far away, Beth reached up and touched his thick hair, and then stood on tiptoes to bring her lips to his.

"And one more thing."

She smiled and brushed her nose to his. "What?"

"I want to spend forever with you," he whispered against her lips.

"And you will," she promised.

"Your forever, not mine."

Beth took a shuddering breath, resting her forehead on his mouth. In a clear voice, she informed him, "Forever is forever, Harrison."

She felt his smile against her forehead as he fiddled with her left hand, something cool and hard sliding along her finger. "I want my forever with you to formally start in two days at the Appalachian Trail, with you as my wife. I don't want to waste any more time."

Shocked joy locked her in its unmoving embrace, and Beth opened her mouth to speak, but nothing would come out. Her pulse was too fast, her mind going blank, and then speeding through questions. Did he really ask her that? Did he really mean that? Was there really a ring around her finger? Beth was scared to look, scared to believe.

She didn't dare to think of such things like marriage and babies, but it was there, in her heart. That need, that want, it was there. The ring felt like a remarkable weight, an anchor of their hearts to one another. Something to keep Harrison tethered to this world, and her. She blinked her eyes as tears formed, and a sniffle escaped.

"Beth?" Harrison angled his head down to meet her eyes, his fingers touching the sides of her face. She felt Harrison's nervousness between them, the air spiked with disquiet. He tried to smile, to joke, but doubt and fear swam in his eyes. "Was the sniffle a yes, or a no? Don't leave me hanging here."

"Yes," she croaked. Beth cleared her throat, smiling against watery eyes and a pinched throat. "A million times yes. I want to be your wife. I would love to be your wife. Now. Right now. Yes, so much yes."

A grin split his face, eradicated the illness in a singular moment of pure ecstasy. Harrison crushed her to him, his heartbeat racing against her chest. He kissed her head before pulling back to say, "There's necessary paperwork to make it official, but I already talked to someone who is ordained, and our parents want to be there. I know it's sudden, and maybe you want something more extravagant, but with us going to the Appalachian Trail, I thought it was—"

"Exactly what I want." Beth grabbed his face and slammed her mouth to his, kissing all of her love for him into his lips. She felt light, and full. Like she could fly away, and never leave the ground. Heat swept through her body, and she let the hunger take over, let it snuff out the fear. Harrison moved back, and she moved with him, falling onto the bed with her on top.

"Are you even going to look at the ring?" he rasped after break-ing off the kiss, his chest heaving as he fought to breathe. *Careful, Beth, be careful.*

"I will, but not yet. It will make me cry, because however it looks, I know it's perfect," Beth whispered against his lips, and kissed him again. Gently. Softly.

He was careful not to deepen the kiss too much, careful, careful, careful. She thought of the story, of their engagement, of their love, of the disease, and she was broken and healed, over and over. Breath-less, she kissed him harder, faster, sealing them as one with their mouths. Wanting to kiss the disease from his very lips. Their love was beautiful, and tragic, and she just wanted it to be beautiful. She didn't want to know that one day Harrison could be taken from her.

"Beth," he rasped, turning his head to the side when she tried to kiss him again.

Beth kissed his jaw, both cheeks, his forehead, all the while Harrison looked up at her, still and silent.

"Beth," he whispered, asking with his eyes what she didn't want to answer. "You're sad about something, and I really hope it isn't the prospect of marrying me."

"I finished the story." She stared down at the stack of white papers near them, tattooed in black with her heart. All of Beth was shredded again and again on the pages, but in the best of ways.

The book wasn't about Harrison. It was them. It was the story of a young woman disillusioned, but still somehow able to dream. It was about a man, weighted down by a fate he could not change, and deciding to change how he saw it. It was their love story, altered into a world where no one died, and no one got sick, and there were only good people. It was the perfect life in a perfect world in a perfect, nonexistent reality.

"It's okay," he told her.

Beth shifted her eyes from the pages to him.

Harrison gently touched her face. "Hold on to it." He stared at her, scrutinizing her features, adoration and strength looking back at her from his eyes. Strong eyes, strong mind, strong heart, weak body. Three out of four should be more than enough, but it wasn't.

"Keep writing my story. Our story. It is obvious you're not ready to part with it. And now you have more to write about, right?" His smile was subdued, the happiness of their engagement taking a backburner to reality.

Her shoulders lowered with relief. Beth could keep writing. She didn't have to give this up. She didn't think she could anyway.

"You don't have to stop." Harrison seemed to realize the gift he was giving her, how ever strange it might be to someone else. "Publish it after I'm gone. Can you do that for me, Beth?"

It was a simple request, asked quietly, and it broke her heart. *After I'm gone*. It was a reality she liked to avoid.

Her mouth trembled. "You know I will. Of course I will."

He nodded, relief leveling shadows from his face.

"But that will be years and years from now. Even decades." Whether it would be or not, that's what Beth chose to believe.

A smile tipped his mouth, grew to his tired eyes. "Wouldn't that be nice?"

"You're sick, Harrison, but you're not dying. You know that."

"I know that," he quietly agreed, but the way he avoided her eyes told her his conviction of that wasn't as strong as hers.

"Beth Caldwell," she whispered to buffer the sadness leaking into the happy moment, and Harrison's eyes lit up like he'd just been told he was cured.

He stroked a hand across her hair. "I like the sound of that."

When Beth sat up, putting space between them, Harrison settled his tall, lean frame on the bed, pulling up the blanket as a shiver went through him. Her stomach twisted, nausea threatening to overtake her resolve. Beth shoved it aside; refused to think of anything other than Harrison's heartbeat. Beating. Always beating. She focused on the beat of his heart.

Only the glow of the lamp on the nightstand offered light, and it silhouetted the man she loved. Made him faint, obscure. Dim. Beth looked at him, blinking against the image of his weakening body, denying the frailty her eyes saw, that which her mind refused to compute.

Her heart only saw Harrison. And he was bright, and mighty, and so, so strong.

"Will you read some of it to me?"

Beth crawled up the bed to him and brushed hair from his forehead. She nestled under the covers beside Harrison, careful to keep one hand always touching him. Reminding herself he was here, with her. Warm. Breathing. Alive. Hers. With his heart beating.

His sweet, clean scent calmed her, brought her peace. He rested his head against her cheek, his eyes closed, breathing softly. She lifted her left hand and studied the silver band with the dainty infinity symbol in diamonds, and tears dripped down her face as she silently cried. She loved him so much. Forever. *Your forever. My for-*

ever. Forever is forever. Beth breathed along with Harrison, pacing hers to his, even as she held back a sob.

"Of course. I'll read it every night. I promise," Beth whispered brokenly, turning her face to press a lingering kiss to the smooth skin of his forehead. "Our story, our world, remember?"

Harrison smiled faintly, his eyes still closed. "I want to live in our world for a little bit longer."

"You will," Beth promised. "Always."

She wiped an arm across her damp face and took the first sheet of paper from the pile, cleared her throat against the catch in it, and read out loud. Her voice wavered at first, but as she spoke, the strength of it grew. It was their story, after all, and she knew it well.

"I met Harrison Caldwell on the first snowfall of the season, and like the fall of the snow, steady and sure, I fell in love with him."

If you enjoyed this book, please consider leaving a review on the site from where you bought it. If you did not enjoy this book, please consider leaving a review on the site from where you bought it. Keep it classy—all hateful posts will be framed and hung on a wall in my home for my kids to read. Please don't traumatize my kids.

Lindy

About the Author

Lindy Zart is the USA Today bestselling author of Roomies. She has been writing since she was a child. Luckily for readers, her writing has improved since then. She lives in Wisconsin with her family. Lindy loves hearing from people who enjoy her work. She also has a completely healthy obsession with the following: coffee, wine, bloody marys, peanut butter, and pizza.

You can connect with Lindy at:

Newsletter signup form: http://bit.ly/1RqPP3m

Facebook Reader Group: https://www.facebook.com/groups/335847839908672/

Google.com/+LindyZart

Twitter.com/LindyZart

Facebook.com/LindyZart

Instagram ZartLindy

Lindyzart.com

Lindyzart@gmail.com

Check out Lindy's YouTube channel: http://bit.ly/1Qs6wXr